Their family. This house. This life.

Bonnie wanted so badly to want the same things Keith did, the things they'd always wanted together.

Their family. This house. This life.

Tied up in knots, she lay there beside him. Did she tell him she hadn't stopped their spontaneous lovemaking because she hadn't *had* to? That it was a safe time for her? The admission would hurt him, ruin the best evening they'd had in months. And for what?

Keith wanted another baby; she didn't know whether she did or not. Even though she loved being a mother. And a wife.

She just had to figure out what she needed to do for Bonnie, the woman, before she committed herself any further. Or figure out how to convince that woman to feel completely fulfilled with the life she had.

But how did she tell her husband that? How could she look into those gorgeous eyes and tell this man that the life he loved, the one they'd built together, wasn't enough for her?

They could lose everything. And for what?

So maybe they wouldn't use protection the next time they made love. Or the time after that.

She loved him so much.

And couldn't hurt him anymore.

Dear Reader,

We're back in Shelter Valley, and I'm awfully glad to be here. To see familiar faces, spend time with trusted friends—to live for just a while in a place where good usually wins out.

This visit hasn't been easy, though. What happens when two good, loving people change as they grow, wanting to travel different roads than the ones they set out on when they started their journey together? Who's right? The person who wants to stay on the same road? Or the person who's looking for something different?

Is the pursuit of personal happiness selfish and wrong? Or is it the biggest right? And what do you do with the love that refuses to die regardless of the unhappiness it brings?

I found Shelter Valley a secure place to explore some of the possibilities. And then I stumbled into a series of alarming mishaps at Bonnie's day care....

The old cliché, "when it rains, it pours," might be apropos— except that Shelter Valley is in the desert and doesn't get much rain!

Anyway, I know I speak for everyone here when I say welcome! We're glad you've joined us....

I love to hear from readers. You can reach me by mail at P.O. Box 15065, Scottsdale, AZ 86226, or by e-mail at ttquinn@tarataylorquinn.com. And I hope you'll visit my Web site—www.tarataylorquinn.com.

Tara

Books by Tara Taylor Quinn

HARLEQUIN SUPERROMANCE (SHELTER VALLEY STORIES)

SHELTERED IN HIS ARMS (a Harlequin single title)

Born in the Valley

Tara Taylor Quinn

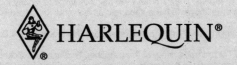

HARLEQUIN®

TORONTO • NEW YORK • LONDON
AMSTERDAM • PARIS • SYDNEY • HAMBURG
STOCKHOLM • ATHENS • TOKYO • MILAN • MADRID
PRAGUE • WARSAW • BUDAPEST • AUCKLAND

ISBN 0-373-71135-2

BORN IN THE VALLEY

Copyright © 2003 by Tara Lee Reames.

Visit us at www.eHarlequin.com

Printed in U.S.A.

For Nancy Lynn Miller and Rachel Marie Reames.
You jumped in with energy and enthusiasm
and made a hard time bearable.
I'll never forget....

THE RESIDENTS OF SHELTER VALLEY

Will Parsons: Dean of Montford University.

Becca Parsons: Wife of Will, active in community.

Bethany Parsons: Daughter of Becca and Will.

Ben Sanders: Former student, father (from previous marriage).

Tory Sanders: Wife of Ben, former abused wife.

Alex Sanders: Daughter of Ben, stepdaughter of Tory.

Phyllis Christine Sanders: Baby daughter of Ben and Tory.

Randi Foster: Sister of Will Parsons, married to Zack Foster. Manages women's athletic department at Montford.

Zack Foster: Veterinarian. Husband of Randi.

Cassie Montford: Veterinarian. Works with Zack Foster and involved with pet therapy. Married to Sam Montford.

Sam Montford: Descended from the founder of the town. Married to Cassie. Successful comic strip artist.

Mariah Montford: Adopted daughter of Cassie and Sam.

Brian Montford: Son of Cassie and Sam.

Phyllis Sheffield: Psychologist. Prominent in psych department at Montford.

Matt Sheffield: Married to Phyllis. Works in theater at Montford.

Calvin and Clarissa Sheffield: Twin children of Phyllis and Matt.

Beth Richards: Found refuge for herself and her son after escaping abusive ex-husband. Married to Greg Richards.

Greg Richards: Sheriff of Shelter Valley. Married to Beth.

Bonnie Nielson: Sister of Greg Richards, runs Little Spirits Daycare, married to Keith.

Keith Nielson: Husband of Bonnie, works at Montford.

Katie Nielson: Daughter of Bonnie and Keith.

Lonna Nielson: Keith's grandmother.

Martha Moore: Friend of Becca Parsons, recently divorced.

Brady Culver: Deputy of Greg's.

CHAPTER ONE

THE STREETS WERE DARK, but she welcomed the darkness. Welcomed the anonymity that wrapped itself around her, allowing her to run as no one in particular, a generic body passing unidentified through the early March night.

Sweating, heart working overtime, Bonnie Nielson concentrated on her rhythm, picking up speed as she reached her stride.

She knew these roads. Knew which houses gleamed bright and clean beneath a noonday sun, which yards grew beautiful flowers, which were the lucky ones with grass, instead of the more common desert landscaping. She knew every neighborhood, every family. In many cases she even knew the families who'd previously occupied these homes. She knew when the street had been paved. When that light went in. She even remembered when the stop sign was erected at the corner of Sage and Thyme.

She knew that an old man had died in that two-story stucco house she'd just passed. His unmarried son had inherited the place and moved in. She knew that the man living next door was divorced. And the one after that, a widower. Sometime during the past couple of years, she'd started thinking of the strip as bachelors' row.

And she knew that what was now a big looming shadow was actually an old gray house that bucked the stucco tradition with its aluminum siding.

Growing up in Shelter Valley she'd always known the neighborhoods. Had taken comfort in that knowledge.

It was different now, though. Now the familiarity distressed her, a moment-to-moment reminder of how very small her world was—and always had been. How insignificant a role she played in this tiny, sheltered part of a planet that was drowning in need.

Yet this town also housed what was most important to her. Keith. Katie. Greg and Beth and little Ryan. Her friends. Her home.

So she ran. And when the Bonnie Nielson no one knew was hidden far enough inside her, she jogged toward home.

KEITH NIELSON was used to having the sheriff of Shelter Valley in his family room. Sprawling on Keith's couch, eating Sunday dinner, baby-sitting three-year-old Katie, Sheriff Greg Richards visited regularly.

But not in uniform.

And never before in an official capacity. There'd been a fire, and Sheriff Greg Richards was there to break the news to his sister.

"She always out this late?" He was standing, hands in his pockets, between the kitchen and the family room—keeping watch on the garage door at one end of the kitchen and the sliding glass door in the family room.

Keith appreciated the look of concern on his

brother-in-law's face. Bonnie and Greg were the only living adult members of the Richards family.

Sitting on the edge of the couch, arms resting on his knees, Keith dropped his head, staring at hands that wouldn't stay still. Staring at the wedding ring that had been a source of joy to him—until recently.

"Not often," he said. But the truth was only partially revealed in those words. If he measured the number of times Bonnie had been out late at night during their whole marriage, it wasn't often. If you measured the number of times she'd been out late since Christmas, it was higher. A lot higher.

Greg leaned back against the wall. "I figured this jogging thing would fade quickly."

Keith thought about that. "Me, too," he answered slowly. "Just like the aerobics and weight training did."

Greg nodded. Glanced toward each door. Keith wished Tuesday was a good TV night. At least then they could pretend to be distracted.

"She's sure looking great."

"Yeah." He'd rather see every one of the twenty pounds Bonnie had lost if he could have back the cheerful woman he'd married almost seven years before.

Keith's head shot up, eyes trained on the garage door.

He thought he'd heard Bonnie come in. He waited, not looking forward to the moments ahead. Little Spirits Daycare had been Bonnie's dream since her early teens. How badly was Greg's news going to affect her? She hadn't been herself for months as it was.

And how much did Greg know about that? Just because Bonnie hadn't been open with him didn't mean she hadn't gone to her brother.

Or maybe Greg hadn't noticed anything at all.

Keith listened and waited. For nothing.

"Katie's sleeping soundly." Greg hadn't straightened from the wall.

Keith studied the grain in the hardwood floor. "Bonnie put her down before she went out."

More silence. More door checking and glancing at watches. She'd been gone twenty minutes longer than her usual hour.

"Ryan's had two dry nights in a row."

Keith grinned at his brother-in-law. "That's great, man!" he said, in a way only two men who were close would do.

Greg nodded, his smile slowly dropping to a frown. "You want to break it to her?" he asked.

"You're the cop."

"I figured you'd say that."

"You've known her longer."

"You're married to her."

Slapping a hand against his jean-clad thigh, Keith stood. "Who the hell would've done this? I mean, set a fire in a *day care*."

"I don't know, but you can be damn sure I'm going to find out."

Keith believed him. Against every conceivable probability, Greg had solved a ten-year-old carjacking/murder that past spring. He'd found his father's murderer.

Keith thought he heard Bonnie in the garage

again. Moved into the kitchen. Ran a hand through hair that was straight and blond and a little long.

He peered into the refrigerator. ''You want a beer?''

''Yeah.'' Greg wandered over to the kitchen sink. ''No, not really,'' he muttered.

Closing the refrigerator door empty-handed, Keith said, ''Me, neither.''

What he wanted was to go to work. Picturing the brand-new bigger studio, his general manager's office, the monitors and cameras and constant activity, calmed him slightly. At MUTV—the Montford University television station—he was in control.

Or, barring work, he'd like to go to bed with his wife. But only if she'd snuggle her body up to him the way she used to.

He couldn't just keep standing there, looking at his watch.

When he seriously considered searching the streets for his wife, knowing damn well he'd see her sooner if he just waited for her here, Keith went in to check on his daughter for the third time in an hour. Bonnie didn't run particular routes. She could be anywhere in town. And unless he got lucky and chose the one street she happened to be on…

Katie was sound asleep, her thumb hanging out of open baby lips, her sweet cheeks plump and red and begging for a kiss. Keith touched the soft curls that were dark like her mother's but still baby-hair wispy. He pulled pink sheets with little princess crowns up over the three-year-old's shoulders and quietly left the room. He worried about Katie. Wondered if she was noticing the changes in her mother.

Was anyone else noticing?

Greg certainly hadn't said anything.

So was it only with Keith that she was different? Was this a marriage thing?

His blood ran cold. God, he hoped it wasn't. Anything else they could beat. As long as they were fighting it together.

Bonnie, sweaty and breathing heavily, was just coming through the garage door as Keith returned to the kitchen.

"What's up?" she panted, looking from one man to the other. She frowned. "What's wrong?" she demanded before either of them had replied to her first question. "It's not Katie...." She glanced at Keith, who immediately shook his head.

She stared at her brother. "Did something happen to Beth? Or Ryan?"

"No." Greg shook his head. "They're fine."

Keith braced himself as Greg's hands dropped to Bonnie's shoulders. "It's Little Spirits."

"What about it?"

She looked damned cute standing there in navy sweats with the bottoms hacked off to fit her short legs, and a white T-shirt under the matching hooded navy jacket. Too cute to be the recipient of distressing news.

"There's been a fire."

"At the day care?" She was hiding her grief well.

Greg nodded, then looked at Keith as if asking for help. Keith, however, was still waiting for Bonnie's horrified gasp. "In the back supply closet."

"Was anyone hurt?"

"No."

Bonnie pulled out a chair, sat down, one arm leaning on the table. "Was there much damage?"

After that initial glance, she had yet to look at Keith, to give him a chance to offer his support.

Dropping into the chair across from her, Greg said, "You lost everything in the closet, but the fire was stopped before it spread any farther."

Because he was feeling superfluous standing on the other side of the room, Keith joined the two at the kitchen table, pulling out the chair next to his wife.

Bonnie was frowning. "I wonder how on earth a fire got started in that closet. There's not even an electrical outlet in there."

"Someone set it." Keith did the dirty work, after all. This was the part they'd known would upset her the most.

"You mean arson?" She peered back and forth between the two men. "Who would do a thing like that?" Then after a long pause, she added, "And why?"

Keith was still waiting for that gasp. For Bonnie's usual intensity. For some kind of emotional reaction. Anger. Sadness.

Bonnie was perplexed.

And that was all.

"I was hoping you might be able to shed some light on who might've done this," Greg told her, taking a notepad from his pocket.

Bonnie didn't know.

They talked for half an hour, considering and dismissing one possibility after another. No matter what angle Greg took, Bonnie had nothing for him to go on, no leads to pursue. She gave her attention to the matter, answering every question thoughtfully, but with an almost unnerving calm.

Where in hell was Keith's emotionally exuberant wife?

Greg finished. Eventually left. And Bonnie went in to shower.

Keith stood at the kitchen window, replaying the past hour in his mind, trying to make sense of a world he no longer recognized.

Bonnie, his protective, mother-hen wife, had just had one of her life's dreams vandalized and had shown not the least bit of outrage—or hurt.

It was as though she didn't care at all.

EVERYTHING WAS WET and charred, and there was a choking stench in the air. Bonnie pulled out a mop she'd used the week before to clean up an orange-juice accident in the classroom for the three-year-olds, while Alice, their teacher, had wiped off the children who'd been caught in the fray. The mop was wet again, but no longer white or orange-stained. Its synthetic fibers were more than half gone, the remaining strands dark gray and smeared with soot. One side of the long handle—the side that'd been burned—was splintery and coal-black.

She held it carefully.

"I can help with that."

Her back to the door, Bonnie turned when she heard the voice of the landscaper and handyman. Shane Bellows was employed by the owner of the building in which she leased space.

"Hi, Shane," she greeted the man who'd once

made her teenaged heart throb—before he'd shattered that heart.

Shane might still look like the high-school quarterback who'd broken up with her their senior year because she was too nurturing and "not enough fun." But the dark-haired man taking the mop from her wasn't even a shadow of the boy he'd been.

The skiing accident that had changed Shane's life forever had left him brain-damaged. His memory was somewhat impaired, and he'd become unable to process more than one thing at a time—which made it difficult for him to make decisions. Or to figure out little everyday details, such as the nuances in people's words or facial expressions.

"I'm sorry I wasn't here last night to clean up for you." Her emotions were touched by the little-boy tone of voice. He wanted so badly to please. "I'm sorry it had to stay like this all day."

She handed him some crusty metal hangers to put in the industrial-size trash can she'd wheeled up to the door of the supply closet. "At least it's out here, away from the kids' rooms," she told him. Her tennis shoes sloshed through puddles on the slippery floor as she stepped forward to clear the bigger pieces of melted plastic that had, the day before, been storage bins, from the now-warped metal shelving unit. "We were able to have school as usual today."

Shane carefully took the plastic, turning completely, holding it over the container before dropping it in—as though making sure he'd aimed right.

"Besides," she added, "it's not your responsibility to clean up my messes."

"I know." He nodded, frowning slightly as he surveyed the charred remains and started on a shelf that was too high for her to reach without the discolored and misshapen stepstool next to the shelving unit. "I just want to help."

"You are helping," she told him, going to work on a lower shelf. "A lot." She wasn't even sure what exactly she was clearing away. There'd been a foot-high metal cabinet with twenty or thirty plastic drawers for screws and picture hangers and other little essentials. The drawers were melted shut. Bonnie tossed the whole thing.

"And, anyway," she told Shane, "no one was allowed in here until the investigators finished up their work this afternoon."

"Okay."

They worked silently until the shelving unit was nearly empty. Having Shane around calmed her. She didn't have to keep up appearances with him.

And being with her seemed to calm him, too.

"This is going much more quickly than I expected, thanks to you."

He grunted, looking embarrassed, and then slowly smiled. "I'm glad I can help you."

Bonnie turned back to the job at hand with a twinge of guilt.

Keith had offered to come and help with clean-up duty after work. Beth had said she'd take Katie home with her and Ryan. Wednesday night was macaroni-and-cheese night, and Katie loved it almost as much as Ryan did. Bonnie had sent Katie home with Keith, instead. The little girl had missed her bath the night before and had had a long day.

And Bonnie had needed a break from them.

She would rather die than have Keith know she was dissatisfied with the life they'd built together—a feeling that had been oddly exacerbated by the events of the past twenty-four hours.

She just needed a little time to get herself back in line.

"Do you know who started the fire?" Shane asked, each word spoken deliberately.

Shaking her head, Bonnie shrugged. "People from the sheriff's office said somebody threw a book of lit matches in through that vent up there." She pointed to the outside wall of the closet.

Shane stared blankly toward the ceiling. "How do they know that?"

"Because it landed on the wet mop and didn't completely burn."

He took a full minute to process that. Then, "Do they know who did it?"

She felt a surge of pity at the obvious struggle he was having. Conversation was difficult for him.

"No," she said. "I guess there was too much fire and water damage for fingerprinting. It was probably just kids, playing a prank."

"Why would someone play a prank on you, Bonnie?"

"After looking at things today, my brother, Greg—who's the sheriff now—doesn't think they were going after me. There's not much chance they knew that the vent led into the Little Spirits supply closet."

"Oh."

Yeah, and an even bigger "oh" was the fact that

Bonnie had been a tiny bit disappointed that Greg hadn't seen the fire as a premeditated act aimed at her. She'd almost had an excuse to move on.

Bonnie stopped, shaking, hands on the edge of the garbage can she was peering sightlessly into.

An excuse to move on? Where on earth had that thought come from?

She had nothing to move on *to*. Nowhere she wanted to go.

She loved her husband to distraction. Would give up her life for her daughter. Little Spirits had been a far greater success than she'd ever dared hope.

And still, she was consumed with a nebulous need for more. It made no sense to her.

How could she suddenly resent the very things she'd spent her life dreaming of, praying for, building?

"Are you okay?" Shane's words pulled her back.

"No," she told him, walking back to the closet.

She couldn't prevaricate with Shane. It would be too cruel to this man who was trying so hard to make sense of an already bewildering world. And she didn't need to pretend with him. In Shane's mind, what was, was. He wanted predictability, craved patterns and rules, but there was no analysis of motivation, no judgmental thought, no opinion of what should be. Only an acceptance of the environment around him.

Most importantly, her confusion wouldn't hurt Shane.

"People were talking to you today like you were sad. I saw them when I was waxing floors."

"I know they were." They were standing, one on

either side of the mangled shelving unit, tilting it to get it out the closet door. "You may not remember, but Little Spirits is something I've talked about my whole life and I've worked really hard to make it successful. Most of the people in this town know that. So they think it would be really disturbing for me to have it intentionally vandalized. Or even damaged by accident."

He stopped, stared at her, his gaze intent. The brown depths of his eyes had always been compelling.

"I remember."

Bonnie didn't know how to respond. When Shane had suddenly reappeared in her life a couple of months before—her new handyman, instead of the high-powered financier she'd heard he was in Chicago—she'd immediately accepted the man he'd become. Never probing for traces of the man he'd been.

Beyond acknowledging to her landlord that they knew each other, they'd never once referred to their personal past.

The two of them deposited the ruined unit by the emergency exit door.

"What do you remember?"

"That you always wanted to take care of people."

Yeah. He was right about that. Was that all he remembered?

"And now you don't?"

Breaking eye contact, she shrugged, dipped back into the closet to start clearing rubbish from the corner. "Of course I do."

He was hauling out what was left of the vacuum cleaner Beth and Greg had bought her for Christmas.

Bonnie scratched her cheek, felt the slimy wetness of soot from her fingers and wiped her face with her shoulder. She'd brought sweats and a T-shirt with her to work that morning to wear for closet gutting. She was glad she had. She'd probably be throwing them away when she got home that night, because of their smell alone.

"What's wrong, Bonnie?"

She piled a few more pieces of unidentifiable trash on her outstretched arm.

"I don't know," she said, sighing as she dumped it into the rapidly filling can. "I love this place. It just…doesn't excite me like it used to. I'm feeling differently about a lot of things lately, and that kind of scares me."

"Different about what things?"

She dumped and gathered more mostly unrecognizable residue. What the fire hadn't destroyed, the sprinkler system had. "My life, my work, my marriage, Shelter Valley." She rattled on as she worked. "It used to be that those things filled my every waking thought. They gave me strength and incentive." Now it almost felt as if they were holding her back.

"I think you wanted to be married and stay in Shelter Valley and take care of people."

His words were slow, deliberate. His work, focused on one task—cleaning everything out of the closet—with no decisions to be made, was quick and efficient.

"I think I did, too."

"Do you like being married?"

"Yes, very much."

"Do you like your husband?" His back was turned as he asked the question.

Staring at those broad shoulders, Bonnie thought of the hundreds of times she'd wanted to tell Shane Bellows what a great man she'd found after he'd left her.

Like the realization of her lifelong dreams, the fulfillment of that wish was hollow.

"I adore him."

Which was why she was finding all this so hard. How could she possibly need more than Keith and the life they'd built together?

Pulling a rag from his back pocket, Shane wrapped it around the sharp edge of a broken jar of buttons she'd forgotten was in there.

"You love the kids," he said after disposing of the jar. "I see you laugh with them a lot."

Those big hands picking up tiny little buttons gave her pause.

"You're right. I do."

"Then are you okay now?"

"I think I'm just tired." Shaking her head, Bonnie tossed some spare floor tile she'd found behind the shelves they'd removed. "I never thought I'd start to resent this place."

"I never thought I'd be a blue-collar worker." Shane's tongue dragged around the last word.

He stopped on one side of the closet, facing her as she stood on the other. The space between them was almost empty, but not quite.

These times, when he seemed as clear-minded as

she, disconcerted her. She didn't know how to respond.

"I used to be powerful," he told her, his voice sounding at that moment as though he were still the man handling fortunes bigger than Bonnie would ever dream of having.

"I know."

"I remember it," he said. "I remember Chicago."

Her heart ached as she listened to him. She couldn't imagine the hell his life must be. And felt miniscule and petty as she stood there, discontented with her own.

"What do you remember best?" she asked, hoping the question was okay, that it wouldn't distress or confuse him.

"All of it."

A more typical nonanswer. Because he couldn't sift through the memories and make a decision?

"I remember going to work," he said, his words slow again. "I remember my office, how I could understand and fix anything that came in. I was really good," he told her with that strange combination of the intelligent and successful man he used to be and the more childlike creature he'd become.

"I know you were. We used to hear about the great things you were doing."

"I still look at the stock reports and know what they mean," he told her. "I even play the market."

Bonnie frowned. "Is that a good idea, Shane? You don't want to blow your savings."

"Now that I can't earn as much?" he asked. He didn't sound bitter. Instead, he sounded like a little boy who'd just been told he couldn't go on the big camp-out. Disappointed. Sad.

"I'm sorry. I shouldn't have—" Bonnie broke off.

"It's okay," he said, his voice switching back to that of the man he'd once been. These sudden changes were disturbing, even after months of getting used to them. "I got some insurance money from my accident." The voice was still deep, but with the tenor of a little boy again. "I just kept some of it for me and most of it my friend in Chicago is handling for me."

Bonnie hoped to God his friend was honest and taking good care of Shane.

"So how've you done with the money you kept yourself?" she asked, smiling at him.

Bonnie's heart lightened when Shane grinned back. "Good," he told her. "I've tripled it so far."

"No kidding!" She stepped closer, laying a hand on his forearm. "I'm proud of you."

"That makes me happy, Bonnie."

"I'm glad." She gave his arm a squeeze. "You know I'm here if you need anything, right?"

"Yeah." Bowing his head, he almost mumbled. "You talk to me, Bonnie. Like I'm a real guy..."

Bonnie replayed their conversation over and over as she drove home more than an hour later. She'd helped Shane, made a difference. And that felt damn good.

CHAPTER TWO

HE'D NEVER WORN pajamas to bed. Just boxers. It was one thing that hadn't changed.

Keith was hard inside his shorts as he climbed in beside his wife almost a week after the fire. It amazed him, that ready reaction, which happened much more often than he would've expected after more than six years of sharing the same bed with Bonnie.

She hadn't been there long. The sheets were still cool.

"'Night," she said softly before he'd even settled in.

The next day was Tuesday. Keith had a governing-board breakfast meeting. And Bonnie was always up at the crack of dawn taking care of Katie and getting to work earlier than the rest of the eight-to-five world.

Still…

He opened his mouth to reply in kind, but then didn't. With every casual good-night, he could feel her slipping farther away.

He lay down. Fought with himself for all of two seconds. Nudged her backside with his hips. The low, welcoming moan that came quietly from deep in her throat righted his world.

"You make me crazy, woman," he growled against the side of her throat, kissing along her neck and collarbone. His hand slid beneath the short cotton top of her pajamas.

And the pressure of her butt against him increased perceptibly.

"What do you want?" he whispered in her ear, feeling her shiver. "Top or bottom?"

Wrapping her arms around his middle, she pulled him on top of her. A silent reply. There'd been too many of those in these last confusing months.

"I love looking at your eyes in the moonlight," he told her. He loved how they glistened with the intensity of her passion.

Tonight she closed them.

Moving past the disappointment, he bent to kiss her, long lingering openmouthed kisses they'd perfected over the years.

Her mouth opened. But her tongue didn't dance.

"Something wrong?" he asked, raising his head only far enough to see her face.

Bonnie lifted her hips against his groin, inviting him. As badly as he needed her, Keith was hesitant.

"Talk to me." He couldn't make out her expression. "Please?"

"I..."

"What's wrong, honey?"

"Nothing's wrong," she said, her gaze settling at about his nose. "I'm just tired."

In almost seven years, tired had never made their lovemaking a silent affair. Not even in those first months after Katie was born and they were both doing double duty with full-time jobs and night feeding. Their conversation during sex was what made sleeping with Bonnie different from the few other women he'd been with.

She pulled him down to her, enticing him with her tongue along the edges of his lips, enticing him with other things.

Keith wasn't sure he should finish what he'd started.

More and more he'd come up against this strange vacancy in Bonnie. This refusal to tell him what she was thinking. But this was the first time it had translated itself into their sex life.

"Bonnie?"

"Yeah?" Her voice was languorous, as though she was giving herself up to passion, as though she wasn't even aware of the chasm deepening between them.

He was tempted to give up for tonight, to enjoy whatever communication remained between them.

"Why won't you talk to me? Tell me what's wrong."

Her hands didn't move from around his neck, her hips still pressing against him. "There's nothing to tell."

He wanted to believe that. "You seem kind of…distant."

"I'm really just tired, babe," she said, her voice full of the intimate warmth that had made him her slave from the very beginning. "I've spent the entire week reassuring parents. They needed to hear for themselves that there really was no danger to their kids, that Greg's official report said the arson was a random act. And no one was satisfied until they'd heard it directly from me.''

She reached up to kiss him and his body started to respond again.

Keith rose on his elbows.

''So I've just imagined the distance growing between us these past couple of months?''

It was a subject he'd broached often.

''I'm right here, Keith. Loving you and Katie every bit as much as I always have.''

Keith stared down at her. That was the kind of frustrating nonresponse he received every time. Instead of giving him a real answer, she countered with something good and affirming.

And he knew from experience that if he pushed, he'd just get more of the same.

''I don't understand.''

She pushed a lock of hair off his forehead, running her fingers through to the ends, which rested at the bottom of his neck. ''Don't understand what?''

''Why I'm battling this fear that things are slipping away and you don't even seem to be aware of anything changing.''

Fear wasn't an emotion he was all that familiar with. Certainly not one he'd ever admitted to before. It was probably only because he was still lying intimately on top of her, her arms around him, that he could own up to it now.

''Keith.'' She held his face with her hands. ''Things are *not* slipping away. You have my word on that. I'm right here. I'm going to stay right here. I love you very, very much. I don't even want to contemplate what life would be like without you. Okay?''

Slowly Keith nodded, all the while feeling a sense of defeat. How in hell did you communicate with someone who refused to acknowledge the problem?

And how could he fix whatever was broken when he couldn't find out what it was?

Or maybe she couldn't acknowledge the problem because it was him? And it couldn't be fixed?

Staring down into green eyes that looked almost black in the darkness, Keith knew he wasn't going to be able to rest easy that night. ''You're sure there's nothing wrong that you aren't telling me? You aren't sick or anything?''

''I'd tell you if I was sick, you know that.''

''And business at the day care is good?''

''Amazingly so, especially considering the fire.''

''What about Katie? Is there something wrong there you aren't telling me about?''

''Of course not! I tell you everything about Katie.''

About Katie maybe. But then, Katie had always been a source of joy between them. Caressing Bonnie's cheek softly, he remembered how Bonnie's pregnancy had brought them so much closer when he'd already thought they were as close as two people could be.

The nights they'd spent creating scenarios of what it would be like to be parents, the doctor's visits, listening to that heartbeat inside her, the hundreds of names they'd picked out only to discard each one and begin again. The countless times he'd rubbed her growing belly with lotion…

"You don't regret having her, do you?" he asked as the horrible thought occurred to him right in the middle of his reminiscing. She sure hated those stretch marks now that she'd lost weight.

Bonnie tried to sit up, which only brought her breasts and hips against him. "Of course not," she said, settling back. Her eyes were huge in the moonlight. "Never! Katie is so special. I'd give up my life for her."

"I still remember the day we found out you were pregnant."

It had been a Saturday and they'd gone together to buy the home pregnancy kit. And then she'd made him wait outside their bedroom while she'd done the test. He'd burst in, anyway, when her thrilled scream exploded throughout the house.

"Me, too," she said, her voice softening. "I was incredibly happy. I didn't have any idea how great it was going to be once I actually held her."

They were quiet for a moment, a contented quiet. A together quiet. Like they used to share.

"Remember all the hours it took to find just the right crib?" he asked, enjoying the escape to a happier time. "It had to be antique white with spiral spindles, only three inches maximum between the bars."

"And the wallpaper." She grinned. "I can't believe how many days I spent trying to decide between horses and rainbows."

"It's a good thing you didn't have to, or the nursery still wouldn't be done." He smiled, recalling how excited she'd been when she'd found a paper that had horses on a carousel with rainbows in the background.

Excited. Happy. *His.* He'd come in from work that night to be greeted by her exuberant ''Guess what?'' as she'd launched herself at him, throwing not only her arms around him, but her legs, too, catching him off guard. Luckily the couch had been behind him and they'd fallen onto its cushioned softness. As he remembered, it had been a good half hour before he'd ever found out what she'd been so excited to tell him.

And then, without warning or forethought, as they lay there intimately entwined, the solution to the undefined problem became crystal clear to him.

''Let's have another baby.''

Hips that had been pressing into his withdrew, not far, but then, the bed wouldn't allow her to move any great distance.

''Katie's three,'' he reminded her. ''Potty-trained. The timing's good.'' He paused, but not long enough for her to reject the idea. ''If we wait much longer, there'll be too many years between the kids for them to have anything in common.''

Her hands had dropped, and she ran her fingers along his arms. ''You said you didn't want a bunch of kids.''

The irony was not lost on him. She'd always wanted a big family. The thought of several kids to provide for, several kids taking his and Bonnie's time until they had none left for each other, had only made him feel trapped.

''I'm not talking about a bunch of kids,'' he told

her, allowing the weight of his hips to rest completely on her. "Just one more."

She didn't say anything. Her fingers were almost frantic as they drew small circles on his upper arms. Her breathing had quickened.

And she wouldn't look at him.

"Is that a no?" he asked, bracing himself for her answer.

She shook her head. And relief swept over him.

With a surge of protectiveness—and feeling very much in love—Keith bent to kiss her softly. "Talk to me, honey."

"I don't know what you want me to say."

"That you want a baby. That you don't." He loved her so much, needed so badly for her to be happy. "Just talk to me. Tell me what you're thinking. Let me in."

"You *are* in," she said, stroking his face lightly, her sweet touch making his desire for her immediate again. It astounded him that a gesture as simple as her fingers on his skin could ignite him. "You're in farther than anyone has ever been."

It should be enough. Goddammit, it should be enough.

"I'm just tired, Keith. After years of struggle with the business and heartache with my dad and worrying about Greg, I'm finally coming down."

She kissed him, a full-tongued, wanton kiss that was meant to take him to the place where only the two of them could go together. Sliding his arms beneath her, Keith pulled her closer, kissing her back with every bit of energy he possessed.

She was hungry. Generous. She wanted him.

"I'm still amazed by this," she said softly. Her eyes were glinting, her lips smiling as she studied him.

She was there. Loving him.

Keith grunted, stripped off her pajamas and explored every inch of her newly thin body.

There was absolutely no doubt that this woman needed him.

Was it possible that the problem was *his?* Had he somehow imagined the change he was perceiving in her? Was his mind taking him down a dangerous road he didn't need to travel? Was this remoteness of hers no more than a small case of emotional exhaustion, just as she claimed?

His heart filled with hope, with a resurgence of the peace he'd begun to take for granted over the past few years.

"Now," she moaned. He drew out the moment, savoring it, her, them.

"Nooowww." Her groan was louder.

He settled his body in the cradle of her thighs, slid up—

"Wait!"

He froze, confused by the alarm in her voice. "What?" he asked, concerned, afraid something was wrong.

"This." She'd reached inside the cupboard behind them and pulled out the condom he'd thought they weren't going to use.

Aroused beyond the ability to analyze anything but his need to have sex, Keith held himself up while she unrolled the condom around him. He plunged inside her before she'd completely finished.

The human body was incomparable. It could accomplish all manner of tasks, from the menial to the perilous; it could also transport, transcend, divert. Keith let Bonnie take him away, his mind wholly on their physical communication.

It was physical. It was exciting. And it was empty.

They weren't making a baby.

And he had no idea why not.

THE THIRD LETTER from Mike Diamond arrived eight days after the fire. It appeared in a pile of mail that also included the insurance forms she had to fill out.

She waited until everyone was busy feeding lunch to a passel of hungry kids before she tore open the envelope with her landlord's return address.

Keeping one eye on the space outside her glass-enclosed office—making sure she was alone—she perused the letter quickly.

The tone was more congenial than she'd expected, considering that this was the third letter in almost as many weeks. But the entreaty was just as insistent.

He wanted her to relocate Little Spirits. He had a buyer in Phoenix for the small Shelter Valley strip mall in which the day care was located, and the deal apparently hinged on the early termination of Bonnie's three-year lease.

According to Mike Diamond, the day-care noise level, as well as the deluge of drop-off and pick-up traffic during rush hour each business day detracted from the strip's appeal. A couple of weeks before, after receiving Mike's first letter, Bonnie had placed an anonymous call to the Phoenix-based management company Diamond had named. She'd found that they did indeed have a policy that precluded day cares from renting in any of their strip malls.

A guffaw of laughter sounded just around the corner from Bonnie's office. She quickly filed Diamond's letter with the other two in a folder at the back of the file drawer in her desk.

It had taken her more than a year to land the right location for Little Spirits. Shelter Valley was a small town, and there just weren't many places that had enough space, private kitchen facilities, the right zoning, an outside play area and met all the other specifications. And although she was doing well, she wasn't making enough to build her own facility.

Which meant that Diamond's continued and very determined hounding should upset her.

Six months ago, she'd have thrown his letter in the trash—after first expending much frustration in tightly wadding the paper. Today she knew only that she wasn't moving. Tomorrow? She couldn't say.

That didn't mean she hadn't considered letting Mike Diamond out of the lease.

Leaning back in her chair, eyes closed, Bonnie thought about the fire that could have solved the problem for her the week before. If only the Kachina County volunteer firemen hadn't been so damn good at what they did—responding so quickly to the call. If there was no building, there'd be no choice to make.

"I saw a letter come in from the Diamond Company. Did they rent that space next door?"

Bonnie jumped as Beth Richards, Greg's wife, stepped into her office. Beth volunteered at Little

Spirits almost every day now that she was a woman free to look at life's options. She'd sold the cleaning business that had kept her and her son fed while they were hiding out in Shelter Valley the previous fall.

"No," Bonnie said, looking over the insurance forms she'd just received. She hadn't told anyone about Diamond's request yet. She knew that her family and friends would want to help her fight, and she had no idea what she wanted to fight *for*. Or if she wanted to fight at all.

"Darn." Beth dropped into the chair across from Bonnie—just as she had all those months ago when she'd shown Bonnie the missing-persons postcard depicting Beth and her toddler son. "It's been what—three months now? I was really hoping something would go in soon. Preferably a bookstore. I hate having to go all the way to Phoenix to buy Ryan new books."

Bonnie smiled at the woman who, while casually dressed in jeans and a short-sleeved sweater, still looked like a fashion model. "You could always open one."

Beth shook her head. Moving to the edge of her chair, she grinned. "I can't run a store and the Montford classical music department, too."

Squealing, Bonnie ran around her desk and hugged Beth. "No kidding? You got the job?"

"Will called this morning."

The happiness she felt for Beth—and for her brother, whose life was finally falling into place—dispelled some of the confusion weighing her down. Her family was settled, healthy, content.

They talked about the logistics of the job for a

couple of minutes. Ryan would be a regular student at Little Spirits, which was something they both agreed would be good for him. And though she'd be giving up her volunteering, Beth would still be able to spend some afternoons with her son.

"You have an odd look on your face," Beth said as the two women walked through the multipurpose room toward the playground where the kids were loudly engaged in an after-lunch recess.

Bonnie shrugged and shook her head, afraid to speak in case the tears she was fighting won despite her efforts. What was the matter with her? She had it all. Why wasn't that enough?

Linking her arm with Bonnie's, Beth pulled her away and out another door. "Let's walk."

Which meant talk.

She should argue. She had work to do.

Or did she? The children in her care were all being watched by competent employees. Paperwork, other than the insurance forms, was up-to-date.

"Tell me what's going on." Beth released her arm as they circled the day care and strolled out to the desert beyond. "And before you say nothing, let me tell you right now that answer's already disqualified."

"I'm just ti—"

"Nope." Beth shook her head. "Tired isn't going to cut it, either. You're the most energetic person I know, Bon, and besides that, I'm not just talking about this week. The guys might not have noticed yet, but you've lost your spark."

"Keith noticed."

"I don't think Greg has, but then, he's not looking. All he knows is that you're married to the man you love, have the child you've always wanted and the career of your dreams.''

"I know."

On the other side of the desert lot was a quiet residential street. Beth took the sidewalk away from town. And said nothing. Bonnie's new sister-in-law, who'd quickly become her closest friend, already knew her well.

"There's really nothing wrong," Bonnie said slowly, wanting above all to present her case honestly. "As you said, I have everything I've ever wanted. And I'm incredibly thankful for that."

Someone needed to clean the gravel out of the cracks in this sidewalk.

"But?"

"I don't know," Bonnie said, frustration welling up inside her. She glanced at the clear, blue Arizona sky—illuminated by a sun that was already heating this March day to Midwest summer temperatures.

She slid her hands into the pockets of her slacks. "Have you ever had the feeling that the role you're playing isn't significant?"

"Of course you're significant, Bonnie!" Beth said, stopping to stare at her. "My gosh! This entire family revolves around you."

"Only because I got here first," she said. "It could just as easily revolve around you."

"But you—"

"That's not really what I meant," Bonnie continued, cutting off Beth's rebuttal. "And you're right. I have no business feeling like I do and I'm just going to stop."

She turned, heading back toward the day care.

"No." Beth grabbed her arm. "Wait. I'm listening now. Talk to me."

Feeling ungrateful and selfish, Bonnie tried really hard to convince herself that if she just kept working on it, she could make these feelings go away.

She'd been trying for months.

"I just feel my life is too small, that I'm not doing enough with it."

Beth started to walk and Bonnie fell into step beside her. "With my education and capabilities, I could be helping the homeless or abused women, making some kind of real difference. Sounds crazy, huh?"

"No. Not at all."

"The world is filled with people who need my help more than the relatively privileged, well-loved kids who come to my day care."

"We don't have a lot of homeless people here," Beth said softly. "And though I'm sure there are some, there probably aren't many abused wives, either."

"That's part of the problem, I think. Shelter Valley is such a protected—and protective—place that I'm isolated from larger realities."

"So you want to leave town?"

"No!" Bonnie ran her fingers through her hair, trying to massage the ache from her head. "Of course not. Maybe I just need to feel needed."

"Which you are, of course, by so many people."

"Yeah, but not in the way I mean." She tried to find words to articulate things she wasn't sure she understood. "Last week, after the fire, Shane Bellows helped me clean up. All I did was talk to him for an hour and yet I left feeling I'd really used my life for a greater good. He was responsive and just so happy to be part of an adult conversation. He needs a friend, Beth, someone who'll treat him like a grown man with something to contribute, instead of the half person he's sort of become. It's that kind of satisfaction I'm missing. I think.''

"Be careful with Shane, Bonnie. You've got a history with him that could trip you up.''

"No worry there. He's not at all the man he once was. That history is dead and gone.''

"From what I understand, even the doctors aren't completely sure how much Shane's mind has been altered.''

"He's completely harmless, Beth, if that's what you're getting at. His doctor didn't think there was any problem with him working around small children, which he certainly would have if Shane posed any kind of threat.''

"Just be careful.''

Beth waved as a car passed. Mr. and Mrs. Mather. They'd been one of her house-cleaning clients, Bonnie remembered.

"You think I'm crazy, don't you.''

Bonnie wished Beth's opinion didn't matter so much.

"No.'' As if by previous consensus, they both turned the corner, slowing their pace as they started down another deserted street. "As a matter of fact, I completely understand.'' She spoke in a low voice, holding Bonnie's full attention.

"You know how I spent my youth, Bonnie. Training to be a concert pianist is completely consuming, draining every ounce of energy you have and then demanding more. I gave it everything and somehow managed to get my business degree, as well. And then, after my parents were killed and I was on my own, I suddenly found myself with skills and discipline and drive, and nothing important to contribute. People were dying every day while I played scales.''

''Hardly.'' Bonnie still got chills every time Beth sat down at the piano. The woman brought something elemental, spiritual almost, to everything she played.

''It's how I felt,'' Beth insisted. ''And that feeling drove me straight into the trap James Silverman and Peter Sterling set.''

It was the first time Bonnie had ever heard her friend mention her ex-husband and his partner. The two men who'd, in the end, contracted a killer to ensure her death.

''I wanted to make a difference, to stand for something, to help save the world in some significant way.''

Taking Beth's arm, a silent support, Bonnie ached for her friend, ached because of the memories Beth would never completely escape.

''The cult allowed me to believe I was contributing something huge, and that feeling drove me for a long time, Bon. Far longer—and farther—than it should have. It drove me into turning a blind eye to things that were not only immoral but illegal, as well.''

Sterling Silver, the cult run by Beth's ex-husband

and his doctor partner, had been shut down the previous year when Greg had gone searching for the identity of the woman he loved. James Silverman and Peter Sterling were currently serving life sentences in separate Texas prisons.

"So you're saying I should just ignore this feeling and be thankful for the life I have."

It was exactly what she'd been telling herself.

"I don't know," Beth said, turning with Bonnie as they reached another corner, heading back toward the day care. "I don't think there are any easy answers."

Bonnie didn't think so, either.

"You said Keith noticed something's wrong. What does he say about all this?"

"Nothing," Bonnie said, kicking a pebble into the street. "I can't tell him I need more out of life than he's giving me, Beth. It would kill him. And it's not fair to him, either. Because there's nothing he can do. Besides, I might wake up tomorrow and be perfectly satisfied again."

"I doubt it."

"Me, too."

They walked on, their silence broken only by an occasional passing car. And there weren't many of those.

"But I still can't tell him," Bonnie eventually said. "I can't hurt him like that."

"I couldn't, either."

"That letter from Diamond today…"

"Yeah?"

"It was the third one of its kind. He's got a buyer for the property, contingent on me relocating. The developer has a rule against day cares in strip malls.''

''Mike Diamond's selling?''

''I guess.''

''Wow. That surprises me. I thought he was planning to expand, not get out.''

''I know. Me, too.''

''So what are you going to do?'' Beth asked, slowing as the day care came in sight.

''I can't move without building a place,'' Bonnie said. ''I'd already exhausted all the other possibilities when Diamond's place became available.''

''Can you afford to build?''

''Maybe. Probably. If Keith and I take out a loan. But how can I even contemplate putting us deeper in debt when I'm not even sure this is what I want?''

''I'm guessing you haven't talked to Keith about it.''

They stopped at the corner across the street from Little Spirits. Bonnie looked at her sister-in-law. ''How can I—without getting into the whole 'I'm not satisfied with my life' thing?''

''So tell Diamond no.''

''I'm planning to.''

''Then why haven't you?''

They crossed the street, the traffic noises not nearly loud enough to hide what Bonnie hated to admit.

''Because I can't quite turn my back on the chance to get out of the two years I have left on my lease.''

CHAPTER THREE

THERE WERE SOME THINGS that just shouldn't change. Stockings was one of them. Lonna Nielson rolled the silky material up her right leg, ignoring the varicose veins she passed along the way, and clipped it into place with two quick pinches of her fingers.

Women had been wearing stockings since before she was born. They hid imperfections. They gave a woman a sense of dress, of polish—a personal finishing that served as an invisible shield between her and anything the day might bring. Those silk stockings told the world that she took pride in herself.

And they had to be *real* silk stockings, pulled up one at a time and hooked to the garter belt. None of that panty stuff for her. There were certain places a woman just needed to breathe.

Besides, everyone knew that garters were far sexier.

Didn't make a whit of difference that she was seventy-six years old or that she'd been a widow for more decades than she'd been a wife. Feeling a little bit sexy was important to her.

Taking a deep breath to prepare for the pull in her lower back, she reached down for the second stocking, her mind sliding over the list of things she had to do that Friday morning. First was the Beautification Committee meeting. Not the most important, perhaps, but those idiots wouldn't get anything right if left to their own devices. She'd been living in this town longer than most anybody else here and knew how to hide her imperfections.

Second stocking in place, Lonna picked up the navy slacks and polka-dot blouse she'd ironed after her five-mile walk and before her granola-and-fruit breakfast that morning. It was almost seven o'clock, and she had to hurry or she wouldn't have time to get over to Grace's, fix breakfast and wait for her to finish eating so she could do the dishes before her eight-thirty meeting.

Missing the cat that had been lying on her bed for seventeen years, Lonna worked buttons through holes that had grown curiously tighter and harder to maneuver over the years. Buffy, her snarly calico, had died six months ago, and while Lonna was probably lonelier than she'd admit, she was loath to start all over again.

Besides, kitty litter was damned heavy to haul around.

Purse over her forearm—navy to match her slacks and low-heeled pumps—she was almost out the door before she remembered the list of new books she was recommending to the library board later that morning. It was still on the printer Keith had installed to go with the computer he'd bought her for Christmas. The boy meant well. And he'd been right. The blamed machine made keeping up with her jobs somewhat easier.

But it was a love-hate kind of thing. Refusing to

look at the screen that revealed more information than Lonna had ever had or ever would have, she grabbed the sheet she'd printed out before going to bed the night before.

The phone rang.

She was late already, and even if she didn't get Grace's dishes done, she couldn't just make breakfast and leave the woman to eat it alone. Grace looked forward to their morning chats.

And Lonna did, too.

The machine could get the phone. She slid the paper into the leather zip folder Becca Parsons had given her for her last birthday, stiffening as the phone rang again.

Someone needed to talk to her.

And who was Lonna to determine that whatever he or she had to say wasn't important?

With an exasperated sigh she picked up the phone.

And three hours later, sitting beside Dorothy's hospital bed, she assured her friend of seventy years that she would not have to go into a Phoenix nursing home. She would not have to leave Shelter Valley or the home she'd lived in all of her adult life. Dorothy's heart and soul were her essence, and they were still in one-hundred-percent working order.

Lonna would help her while her broken hip healed.

She'd find the time.

And the energy.

She always had.

THE FILM WAS EVOCATIVE. Intense. Full of energy. Keith just wasn't sure that what it evoked had anything to say to their audience. Or to anyone except maybe the people involved. Or people like them.

Of course he'd been preoccupied with the conversation he'd had with his grandmother earlier that day. He'd been trying to talk her out of a trip to Phoenix by herself. Friday-afternoon traffic was hell. He'd told her Dorothy would be just fine until later that day when he could take Lonna Nielson to the hospital to see her friend.

Had his grandmother listened?

Of course not.

She'd climbed into her Buick and sped to her friend's side.

This seemed to be a pattern in his life. His word apparently had little value to the women he cared about.

"You don't like it."

Keith glanced at his new program director and smiled. Martha Moore, at least, respected his opinion.

"I didn't say that," he said, smiling at her before turning his attention to the monitor.

"You don't have to say it." Her words were soft as she, too, focused on the film they were previewing. It was a work a student had found and suggested for the following week's Fine Art feature on MUTV.

The piece was a dance performance. Sort of. It was a depiction of a human condition, one that every human being eventually faced.

An excellent depiction as far as Keith could tell.

He just had no idea why people would choose to watch other people act out the process of dying. It wasn't something *he* wanted to put himself through.

But Martha was riveted. Her whole body leaned toward the monitor, almost as though she was going to jump on that stage with those writhing, painfully weak bodies. Eyes drawn to the slim neck exposed by her short black hair, Keith wondered why Martha was still single. Her husband had left more than two years before, and other than a few dates with the architect who'd done some work at Montford, Martha's love life had been nonexistent.

As far as Keith knew, anyway.

And he couldn't understand that. Not only was she slim and sexy and down-to-earth, the woman had a way of making a guy feel she honestly enjoyed his company. He wondered if she had anything planned for the weekend ahead; if so, he hoped it would involve something for her and not just for the four kids she was raising alone.

"What?"

She'd caught him staring.

"Nothing." Jaw set, Keith turned back to the screen.

Keith made it a priority to support student initiatives as often as he could. Part of the MUTV mission was to give the students running the new digital cable station opportunities to recommend and even develop programming. His television motion-picture students had been the driving force behind Keith's initial idea for the Montford University television station. Unlike many college and university stations, MUTV was not an education-access station.

They were in control of their own programming.

But this particular piece...

Bodies in nude-colored body things, showing the most godawful suffering...

"I think we're going to have to give this one a miss," he said.

"No!" Martha's head spun toward him. "This is what we're all about, Keith! We *have* to do it! This is absolutely the best thing we've seen in the six months we've been here!"

"We're about positive educational experiences," he reminded her. "Our programming enriches peoples' lives in positive ways."

It didn't matter if they were showing actual college classes, university sports or a full-length feature film, the goal was the same.

"And it doesn't get any more uplifting than this," she insisted. Her brown eyes were turned to the screen again.

Keith stared at her. "It's the most depressing thing I've ever seen! Those people are dying of AIDS!"

The depictions were real—performed by people suffering from the deadly virus.

"They're alive, Keith." Martha's tone was low, but carried so much conviction Keith had to take another look at the screen.

"Think of the hours of rehearsal they put in here. Listen to the documentary. Hear the laughter. The love these people have grown to share. That's what living is all about. No matter what," she continued softly, slowly, "life isn't over until it's over."

Okay. He supposed that was true.

So how come all *he'd* seen was dying people writhing on the floor?

"You can't just watch something like this with your analytical mind, Keith. You have to see it, feel it, with your heart."

A young bald man was making motions, as though he was grooming himself, but kept getting interrupted by an imaginary sore on his hand that wouldn't stop bleeding.

"It's horrible," Keith said, wishing he had the guts to get up and leave.

"Look at the expression on his face." Martha's voice was soothing. A balm amidst the tragedy seeming to engulf the small room they used for viewing.

Keith looked.

"He's alive. That sore or whatever it is isn't stopping him. He's still doing what he set out to do. Still accomplishing things."

"Still living," Keith said slowly, relaxing slightly as his focus changed, seeing, instead of the tragedy, the determination in the performer's eyes.

And the deep-seated satisfaction as he completed his task.

"Victory," Martha said.

Her eyes were filled with tears.

Keith had the most bizarre urge to hug her.

HUGGING HERSELF, Bonnie stared at the water at her feet, remembering Mike Diamond's letter. Still, the flood seeping into her tennis shoes could easily pass for nothing more than bad luck. Toilets broke. Seals gave way. Curious children conducted flushability experiments with assorted toys and other nonbiodegradable items. The insurance form was already mentally half-written.

"I can help you." She heard Shane's thick, deep voice behind her. She hadn't noticed the slushing of his tennis shoes in the inch-deep water pouring out into the hallway.

He was carrying a mop in one hand, pulling a wringer and bucket with the other.

"The toilet exploded."

He nodded, started to mop. And then to wring.

Bonnie glanced back at the tile floor in the private teachers' bathroom. With the wallpaper and area rug, the matching curtains and towels, wastebasket and soap dispenser on the sink, the wood cabinet in which the sink sat—the one she'd saved two months to buy—the place looked like home. Or it had. That cabinet wasn't going to escape unscathed. She could already see the wood at the bottom starting to warp.

Another insurance form to fill out.

"I turned the water off," she told Shane. And that was all she'd done. Except feel relieved that her husband had picked up their daughter a couple of hours before. She hadn't even called Keith yet to tell him about this latest disaster, let alone phoned a plumber. Six o'clock on Friday night wasn't a good time to get someone in, and it wasn't as if this was a real emergency.

With one easy flick of the wrist, Shane pulled the lever to bring the rollers down over the mop and release the dirty water into the bucket beneath.

"Can you pick up that rug?" he asked, speaking slowly.

Bonnie hurried to do as he'd asked. The little rug

was heavy with water. She dropped it into the sink and then got out of Shane's way.

"Are you okay?" he asked.

"Yeah," she said, touched that in spite of his limited capabilities, he was such a good friend. "Accidents happen."

"But you just had a fire."

"Yeah, maybe someone's trying to tell me something," she said wearily, trying to smile.

"Tell you what?"

"Nothing." She shook her head and moved aside as he worked. "It's just an expression, but much more of this, and parents are going to wonder if it's safe to bring their kids here."

"And your business would be in trouble."

So why didn't that thought strike terror in her heart?

He mopped and wrung, bending down to wipe a bit of debris off the baseboard behind the toilet with a paper towel he'd pulled from his back pocket.

"I'm really sorry about this."

"It's okay, it's my job."

The simple statement brought tears to her eyes.

Bonnie didn't know what was wrong with her. She didn't seem upset about what was happening to her day care—her life's dream. And Shane Bellows's mopping made her cry.

"I'll go call a plumber," she said, and escaped to her office before she could do something else she didn't understand.

Like ask Shane to have dinner with her so she could figure out a way to help this shell of a man with whom she'd once been so in love.

Or use the flooded bathroom as an excuse to call her husband and tell him she couldn't come home.

KEITH WAS LYING on his stomach, propped up on his elbows, three-year-old Katie astride his upper back. She was leaning forward with her chin near his ear as her green eyes intently followed along in the big book of children's stories her father was reading to her.

If one could refer to Keith's dramatic rendition of each scene as simply reading.

Closing the door from the garage into the kitchen, Bonnie stood and watched the two of them, filled with so much love she ached. Keith's voice rose and fell, his head turning or nodding, his shoulders rising and falling, with Katie riding right along with him, her body responding to each change of cadence. Her little hands clutched her daddy's sweater and patted his shoulders in excitement. Her eyes grew large. She laughed. Her dark curls seemed to dance. Then, as the story grew more serious, she listened quietly again.

Keith looked up as he played the part of a frog turned into a prince and caught Bonnie standing there. The grin on his face froze; his voice died. Katie looked up then, too, her wriggling body stilling immediately as she saw her mother. And the questioning look in the little girl's big green eyes shocked Bonnie. It was as though, like her father, Katie was assessing the situation.

"Hi!" Bonnie dropped her purse and briefcase on the table. "Don't stop," she told Keith. "You were just getting to the good part."

His face softened as she joined them in the family room. "How was your day?"

She thought of the flood. Of Shane.

"Fine." She didn't want to spoil the fun Katie and Keith were having.

Keith watched her for a minute more and then, without letting her see his thoughts, turned back to the book.

The tales continued and eventually, as Bonnie relaxed and laughed along with her daughter when Keith tried to play the wolf huffing and puffing at the straw house, Katie slid down from her father's back and crawled onto her mother's lap.

As she hugged her little girl close to her heart, savoring Katie's warmth, and shifted just enough to let her toes rest against Keith's thigh, Bonnie swallowed hard.

GRANDMA NIELSON called just as they were finishing the pizza Bonnie had made for dinner. Katie had sauce smeared on her nose, rimming her pert baby mouth, over her chin and on her chest. Bonnie couldn't see Katie's booster chair under the table, but there was probably sauce mixed in with a pile of crumbs on her lap, as well.

"She just got back from Phoenix," Keith said, hanging up the phone.

"At eight o'clock? She drove home in the dark?"

Her husband frowned. And nodded. While he accepted his grandmother's right to live her life the way she wanted to—encouraged it even—her health and well-being had become a constant worry to him.

"How's Dorothy?" Bonnie asked, getting a damp cloth to wipe Katie's cheeks.

"She doesn't need a hip replacement." Keith didn't look too happy.

"That's good news."

It was testimony to the changes in their little family when, without a fuss, Katie lifted her face and only blinked when Bonnie wiped her clean.

"She'll be home next week."

Bonnie set Katie on the floor before tending to the mess on the booster chair and table. "Wow," she said to her husband, never missing a beat in their conversation. "That's a fast recovery, isn't it? She'll be able to get around that soon?"

"No."

Cloth in hand, Bonnie stopped. "No?"

"The doctor suggested long-term care. Grandma's determined to bring her home."

"Who's going to…" Bonnie didn't need to finish the question. She knew the answer. Lonna Nielson was.

"She says she's sure she can get people to come in shifts—at least for meals."

And who would do the rest? Bonnie's heart lurched when she thought of her adored grandmother-in-law doing any lifting or carrying while her old friend recovered. Hips could take months to heal.

"Is she coming over?" she asked Keith, satisfied that Katie was safely ensconced in front of her favorite animated video before she started the dishes.

Grandma usually joined them for a game of canasta on Friday nights. Maybe she could talk to her.

"She says she has paperwork to do."

"You going to get her?"

"Of course."

Bonnie grinned, her troubled heart filled with warmth as she heard her husband's exasperated tone. It was always the same.

When Keith started college, his parents left Shelter Valley on a church service mission in Cairo. His father was Grandma's only child. Consumed by their jobs as house parents at an orphanage there, they'd returned to Shelter Valley just once in fifteen years. Their deaths in a bus accident shortly after Katie was born had left Grandma and Keith as the only surviving members of their family. But no matter how lonely Grandma might feel, or how much she might want to be with the kids, she always made excuses. When Bonnie and Keith got married more than six years before, Grandma had determined that she would not interfere with their lives. Which was why her car was never seen in her grandson's driveway. Whether for Sunday dinner, Friday-night canasta, holidays or anything in between, Keith more often than not had to go and get her or she wouldn't come.

Wet hands in the sink, Bonnie looked over her shoulder, her eyes meeting his.

"You're a good man, Keith Nielson." The whispered words came from her very depths.

Almost as if they drew him, Keith moved toward her, then bent to press his lips to hers. The wealth of love she'd been feeling since she'd walked in the door that evening just continued, fueling the kiss. God, she loved this man. Wanted him.

There was never any doubt about that.

"Gotta go," Keith muttered, obviously reluctant.

He kissed her again, raising a longing in Bonnie that could easily have consumed her. A longing for life to be only this. A sure knowledge of what was.

He pulled back slowly, his eyes searching hers.

"I'll, uh, make brownies for when you get back." She stumbled over the words.

They were the right ones. Keith's face softened, the question in his eyes fading as he nodded, grabbed his keys and strode out the door.

Making brownies. Kind of a code.

It had all started that first time she'd made brownies after they were married. They'd been in the kitchen of the little house they'd rented on the back of the Weber property. The Webers were the owners of Shelter Valley's only department store, and their son, Jim, had graduated from high school a couple of years behind Bonnie.

It hadn't been after dinner then, but fairly late on a Sunday morning. She and Keith had missed church because they'd been unable to keep their hands off each other long enough to get out of bed. But they couldn't miss the lunch Grandma had invited them to share with her, and Bonnie had promised to bring brownies.

She'd started the project fully dressed in a completely respectable, unsexy pair of sweats and a T-shirt. She'd even had a bra and panties on underneath.

And then Keith had announced that for every ingredient she added to the brownies, she had to take something off.

She'd been using a mix and had ended up naked when all the ingredients were in the bowl.

The batter had been delicious.

They'd had to stop and buy brownies at the grocery store on their way to Grandma's.

Pretty much ever since, whenever she made brownies, they also made love.

Bonnie finished the dishes, a smile on her face.

CHAPTER FOUR

GRANDMA DISCARDED the two of diamonds. And she had no meld. When she'd picked up a couple of fours and then discarded a four, Bonnie had wondered—in canasta you could never have too many of whatever you were saving. But to discard a wild card without a meld...

"You want to skip the rest of the game and go straight to the brownies?" Keith asked her.

"I can finish."

"But do you want to?" Bonnie pushed. Though she'd obviously freshened her makeup, Grandma still looked exhausted. Her slacks and blouse were wrinkled, her shoulders slumped, and her gaze not as open and clear as usual.

"Yes, I want to." But she obviously didn't.

Sending her concerned husband a reassuring smile, Bonnie packed up the cards and cut the brownies. Grandma asked about Katie, who'd been going to bed when she'd arrived, asked if Bonnie had seen Becca Parsons that day and if Becca had said anything about a long-range planning committee meeting the next morning. She asked about Keith's work.

And she avoided Keith's attempts to tell her to

slow down. When they asked about Dorothy, her answers were brief and seemingly carefree.

After two brownies, Grandma was ready to go home.

Keith rose to get his keys.

"Why don't you stay and finish up in here," she told her grandson, waving toward the dessert plates and napkins, half-empty milk glasses and score card still on the table. "Bonnie can take me home."

Exchanging one more silent look with her husband, Bonnie followed the older woman out the garage door to her van.

"YOU'VE GOT TO TELL that grandson of mine to let up on me."

Bonnie hadn't even backed out of the garage before Grandma spoke.

Easing the van into the quiet street, she flipped on her headlights and put it in drive. "He just cares about you, Grandma."

"I know that. I care about him, too. Far more than he'll probably ever know. Which is why it's so hard to keep fighting him. I have enough to do without expending energy fighting with him." Bonnie was amazed at how the older woman could take a much-repeated grumble and speak it with such convincing authority.

"He won't listen to me on this one." Bonnie said the same thing she always did.

"I mean it, Bonnie. I need his support right now."

Turning a corner, Bonnie slowed and glanced at Grandma, a knot in her stomach. "What's up?" she asked.

"I will not turn my back on my friends."

"I know that."

"I'm seventy-six years old, not dead."

"I know that, too."

"But *do* you?" Grandma asked. Bonnie had pulled into Grandma's drive, but the old woman made no move to get out of the car. She stared at Bonnie through the semidarkness, her eyes faded and watery. "Do you have any idea how it feels to have lived a full, productive life and then to discover that because you've had one too many birthdays, everyone suddenly thinks you no longer have anything significant to offer?"

Grandma's words, though softly spoken, reverberated through the van, knocking the breath out of Bonnie.

"I think I do," she whispered. She didn't know which was worse—thinking that you were giving nothing significant, or having others think you were incapable of giving.

She wasn't sure it even mattered.

"I'll talk to him."

She watched Grandma to her door with a new understanding, one that effected a change she wasn't sure she fully grasped. Grandma wasn't the only person who got older. There was an entire community of elderly citizens in Shelter Valley.

She wondered how many of them were fighting the same frustrations she'd been fighting these past months. The need to be needed. Or to make a difference in a world that cried out for help.

And wondered if there were answers for any of them.

KEITH WAS WAITING for her when she got home. Only the small light over the kitchen sink was glowing. Pachelbel's "Canon in D" played on the stereo behind her.

Bonnie smiled.

He walked toward her, unbuttoning his shirt. His longish blond hair was mussed.

"Got Grandma home safe and sound?"

She nodded. That short car ride had left her with too much to think about. And no conclusions other than a determination to somehow talk Keith into letting Grandma do what she had to do, even if it killed her.

Later.

Forcing thoughts of the disturbing conversation from her mind, Bonnie focused on the lithe male body slowly approaching.

As always, a rush of delicious anticipation leaped in Bonnie's abdomen. This man had the power to change her in some elemental way. And if, tonight, there was a bit of desperation in her eagerness for him, it wasn't something she was going to dwell on.

She unbuttoned her blouse, as well, exposing the teddy she'd slipped on when he'd gone to get Grandma.

"Oh, God, Bon, you're so beautiful it hurts."

She ran her fingers up his chest, his throat and into his hair, every nerve in her hands heightened so that she felt each silky strand slide between her knuckles and fall across her skin.

"Kiss me," she begged, standing on tiptoe to reach for his mouth as she pulled his head down to hers.

He did. Again and again. His hunger was insatiable. His taste excitingly familiar. *Hers.* Bonnie groaned. There were so many feelings pulsating between them, so much to say.

Love into eternity. Trust and an honest desire—stronger than self—to provide happiness. Forever.

Keith had always aroused her. But tonight, as he loved her urgently, his body was perfect, in tune with every physical sensation she had. And his spirit was there, too, communicating without using the words she was so afraid to speak.

Words were too messy. Left too many things unsaid, or said wrong. But this—this all-consuming absorption in each other—was more vital than any conscious thought.

By the third time they made love, they were stretched out on the family-room carpet on a quilt pulled from the back of the couch. Keith had turned on the gas fire and flames danced lazily in the fireplace in front of them. This time their loving was traditional, slow, soothing raw places deep inside Bonnie's heart.

Bonnie savored the love she knew she was so lucky to have.

''You've brought me to my knees, woman,'' he grumbled beside her on the carpet. ''I love you so damn much.''

''I love you, too.''

He rolled to his side, head propped on one hand. ''Thank you.''

His words startled her. She was the one who should be expressing gratitude.

''For what?''

"Tonight."

She kissed Keith gently, wishing she wasn't too exhausted to make love again. She didn't want this feeling to end.

And knew that it would.

Her stomach tightened. She'd be kidding herself if she thought her dissatisfaction with life would just disappear when she woke up in the morning.

Settling down onto the quilt, she pushed herself up against Keith so that his hips were cradling her bottom, his arms around her.

"You know, that first time in the kitchen tonight, while I wasn't thinking about anything but getting inside you, it still hit me hard that you didn't insist on using protection. I had this huge urge to laugh out loud."

He paused and Bonnie lay frozen, willing him not to think what she knew he was thinking. "Of course, other urges were much stronger than laughter...."

She chuckled with him and felt no laughter at all.

"I know it took a while for us to get pregnant with Katie," Keith continued, his voice sleepy, content, happier than she'd heard him in far too long. "I'm not expecting anything to come of tonight. I'm just glad we're getting started."

Bonnie moved her head. It could have been a nod. Or a protest. She wanted so badly to want what Keith wanted, what they'd always wanted together.

A family. This house. This life.

Tied up in knots, she lay there beside him. Did she tell him she hadn't stopped an incredibly spontaneous moment because she hadn't had to? That it was a safe time for her?

The admission would hurt him, ruin the best evening they'd had in months. And for what?

She wasn't sure she *wasn't* going to have another child. And didn't want him to think she didn't want one. Because maybe she did. She loved being a mother. And a wife. She just had to figure out what she needed to do for Bonnie, the woman, before she committed herself any further.

Or figure out how to convince that woman to feel completely fulfilled with the life she had.

But how did she tell her husband that? How could she look into those gorgeous blue eyes and tell this man that the life he loved, the one they'd built together, wasn't enough for her?

They could lose everything. And for what?

So maybe they wouldn't use protection the next time they made love. Or the time after that.

Rolling over, she studied Keith's familiar features. Those eyes, half-closed, slumbrous and sexy, the jaw with the familiar dark shadow, a mouth that wasn't quite grinning but somehow expressing complete satisfaction. She loved him so much.

And couldn't hurt him anymore.

"I SAW THIS FILM in the studio today."

Keith and Bonnie were sitting up, wrapped in the quilt. Reflection from the flames swayed across Bonnie's skin, clothing her in a mysterious beauty. It was after midnight and they both had to work early, but Keith had absolutely no desire to go to bed.

"Previewing?" she asked, glancing sideways at him.

He nodded. It wasn't often a film stayed with him, coming to mind again and again, as this one had.

Keith wasn't sure if it was the film itself or Martha's reaction to it that was nagging at him. While he appreciated what the dancers and the filmmaker were saying, he still didn't think it fit their programming mission.

"It's bothering you?" Bonnie asked, understanding, even though he'd said nothing.

He nodded a second time, his gaze moving from her face to the fire.

He told her about the suffering he'd seen. The death and hopelessness that pervaded the film. "It was too much."

"The movie showed them dying?" Bonnie asked.

"No." And then, "They were dancing."

"Dancing." He could feel her looking at him. "Even at the end? They were dancing?"

"Yeah, but you had to see it, Bon. These guys were like shells of men, their bodies so thin you wondered how they had the strength to move."

"But obviously they did have the strength, or they wouldn't have been able to dance."

She'd know about that, having been a dancer for years before she'd stopped to study early-childhood education.

"Yeah." Elbows on his knees, Keith stared down a particular feisty flame.

"I think that's inspiring. Like they weren't going to quit until it was over."

"So you think it would be okay to broadcast?"

"Of course!"

Keith turned his head to see Bonnie frowning at him. "Don't you?" she asked.

He shrugged. "Yeah, I guess." More so now.

"What did Martha have to say about it?"

"Pretty much the same thing you did."

"I'm not surprised. We think a lot alike."

Keith nodded.

He'd noticed that, too.

SHANE BELLOWS'S HEART sped up as he walked down the deserted hallway in Little Spirits. A light was still on in the playroom. That meant Bonnie was there.

According to the note he'd left on his mirror last night, she'd mentioned that she planned to move the reading corner to the other side of the room today.

He could help.

He could talk to her.

"Hi," he said, trying to force his voice to respond to the commands he was giving it—trying to sound the way he had when he'd spoken to her during high school.

She'd wanted him then.

Facing a ceiling-high shelf, her arms full of the books she was pulling down, Bonnie turned to look at him over one shoulder.

"Hi, Shane." Her easy grin settled so much of the uncertainty that was constantly there inside him.

He wanted to grin back, but was afraid his mouth would get that crooked hitch that came and went for no reason he could figure out. He didn't want her to see that stupid look. Not ever.

"I can help," he said, keeping his words to a

minimum, as he always did around her. He hated the way his speech slowed and slurred. He'd never get used to that.

"You don't have to," she said. "You've been working all day."

"So have you."

She'd let him stay. She always did. And she always talked to him. Bonnie was the only person in his hometown who still treated him like a man.

She didn't smother him with the pity that stripped him of what little pride he had left.

He removed some books from the shelves, taking care to keep his movements slow so he could control them. Bumbling around in front of Bonnie was humiliating.

"It's not quitting time for you yet, is it? You've still got your own work to do," she said, her brows knitting together as she watched him.

"I got it done." So that he'd have this time with her. He'd come in early, rearranged the order of a couple of jobs to be more efficient. He'd figured that out on his own and was really proud of himself that it had worked.

He might be an idiot now, but he could still plan things if he concentrated really hard.

And left himself notes. He'd written at least ten of them since yesterday afternoon, reminding himself about today's events.

The doctor who'd told him about his neck injury, about the severing of receptors that used to allow him to process his thoughts in logical order, had suggested the notes.

Shane continued to remove books and pile them

in the box she was filling, glad that most of the jobs Bonnie did after the day care closed were easy. There wasn't a lot of figuring out to do about moving shelves. Mostly what Bonnie needed when she was here alone was muscle, and that was something he had plenty of. And she didn't.

He had something of value to offer her.

Feeling happy, Shane stepped up to the shelf a little faster, grabbing more books than he had the first time. And stumbled.

Hot with embarrassment, he froze. *Why didn't I die on that ski slope?*

He just couldn't get used to this big, unwieldy frame he carried around. He kept forgetting how long it took for his body to do the things he told it to.

Remembering details was confusing.

"I had the strangest urge to drive to Phoenix today," Bonnie said, her back to him as she continued to collect books as if she didn't care at all that he was a bumbling idiot.

"Why? Did you need to buy something?" His voice faltered; he was upset now. They'd told him at the hospital that when he got this way, he just had to calm down and the feeling would leave.

It was hard, sometimes, to be calm around Bonnie. Even though he felt better around her than anywhere else.

"No, I wasn't thinking about shopping," she said. "Though I should make a trip to my favorite linen shop to replace the throw rugs that got ruined in the flood last Friday. I can't believe it's been a week already."

He nodded. He was sorry her rugs had been ruined.

He'd cleared the top shelves of both cases. Bonnie had finished all the lower shelves. She was doing the videos now.

And the job was going really fast. Shane would rather it went slowly.

"There wasn't anything in Phoenix I wanted," Bonnie said. Shane frowned, confused for the minute it took him to remember that she'd been talking about wanting to drive to the city.

"Then why go?"

"That's just it," she said with a little laugh that didn't sound amused. "I have no idea. I think because there's a freeway to L.A. there."

Shane's heart started to pound. "You're going to L.A.?"

"Noooo. No, I'm not."

His shelves were empty, but hers weren't. So Shane started gathering videos, hating that his hands were shaking and worrying she'd notice.

"I'm not going anywhere."

Okay. Because he wanted her to be happy in Shelter Valley.

"It's just weird, you know?" she asked. They were both bending toward the same shelf and she turned her head and looked at him.

Shane felt as if he'd just dived into a swimming pool. Shocked. Invigorated. And feeling like he wanted to get out and do it all over again.

"I just keep thinking about the people there who need me. The jobs I want to do."

"In Chicago I was the boss and the work was

good.'' Kneeling, Shane frowned, concentrating so he could connect all the pieces of the thought he was trying to express. ''But I had to go ski.''

''You had what you wanted, but you still felt the need to escape.''

Wiping the sweat off his upper lip, Shane neatly stacked a row of videos in a box in the same order they'd been on the shelf. ''Yes,'' he said.

''Why?''

''I don't know.''

''Do you think maybe you didn't really love what you were doing?''

''I don't know.''

Kneeling beside him, Bonnie watched as he finished the last shelf. She was rubbing her hands up and down her legs.

Without warning he was in high school again. She had on a short skirt and he wanted to touch her legs.

''Little Spirits has been my dream since I *was* a little spirit,'' she said.

Confused, Shane looked at her. Her eyes were big and green and gave him that feeling in his gut he couldn't do anything about. ''I love these kids so much,'' she said in a quiet voice.

''The kids love you, too, Bonnie,'' he said, his conviction so strong that the words came out faster than usual. He was always surprised when he heard himself sound like the man who'd once run a successful business.

''I know,'' Bonnie said, still kneeling there beside him. She was so beautiful Shane's midsection started to hurt. ''Is it selfish of me to want to do more with my life than be here with them?''

He panicked when she waited for him to answer. His mind went blank.

"I wish I didn't feel this…this drive," she said.

If she cried, he was going to have to put his arms around her. And he was pretty sure that was something he couldn't let himself do.

"I'm scared I might lose everything that means the most to me."

And suddenly Shane knew what he could say. "I get scared, too, Bonnie." The words were slow, but he had a complete awareness of the importance of this thought. "Since I came back to Shelter Valley," he felt compelled to add. "Because, you see, I'm not the boss anymore."

"Of the business in Chicago?" Last she'd heard, he'd been in top management at a large financial firm.

"No." He shook his head and stood up to carry a couple of the boxes they'd filled across the room. "I'm not the boss of me."

Which reminded him of something. He just couldn't remember what. He'd heard something that day, something he needed to tell Bonnie. He made a couple of trips with boxes and tried until he was sweating to remember what he'd heard.

Back and forth across the room and he couldn't focus. Too many thoughts vying for limited capacity. His mind went blank again. Blank and helpless.

Just like Shane.

CHAPTER FIVE

"HEY!" KEITH SAID, looking up from the table in surprise when Bonnie walked in half an hour later. "I didn't expect you so soon." He was eating store-bought pudding from a plastic cup—and supervising Katie while she had some of her own.

"Packing the books went much faster than I expected," Bonnie said, giving Katie a noisy kiss on the cheek, one that made the little girl laugh with a mouth full of butterscotch.

Bonnie savored the sight, the sound.

"As a matter of fact," she continued, dropping her things on the counter and pulling out a chair to join her family while they finished the snack that would tide them over until dinner. She'd suggested it earlier when Keith came to the day care to get Katie.

"As a matter of fact," she said again, "we don't need to go back tonight to move the reading center. Shane brought in his dolly and the whole thing's done, shelves and all."

Cup tilted in one hand while he reached his spoon in with the other, Keith said, "He sure seems to be spending a lot of time at Little Spirits."

"I'm sure he spends equal time everywhere on the property." She took the bite of pudding Katie offered, smacking her lips as she swallowed. "It's not like he has a life to go home to," she added. "He lives alone, except for the housekeeper who takes care of things for him. But I don't even think she shares his meals. Just prepares them and leaves him there to eat by himself."

Katie started to sing a song from her current favorite video—the fifth in the *Baby Shakespeare* series. Bonnie smiled her encouragement, bobbing her head to the beat.

"It's good that he can live alone," Keith said over the noise. He stood, tossing his pudding container in the trash and then throwing out Katie's. "I just think you should be careful. With you spending all that time with him, he could get the wrong idea."

Bonnie jumped up to grab a cloth and wipe pudding off the little girl's face and curls before setting her loose on her toys in the family room.

"Don't be silly, Keith. Shane can't even remember half our conversations ten minutes later. I don't think he'd remember an idea if he had one."

"His mind was injured, Bonnie, not his emotions or his desires." Keith was at the sink with her, dropping spoons in the dishwasher as she rinsed the cloth she'd used on Katie.

"Don't worry, Keith," Bonnie said, trying not to feel defensive. "I'd know if Shane was getting any ideas."

She couldn't let Keith get in the way of her relationship with Shane. He was alone and he needed her.

But neither did she want to fight with her husband.

Raising her face, she invited his kiss, opening her mouth to deepen the caress.

Sex wasn't an answer.

But it helped.

NOT QUITE THE EVENING he had planned, but as Keith sat with Bonnie at Rustler's Roost Saturday night, he was optimistic.

Bonnie had been tired last night after moving the reading center. That was on top of a busy week at the day care, parent-teacher conferences and a visit with her accountant in preparation for filing taxes.

And she'd been visiting some of Grandma's friends, lightening Grandma's load where she could.

Even Bonnie's need to jog the night before, right after Katie's bath, had been easy to understand. She'd missed a couple of times earlier in the week due to the meetings with her accountant, and that regular exercise had become vital to his wife's mental and emotional equilibrium.

And he'd known they had tonight. Greg and Beth were keeping Katie—much to Ryan and Katie's delight—and Keith had made plans to surprise his wife with a picnic in the desert, something they hadn't done since before Katie was born.

She'd surprised him, instead, with dinner at Rustler's Roost in Phoenix, a meal made all the more delicious by the fact that dinner came with a room for the night at the resort where the famous restaurant was located.

"More wine?" he asked, lifting the bottle over the glass she held.

"Yes, please." The black dress she was wearing,

one he'd never seen before, added to the night's fantasy. Demure with its high neck and long sleeves, the figure-hugging dress outlined in tantalizing detail a figure that couldn't have been more perfect and when Bonnie stood, sported a slit all the way up her thigh.

He felt grossly underdressed in his black Dockers and white oxford shirt with the sleeves rolled up to his elbows. He poured the wine.

It was her second glass, and they'd just finished their salad course.

He hoped the cooks were particularly efficient that night, as he wasn't sure how long he'd be able to stand sharing his wife with a room full of people.

"Cassie called," Bonnie said.

"Cassie Montford? When did she call?" Keith wasn't sure he cared at the moment—in fact, he was sure he didn't—but he applauded Bonnie's attempt to turn down the steam long enough for them to get through dinner.

"This afternoon while I was at Little Spirits. She's finally ready to put Brian in day care."

"Getting a bit difficult to keep up with him at the clinic now that he's walking, eh?" Keith asked.

Taking a sip of her wine, Bonnie chuckled, infectious mirth in her eyes. "Apparently he decided that taking the temperature of one of the clinic cats was more interesting than the video Cassie thought he was watching."

"Ouch!" Keith's guffaw of laughter earned him curious glances from several of the other patrons.

"Yeah, well, as it turned out he'd only been missing for about sixty seconds before Cassie noticed, so he didn't have time to do more than formulate the plan.''

"Lucky cat.''

Bonnie shrugged. ''He's fourteen months old. He should start interacting with other kids.''

Keith grinned at the woman he'd adored since he'd first set eyes on her. Mother to all. Sex goddess to him. ''And you've been dying to get him into your clutches,'' he teased.

''I…'' Bonnie started to protest and then smiled. ''You're right. Bethany and Katie are in the same class, and it's so great to see them growing up together. Tori's little Phyllis and Randi and Zack's son are both in the one-year-old class, which is where Brian belongs. I'd like him to be a part of things from the very beginning.''

''I doubt he'll remember, hon.''

''It makes a difference, Keith, whether he has specific memories or not. You know that. Part of Shelter Valley's magic is that those of us who grew up here have been part of each other's lives since the day we were born. That's how we've all become a family. We stick together through whatever crisis life might bring us.''

He did know that. He'd been born and raised in Shelter Valley, too, just a few years ahead of Bonnie. But it was damn good to hear Bonnie standing up so adamantly for the town they both loved.

''Like when Beth was in trouble last year…''

''Yeah.'' Bonnie's voice grew soft. ''I'll love the people of Shelter Valley forever because of what they did for Greg, risking their own lives to save

Beth's, even knowing that she was wanted by the law.''

The relief her words instilled was somehow more potent than the wine he was drinking.

They came straight from the heart of the woman he'd fallen in love with.

He hadn't realized how afraid he'd become that Bonnie wasn't happy in Shelter Valley.

Two waiters arrived with their steaks, more bread and another bottle of wine. The meat was succulent, decadent, teasing senses that were already heightened beyond anything Keith had experienced in years.

"Remember John Strickland?'' Bonnie asked as she raised her fork and poked a chunk of meat between lips he couldn't wait to kiss.

Only because Martha had mentioned him. Keith's program director had dated the architect for a while, shortly after her husband left.

"Will Parsons's friend, right?''

"Yeah,'' Bonnie nodded. "Cassie told me today that he and Lauren Randall are getting married.''

"No kidding!'' Keith was happy for the Montford women's softball coach. He'd worked with Lauren a few times, filming games, and liked her a lot. He also wondered if Martha knew. And what the news had done to his friend, who continually found herself alone.

"So you got the reading corner the way you want it?'' Keith asked as the waiter cleared away their half-empty plates.

Bonnie didn't usually work on Saturdays but had gone in that day just to take in some rugs and rearrange the books Shane Bellows had put on shelves the night before.

She nodded. "Everything's ready to go."

"Was Shane there?" he couldn't help asking. The guy bothered him.

And he wasn't the jealous sort.

"No." She sipped her wine. "And I'm telling you, Keith, you're worrying over nothing. You don't know Shane. He's just struggling to cope with day-to-day living. There's no way he'd be thinking about trying anything with me."

He didn't want to argue with her. Especially not tonight.

And maybe she was right. Bonnie was a good judge of people.

And he was, admittedly, a little oversensitive where she was concerned.

He tried to let months of tension slide from his shoulders as he walked with his lover through the beautiful grounds of the South Mountain resort to their condo-style room.

"You want to take a dip in the Jacuzzi?" Bonnie asked as, with a not quite steady hand, he slid the card key into its slot and pulled it back out.

He would if she really wanted to, but...

"This time of night, there might be kids using it," he ventured.

"Uh-uh." Bonnie shook her head. "I guarantee not."

They entered their unit. "You have your suit?" He made a last-ditch effort to keep her there. Could he hope that she'd forgotten to pack it?

"Uh-uh," she said again, turning her back as she

slipped off her dress. She glanced at him over her shoulder. "You don't want to join me?"

Keith's throat was dry. He looked in the duffel she'd pulled from the trunk of the car when they'd arrived at the hotel just before their dinner reservation that evening. They'd barely had time to drop the bag in their room before heading out to Rustler's Roost.

"I don't see my suit," he said, trying not to sound too happy about that.

"That's because it's not there."

Bonnie turned, wearing only a black thong and the new high heels she'd bought to go with the dress she'd worn to dinner.

His eyes met hers and his fingers moved to the buttons on his shirt, slowly undoing them.

He knew Bonnie couldn't possibly expect them to traipse naked out to the hot tub in the enclosure they'd passed just a few steps from their room. Still, he was intrigued enough to play along.

Her gaze still holding his, she slipped off the panties.

Keith was only minimally disappointed that he didn't get to do that himself. There was nothing demure about those green eyes now.

"Come on," she said. Still wearing her heels, she moved to the sliding glass door in the back of their room.

Losing his pants on the way out, briefs and all, Keith followed her.

And found himself standing beside a bubbling tub on the patio of their suite. The night air was cool, the dark sky filled with a million twinkling stars, and

Bonnie was naked, stepping down into their own private hot tub.

She'd gone to one hell of a lot of trouble.

Dared he hope this was a new beginning for them?

"Coming in?" she asked, her voice as sultry as the look in her eye.

Keith hadn't needed the first invitation, let alone a second; he just needed time to absorb every detail of the moment. He had an idea that once he joined her in the sensuous bubbles, everything except Bonnie was going to escape him.

If the past months had been hell, this night was heaven.

LONNA LET HERSELF IN, and without even bothering to turn on the light, made her way through the darkened house to the bedroom she'd been using for more decades than she could remember. She barely got out of her clothes before she fell onto the comforter. She knew she should eat—and she would. It wasn't sensible to skip meals at any age, and certainly not when she was having to make do with a seventy-six-year-old body.

So she'd eat. Right after she took a nap.

Despite her willing, weary bones, her mind didn't cooperate as readily as she'd decided it should. Instead of finding the respite she needed as her eyes drifted shut, she saw images of the day, of the past several days and weeks and months, playing themselves out in her mind. She couldn't stop herself from thinking about the next days and weeks and months, either. There was so much to do.

Breakfast for Grace. Dorothy's care schedule—

creating and managing it, as well as fulfilling her own duties on it. The library board. City council meetings to attend to make sure the voices of the people were heard above the ruckus of the Smith family—Shelter Valley's well-to-do mayoral family, who served more as a tradition than because they had anything of value to contribute to the town's governance. Then there was the welfare assignment at church and Shelter Valley's long-range-planning committee. And today, a day she'd been planning to spend at least partially at home to get caught up on her computer work, she'd had a cancellation on Dorothy's bath and evening meal and had to fill in herself.

Lonna didn't pay much attention to the tightness in her belly as pictures continued to appear in her mind, moving from one to the next in quick succession. She wasn't one to worry much about her health. She was just tired.

But determined. And with enough strength to move mountains. As soon as she had a rest. And then a meal.

The tightness moved to her chest, and as it slowly dissipated, she finally relaxed enough to sleep.

BONNIE HAD a pretty good understanding of the divine plan for sexual intimacy. Besides procreation, of course. It was a bond that two people shared only with each other, something that drew them closer. A way to communicate more deeply than words.

A way of gluing together a relationship that might be straining in other areas.

Like a hero from a historical romance novel, Keith

gave her no mercy in the Jacuzzi that night. There was more talk. Kisses that would have been pornographic had they not been alone. Touching and teasing that was driving them both wild.

Wild enough to forget where their passion might lead? This wasn't a safe time for her. She'd known that when she'd planned this night of healing.

And she'd been praying all day that she'd have the faith to be with her husband and accept whatever consequences might result. She adored children.

She wanted this marriage.

Falling back against her husband's chest, helpless, she gave herself up completely to the water—to him.

When she was trembling and weak with need, he turned her around on his lap, positioning her.

The wave of tremors that had begun low in her abdomen disappeared. Instantly. Without warning.

Replaced by panic. If she got pregnant, her choices would be even more limited!

The woman who needed to be more than she was went into survival mode.

It was all she could think about. All that motivated her.

"Wait!" she cried in a voice she could neither stop nor control. Fumbling, she reached for the shoe she'd removed at the edge of the pool, dug her fingers into the toe, and when she came up empty, reached frantically for the other shoe.

Only when her fingers encountered the small packet she'd placed there—just in case—did she calm down enough to realize where she was and what she was doing.

But it was too late to stop. To remember.

"You want me to wear a condom." Keith's voice was colder than she'd ever heard it.

She couldn't look at him. Holding it out to him she said, "Please."

Without another word he took the packet. She heard it rip. Felt movement in the water as he sheathed himself, and then, with her knees on the seat of the tub, her weight braced on the tub's edge, she helped him as he gently entered her.

He was behind her where she couldn't see him, his hands on her hips, so, other than at her midsection, she was separate from him. He didn't say a word. With the water bubbling around them, she couldn't even hear him breathe.

It didn't take long. It couldn't, after all the hours of buildup she'd subjected him to. When he was done, Keith quietly left the tub, and her, and went in to take a shower.

CHAPTER SIX

BONNIE STOOD in the shower alone, water sluicing over her sensitized body. The suite had a bathroom as big as her bedroom back home. Too big for one person. But as lonely as she felt there, she wasn't in a hurry to get out.

She'd long since soaped, shaved, washed hair that wasn't dirty, let the warm water flow over muscles that had already been massaged in the Jacuzzi, and still she stood there.

Were they going to stay the night?

Was he even out there waiting for her? He wouldn't have left her stranded, but he could've called a cab or walked somewhere or...

"Bonnie?"

He was right outside the shower curtain.

"Yes?"

"Greg just called." His voice was soft, serious, full of bad news.

Oh, God. Tearing open the shower curtain, she stared at her fully dressed husband, her fingers dripping water all over his leather shoes as she clutched his arm. "What happened? Katie?"

He shook his head. "It's not Katie."

Thank God. Thank you, God. Bonnie grabbed a

towel, did a haphazard job of drying off. "Is it Ryan?" she asked. "Or Beth?"

Keith shook his head. "No one's hurt, Bon. It's Little Spirits. There's been another fire...."

SHERIFF GREG RICHARDS stared at the smoking embers, wrestling with a mixture of anger and perplexity. And fear. While the fire hadn't been as easily contained as the first one and the damage was more extensive, the craft room in which it had burned was far enough away from the rest of the day care to allow for business as usual on Monday.

The fire appeared to have been started by a toy rocket with a lit fuse, sent through the window. There just wasn't enough of it left to know for sure. Fire Chief Martin had made those assumptions from the break in the glass and the pieces he'd been able to put together.

"Makes that first fire look like more than the prank we assumed," Greg said, moving out of the way as a couple of volunteer firemen pulled hose through the room and out the window through which they'd entered.

"Or one hell of a coincidence," the fire chief said, his face dark with a day's worth of stubble and dirty sweat. "And you know how much I believe in coincidence."

About as much as Greg. In other words, not at all.

Greg took one last walk around the burned-out room, hoping to uncover some relevant information.

Had the first fire been more than a prank?

Who would do this to his sister? Bonnie was the sweetest, most giving person imaginable. She'd been serving the people of Shelter Valley her entire life, loving their children as her own. Why would someone want to hurt her?

After a quick goodbye to the Kachina County fire chief, who was supervising his men as they partitioned off the room with yellow caution tape, he headed out to his cruiser. Bonnie and Keith should be back soon. He was meeting them at their house.

What a fool he'd been to blithely shrug off that first fire as random teenage vandalism. He'd tried to find the culprits of course, but hadn't really expected to. Every generation of Shelter Valley boys pulled pranks. Came with the territory: the limitations of small-town life; the need for testing limits—and for creating a bit of the excitement that didn't happen naturally in a place like Shelter Valley.

But twice in one place wasn't random. And the ante had been upped. From supply closet to classroom. He didn't even want to consider what could be next. This time he was going to get answers.

HE'D HAD A COUPLE of hours to calm down. Maybe the crisis helped, but Keith was no longer seething with hurt and frustration by the time he and Bonnie were sitting with Greg at their kitchen table late Saturday night.

Or maybe it was the coffee Bonnie had made for them. After the wine and the hot tub, caffeine was in order. And his wife made great coffee, using just the right quantity of beans, freshly ground, and adding a pinch of cocoa.

"Think, Bon," Greg was saying, his forearms on the table as he leaned toward his sister. Since he'd been called from an evening at home, Greg was wearing jeans and a flannel shirt, instead of a uniform, but his stature was no less imposing. "There's got to be *something*. Some parent who thought his kid got a bum rap. Even a kid on a waiting list who inadvertently got overlooked?"

Bonnie shook her head, her riot of curls the only lively thing about her. She could've been made from cardboard, sitting there so calmly. "There is no waiting list. I find room."

"How about someone who tried to pick up a kid without authorization?"

"In Shelter Valley?"

"It could happen."

"I have no idea who did this, Greg."

Nor did she seem driven to find out. It wasn't like her.

"So what aren't you telling me?"

Keith watched brother and sister, envying them their easy closeness that was apparent even while they were at odds. How had he and Bonnie lost that?

"I'm telling you everything I know."

"I know what you're telling me," Greg persisted, his lips tight. "What I need to know is what you *aren't* saying." He spoke like someone who wasn't going to settle for less.

They'd come through a lot together, Greg and Bonnie—the death of their mother, their father's carjacking, brain damage and ultimate death, Greg's love for a woman who turned out to be a fugitive.

"It has nothing to do with the fires."

The cloud of doom that had been hovering over

Keith for months descended without warning. "What is it, Bon?" he had to ask.

Green eyes unusually evasive, she looked quickly from one man to the other. "Mike Diamond wants me to relocate."

Greg sat up. "Since when?"

"About a month."

"Before the first fire."

"Mike Diamond is a responsible businessman. I'm sure he doesn't go around tossing books of matches and toy rockets."

"Why does he want you to move?" Keith asked, when what he wanted to demand was why she hadn't told him. A whole month and she hadn't said a word!

His attempt at understanding and support was vying with an anger that was relatively new to him.

"He has a buyer for the strip, but it's a developer who has an anti-day-care clause. He says they're disruptive to other tenants and force him to rent to less-desirable people."

Greg turned to Keith. "You didn't know about this, either?"

Keith forced a brief shake of the head.

Greg frowned, facing his sister. "Why didn't you say something?"

She shrugged and Keith's anger escalated. How could she be so nonchalant about something so serious? Why hadn't she mentioned such a critical issue, discussed it with him? Six months ago she would have.

"Because I don't know what I'm going to do."

''Since when do you make all your decisions alone?'' The words exploded from Keith.

With eyes that pleaded, and apologized, she looked at him. ''I don't,'' she said softly. She glanced quickly at Greg and back, then continued, ''I'd fully planned to speak with you before I did anything. I was just taking some time to think about my career plan, to reassess.''

''Think about it how? You've done exactly what you set out to do.''

He wished they were alone.

''Thinking about the big picture.''

''In terms of relocating?'' Why did everything she say these days seem like a threat to him?

She shook her head. ''I'm not moving.''

''Then you've made a decision.'' Without him.

''I guess.''

Damn her.

''YOU SHOULD'VE SEEN IT, babe,'' Greg said just after midnight. ''They were like strangers sitting there....''

Beth had waited for him to come home and, in spite of the cool March weather, they were sitting outside by their pool.

''Shock from the fire?'' Beth suggested, hoping. She'd been worried about Bonnie since their talk the previous week.

She snuggled into her sweatshirt and slid a foot across her lounger to rest against Greg's calf.

''I don't think so.'' He leaned to one side, flipping the switch to illuminate the water in front of them.

The pool was where they'd had their first kiss.

And it was where they usually ended up for the talks that turned out to be difficult. Beth had a feeling this was going to be one of them.

"Are you worried about the fire?" she asked her husband.

"I'm concerned. So are they, but this is more than that."

"You said she told you guys about Diamond."

"Yeah." Greg glanced at her. "You didn't seem surprised to hear it."

Beth wondered how much of what she knew—and surmised—she should tell Greg. She and her sister-in-law had grown closer than most sisters during the past months while Beth struggled to recover from the horrors of mental manipulation and physical abuse that had finally driven her to break the law in an attempt to save both her own life and that of her small son.

She owed Bonnie some loyalty, but Beth had learned the hard way that keeping secrets from Greg was not a good idea.

"Do you think Diamond is behind the fires?" She turned her head to look at the man who had given her back her life.

"No." He shook his head. "Doesn't make much sense for a man to damage property he's trying to sell."

"You don't think Bonnie has anything to do with them, do you?"

"Of course not. But something's up with her."

Beth's guess that this wasn't going to be a quiet unwinding before bed was obviously correct. She looked at the baby monitor on the sill behind them, making sure the light was glowing.

"She's talked to you, hasn't she?" Greg asked softly.

"Yeah."

"Is she in trouble?"

"Not in the way you mean."

His grin held more warm affection than humor. "How do I mean?"

"With the law, someone blackmailing her, her health."

"So what kind of trouble is she in?"

The night air was quiet.

"She needs more out of life than she's getting," Beth finally said.

"What in the hell is *that* supposed to mean? Keith isn't good enough for her anymore?"

"Of course he is," Beth said, hating this. "She's just…feeling the pull of a world in trouble, and she's bothered by her inability to do much about it. She feels that in the big picture, she's insignificant. She needs to make a difference."

"You're telling me my sister suddenly thinks she has to save the world?"

"No." Beth studied the sedate ripples in the pool.

"She's got a great life," Greg said, his frustration evident. "A husband she loves who loves her back. A healthy, beautiful daughter. A successful career, doing exactly what she always wanted to do."

"But she's capable of doing a lot more than she's doing and she knows that." Beth's heart went out to Bonnie. Her sister-in-law was caught—needing to save her marriage, the life she'd built, and save herself, as well.

Because without one, the other meant nothing.

"The day care practically runs itself at this point. Katie's going to grow up and have a life of her own. Keith's got the station. Bonnie plays a supporting role in all of that, as she should. But she needs something else, too."

"Sounds to me like a midlife crisis."

Anger flared in Beth. And quickly died. "It's so much more than that, Greg." She tried to help him understand, not only for Bonnie's sake, but for hers. "These needs Bonnie's describing are almost identical to the way I felt at the time James and Peter approached me about Sterling Silver. I ended up in hell because I was so desperate to escape the feeling that I was unworthy of the life I'd been given. I'd begun to feel like my life was a waste."

"Bonnie's life is not a waste. Hell, she holds this family together!"

"I know that."

"So she's going to throw it all in the toilet? Leave Keith, Shelter Valley and go make some huge difference for people who don't give a damn about her?"

"No. She has no intention of leaving Keith. She loves him as much as she always has."

"Then why hasn't she talked to him about this?"

"*You* don't understand her. Why do you think *he* would?"

"I'm not saying he will, but she's his wife. He has a right to know what she's thinking. Feeling. I'd sure as hell want to."

"For one thing, she doesn't want to hurt him. And she knows that as soon as she tells him she's dissatisfied with her life, he's going to be crushed."

"Like he wasn't disturbed tonight when he found out she'd known about Diamond for an entire month and hadn't told him?"

"I think she's also afraid that if she tells him she's feeling so discontented, it might jeopardize her marriage, which is the last thing she wants. Just like you, he'd assume this means she wants to leave, go out and immediately change everything in her life. He'll be trying to solve things, and that just might push her into something she doesn't want."

"You think she's met someone else?"

"Of course not. But I'll bet she's afraid Keith will think so." Beth hesitated, then added, "She hasn't said a word to me about this, Greg, but I wonder if one of the reasons she's afraid to talk to Keith is that she's afraid of losing him. To someone else."

"You think he's having an affair?" Greg sounded more hesitant than shocked. Beth's concern for her sister-in-law grew.

"I hope not."

"I've seen him and Martha Moore together more than once."

"She's his new program director." Beth had only met the older woman a couple of times, but she'd liked her and admired what she'd heard about her.

Still… A lonely woman, a good-looking man, spending many hours together in a studio…

"I can't believe that of Keith," Greg said, a leg on either side of the lounge as he sat forward. "He's a good guy. Besides, I think I'd know if he were cheating on my sister.''

Greg had so much faith in people.

''So what are you going to do?'' she asked, looking skyward as she thanked the stars that this man, the sheriff of Shelter Valley, was her husband. And hoped he wasn't setting himself up for disappointment.

''For now, figure out who's setting these damned fires.''

Beth didn't doubt that he'd find the culprit. She wished she felt as certain about Bonnie's chances of finding the answers she was seeking.

TUESDAY AFTER WORK Bonnie and Katie stopped by Grandma Nielson's house. Keith was playing basketball with some guys from the university—filling in for a professor who had the flu—and they were worried about Lonna. With good reason, it turned out. Lonna was just leaving as Bonnie pulled in, her car loaded with food for Grace and Dorothy.

Though she was wearing hose and pumps, her slacks were wrinkled and her face looked as though it'd developed more lines in the two days since they'd seen her.

The weariness in Lonna's posture scared her.

''I'd love to stay and play with the little miss,'' Grandma said, the longing in her voice apparent as she caught sight of her great-granddaughter strapped in her car seat. ''But if I don't get these meals delivered…''

''It's okay, Grandma,'' Bonnie said. ''Why don't

we just load up that food in the back of the van and I'll drive you around?''

Grandma hesitated, an indication to Bonnie that she wanted to accept.

"I can't," Grandma said. "I have to stay and visit with Grace. I didn't have time this morning."

"You were there this morning, too?"

"Before my long-range planning meeting," Lonna said, preoccupied as she peered at the food in the back seat of her car. "I hope I have everything."

"I don't mind if we stay and visit Grace," Bonnie announced, figuring they could make a quick stop at home to get a snack for Katie on the way.

"If you're sure…"

"I'm sure."

Bonnie wasn't. But there was no way she could leave Grandma to help her friends alone when she was so clearly exhausted. She just prayed that Katie, who'd had a long day herself, continued to behave until they got home.

As it turned out, she needn't have worried. Instead of being a problem, Katie made the impromptu journey a success, first with her great-grandmother, regaling Lonna with a mostly absurd tale about her day in school, and then as they visited Grandma's friends.

When Katie saw Dorothy propped up with pillows on her couch, the little girl walked over, patted her arm and whispered that Mama would make her all better.

Instead, it was Katie who did that, bringing light and life into a home that was quiet and lonely. Dorothy's eyes were sparkling by the time the three Nielson women took their leave.

And Bonnie had fallen in love with her little girl all over again.

"I'M OBSESSING, Pastor." Bonnie sat in the office of the minister she'd known for more than twenty years.

"About what?"

Bonnie looked down, ashamed to voice the words.

"About money?" he asked softly.

She wished. "No."

He coughed, leaned forward, his hands folded on top of his desk.

"Is it about sex? Another man?"

"No." Another time she might've been shocked at the thought. Now, in spite of her negative reply, the question seemed almost reasonable.

"Things are okay between you and Keith, then?" The words were uttered gently by this soft-spoken man. There was nothing "fire and brimstone" about Pastor Edwards.

"No." Which was why she was having her first ever pastor-parishioner consultation that Thursday evening. Before the previous Saturday, she hadn't been open with Keith. Since that night's revelations, he was hardly speaking to her.

Something had to give.

And because she was the cause of it all, it was going to have to be her.

"In what way are they bad?" The kindly, graying man sat behind his old-fashioned desk, the epitome of every father figure she'd ever known, even though he was probably only in his early fifties. "Is there abuse?"

"No!" Bonnie couldn't have him thinking that. The idea was ludicrous. "We just can't...find each other. Can't communicate."

"Have you tried marriage counseling?" Pastor Edwards asked.

Twisting her hands in her lap, Bonnie shook her head. "No."

"Well, then, it would seem to me—"

"The marriage isn't the problem," Bonnie blurted, frustrated by her inability to speak, to explain, to break out of the prison she'd erected around herself. "It's me." Suddenly the words exploded passionately from her. "I feel like my life here is holding me back."

"From what?"

"I don't know. Using myself, my talents and abilities, to their fullest."

Sighing, Bonnie relaxed in the chair, releasing some of her earlier tension.

With a look of compassion, Pastor Edwards sat back, too, folding his hands across his stomach. Bonnie waited for more questions.

There were none.

"I love Shelter Valley," she told him. "But I feel almost as if this town, with all of us looking out for each other, protects us from the harsher realities of life—and from our responsibilities to other people outside our own safe little haven."

The minister stood, coming around to lean against the corner of his desk.

"What about Keith and Katie? Do you want to leave them?"

"Absolutely not," she replied without hesitation. "They're my life, Pastor. Of that, I'm sure."

Spreading his hands, he said, "Well, you've certainly got the most important things in place."

Disappointed, Bonnie looked up at the tall man, suspecting that he didn't have the answers she'd been hoping to find here.

CHAPTER SEVEN

"YOU THINK I should just count my blessings?" Bonnie eventually asked the minister.

"No." Pastor Edwards shook his head. "But did you ever stop to consider that maybe you're just going through a very natural period of adjustment in the process of life?" He leaned forward with a hand propped on his knee. "I think women, in particular, face this kind of thing again and again," he continued. "You reach a point in life where you've met your immediate goals and then feel as though you aren't needed anymore."

He was in preacher mode, and Bonnie waited for the words of wisdom for which she'd come.

"It's a form of letdown," the pastor explained. "A very real lessening of the energy it took to keep going while you fought your way in the world. Granted, I usually see it when kids are leaving home and mothers aren't sure how to fill their time and the empty spaces in their hearts, but you're a unique woman, Bonnie. A nurturer through and through. And you've been fighting an uphill battle for most of your life, carrying burdens far too heavy for one as young as you...."

Bonnie stared at him, afraid to blink in case she spilled the tears that were slowly filling her eyes.

"You were still a kid—what, twelve?—when you took on caring for your father and brother."

"I loved them! I was glad to be able to care for them. It helped me with my own grieving. Made me feel good, safe, like we were still a family."

"Exactly. Because you're a nurturer. But now your father's gone. And your brother has Beth. The day care is doing well. It doesn't need you in there fighting tooth and nail for its existence. Keith is happy at work. And little Katie is a model child."

Seemed she should be happy, right?

"Do you think I need counseling?" Bonnie held her breath. She didn't want to think she was that messed up.

He shook his head. "A counselor's role is to help you think things through, to discover what's going on inside you, and I think you're already doing that," he said. "You aren't having problems figuring anything out, Bonnie. You're just learning to recognize and understand a new set of feelings.

"Of course, I can recommend some counselors if you'd feel better talking to someone else."

Quickly shaking her head, Bonnie tried to find the ready smile that had been her trademark her entire life.

"Give yourself some time," Pastor Edwards said. "And some of that compassion you give everyone else."

Bonnie stood, nodding. "And what about Keith?" she asked.

"Talk to him. Tell him what you've told me. You're his wife—he's your life partner. And this is one of life's situations."

She nodded again. "Okay." As much as she didn't want to hurt Keith, she'd pretty much decided to speak with him. Because she *was* hurting him. Saturday had shown her that silence had as much power to do harm as the truth.

Still, it was good to hear her own conclusion validated.

Holding out her hand, she was comforted by Pastor Edwards's warm grip, if not his counsel. She appreciated his compassion, but he hadn't told her anything she didn't know.

He walked with her across the beautiful tapestry rug that covered the front half of his office.

"I'll keep you in my prayers."

Bonnie wondered if even his prayers would be strong enough to hold her marriage together.

She smiled at the woman sitting in a chair out in the hall, waiting to see the pastor. Mrs. Emily Baker. Maybe twelve years older than Bonnie, the woman was more beautiful than Bonnie had ever been. Married with a couple of mostly grown kids, she and her family had been in Shelter Valley for at least a decade.

And still felt like newcomers to Bonnie.

She hoped that Mrs. Baker's business with Pastor Edwards was a lot more productive than her own.

Tempted to stop by Little Spirits on the way home, to see if Shane was there, Bonnie turned her car toward Keith and Katie, instead. The day care was closed and she belonged with her family.

After Katie was asleep, she did a couple of extra loads of laundry, cleaning out the kitchen drawers while she waited for the washer and dryer to finish their cycles. Keith was in the office, working at his desk, probably paying bills, but Bonnie wasn't sure. She hadn't ventured close enough to ask.

She'd called Beth. Told her what Pastor Edwards had said. Beth had said Greg had told her pretty much the same thing.

She had to talk to Keith.

She emptied leftovers out of the refrigerator.

She was stalling and she knew it.

So much was at risk. Either way.

"I'm going to bed."

In denim overalls and a white T-shirt, Bonnie was in the laundry room, matching socks on top of the dryer, a job they usually shared. Keith had come to stand in the doorway, but didn't offer to help.

"Keith, wait."

He turned back, shoulders hunched in the black T-shirt he'd changed into after work. "What?" His eyes were dull.

"Can we talk a second?"

"Okay." Hands in the pockets of his shorts, Keith leaned against the doorjamb, one foot crossed over the other.

Bonnie continued to match socks.

She took a breath. And then another.

Keith didn't move.

"I went to see Pastor Edwards after work today."

Her husband didn't say a word.

"I hoped, foolishly I guess, to find some magical answers there."

"He's just a man like the rest of us."

"I know." Little and white with ridges. Little and white with bows at the top. Little and white but smooth. Katie had too many white socks. And not enough that matched. "His only advice was what I'd already determined myself. To talk to you."

Keith's hand appeared out of nowhere, tossing her a little white sock with a bow.

Bonnie twisted around. "I love you, Keith. So much."

He looked at her and then away. Bonnie turned back to the dryer.

"I just want you to know that."

"Okay."

An "I love you, too" would have helped. A lot. Big black socks with ridges. Big black socks, smooth. Casual. Dress. Why did everyone need so many different socks?

"I'm not sure how to explain so you can understand how I feel without taking it personally."

Or so he'd understand at all. According to Beth, Greg hadn't.

"This is about me, then?"

"No!" She swung around, catching his gaze, but only briefly. "It's all me, but I'm afraid you'll think it's a reflection of you, or us, and it's not," she said, resting her belly against the warmth of the dryer as she grabbed another handful of socks from the laundry basket. "It's completely separate."

"Okay." A blue sock appeared, a match to one she'd had sitting alone on the dryer.

She took a deep breath, then let it go. "I'm not happy." They weren't the words she'd chosen any of the times she'd run through this moment in her mind.

"No kidding."

"I mean, I *am* happy—bone-deep happy—with so many things in my life. Yet…it doesn't seem to be enough."

"I don't understand. What do you want that you don't have?"

Another little white sock. Some yellow and green ones. Her running socks. Two different brands of white sport socks, some with gray toes and heels, some with just gray toes. She should've run tonight. Running sounded really good. Free.

"To matter more."

"You think I don't love you enough?"

"No!" She turned. "Yes! You love me far more than I deserve. I told you this wasn't about you."

"Then tell me what it is, Bonnie, because I'm not getting it."

"I think I've made all the difference I can make."

Had he edged away from the door? Or was she just imagining his withdrawal?

"That doesn't even make sense, Bon. You have a three-year-old daughter sleeping down the hall who's counting on you to make a lot of difference between now and her eighteenth birthday. And beyond that, as well."

Head averted, Keith reached for a green sock of hers from the laundry basket, tossed it next to its mate on the dryer. "I was counting on that, too. For her. And for me."

Dropping the pair of blue socks in her hand, Bonnie folded the green ones. The dryer stopped. She missed its soothing vibration.

"I plan to be there to do all that, Keith, but what about the rest of me? Taking care of you and Katie is a given, but what do I do with myself when you're both living your lives every day? Especially as Katie gets older?''

"Are you forgetting you own a business?"

"It practically runs itself."

"I don't get it, Bonnie. It sounds like none of us is good enough for you. Or…enough for you, anyway."

She didn't know which of them was more frustrated. "Katie and I wouldn't be enough for you, either, Keith. Not by ourselves. You've got the station to challenge you every day. And the opportunity there to reach thousands of people with whatever message you choose to send them."

"And you're helping to shape young minds in their most formative years. Teaching them not only about shapes and colors, but about love and sharing. Setting examples of honesty and fairness."

"All things this town will show them on its own," she said more sharply than she wanted to. She wasn't getting through to him at all. "I embody what Shelter Valley has given me. The kids at Little Spirits are already well loved before they come to me. And the feeling of safety and security I give them…well, they get that everywhere in this town."

"So Shelter Valley *is* the problem."

Sighing, Bonnie felt some of her anger deflate. "I don't think it is," she said. "I love this town. I really do. I love the sense of belonging, of family, I feel here."

"Just tell me what you want, Bonnie."

"I'm not sure I can answer that. Other than sparing you and Katie the unhappiness I seem to be bringing us all, the last thing I want is to get away from you.

"And before you ask, I love Little Spirits and Grandma Nielson, and all the children in this town, too. Yet, there doesn't seem to be enough here to satisfy me. I'm just so aware that there's a whole world out there, a world in trouble, and I'm not doing a darn thing about any of it."

Throwing two socks together, Bonnie folded them and put them on top of the washer.

Keith was behind her, reaching around one side of her for those socks and around the other for a lone sock on the dryer.

His warmth, the way he almost had his arms around her, made her lips tremble.

"Those don't match," he said, fixing the problem and returning the correctly folded pair to her pile.

Instead of going back to the door, he stood beside her in front of the dryer, the laundry basket between them.

"It sounds to me like you're having a midlife crisis and we just need to wait it out."

Bonnie bit back the retort that flew to her lips. And blinked back the tears, too. He still wasn't getting it. "I'm having a crisis, all right," she said when she trusted herself to speak calmly. "But this is not about midlife, Keith. Hell, I'm not even forty. I'm certainly not through my child-bearing years and our daughter isn't in kindergarten. This is about needing to be *needed*, about waking up in the morning knowing I have to get up because something necessary won't get done if I don't."

She was just repeating herself. And judging by the

expression on his face, not explaining things any better.

Hands on the dryer, Keith turned, his blond hair endearingly mussed as he looked down at her. "Can you tell me, from the heart and with complete assurance, that you want to stay married to me?" he asked.

"Yes."

"But?"

"But there's something out there calling to me, Keith. I don't know what it is, but I have to find it." She said the words quickly.

His head dropped. "Then all I have to say, Bon, is that if you ever figure it out, you think long and hard about what our marriage means before you act."

"You're so sure that whatever it is, I can't do it and have you, too?"

"What exactly are we talking about?" He sounded as frustrated as she felt.

"I have no idea. I just know I need to help people. There's a convention in Phoenix next Thursday and Friday I'd like to attend. It's being sponsored by the city and has to do with public facilities to help the needy. I've been asked to speak on caring for young children."

"They just asked you and it's next week?"

"There was a cancellation."

"And you think you'll find your answers there?"

"I don't know. Maybe."

"Then you have to go."

He gave his blessing fully, but then, she'd expected nothing less. Of course he'd encourage her to attend professional seminars if she wanted to, as she would him. It was all the other stuff that scared her.

"So, what if I find an opportunity to run some facility or program…"

"You think that would make you happier than being my wife or Katie's mother? To direct a program somewhere? In some other city?"

"No."

Keith sighed, dropped the last pair of matched socks on the pile. "My life is here in Shelter Valley. I'm not saying I wouldn't be willing to consider a move if there was some powerful reason for doing so, but it would have to be pretty damn good to weigh against everything we have here."

"I'm not asking you to move."

"I think I realize that, but then, you probably didn't intend to be feeling this way, either, so who knows what's ahead?" He resumed the sock-matching.

"You're giving up on us?" Fear suffocated her.

"No. I'm just trying to be prepared for whatever the future brings. I can't live forever with the threat that you might leave hanging over my head."

"Of course you can't! I'm not going to leave."

"You don't think you will, but who knows? What kind of program will you find to direct here in Shelter Valley? Other than the one you're already directing? In case you haven't noticed, there aren't a whole lot of homeless people here. And you just said that helping people who are well loved isn't enough for you anymore."

"I'm not leaving you," she said, stamping her

foot. She couldn't remember ever having done that before.

"Okay."

"Don't give up, Keith," she pleaded, tears springing to her eyes. "Please don't quit believing in us." Bonnie wrapped her arms around him, holding on even though he didn't immediately envelop her in his comforting embrace.

"I'm not going to quit believing, Bon," he said, eventually doing what she craved and pulling her close. "At least not yet." His chin moved against the top of her head as he spoke. "I can't. I love you too much."

There was no joy in the declaration.

"And I love you, too."

"Then chances are we'll get through this."

She hoped so. Oh, God, more than anything else on earth, she hoped so.

GREG HAD INSPECTED every inch of the Little Spirits craft room before he'd let Bonnie start cleaning it up.

He'd had every single suspect particle inspected by his top lab people. And still, a week and three days after the second fire, he had nothing more to go on.

Someone had launched a toy rocket through the window. A mistake? A boy with bad aim who didn't even know where his rocket had landed?

Maybe.

Not likely in Shelter Valley, though. Everyone knew about the fire. Even if a boy didn't have the courage to come forward, very likely the parents who'd purchased the rocket would.

Except that, judging by what remained of the rocket, it didn't appear to be purchased. Greg's lab people were pretty sure it had been homemade.

And Greg was pretty sure its launch hadn't been an accident. The window to that craft room was in an alcove at the back of the strip mall. Its accidental landing in the craft room would be pretty remarkable, considering its very limited flight pattern. He was sure of one thing: whoever set that fire had been in the alcove and aiming for that particular window.

But who?

In the past week Greg had talked to Bonnie, to Beth and Keith, Becca Parsons, Phyllis and Matt Sheffield, the parents of Bo Roberts, the little Down syndrome boy, Randi and Zack Foster, Tori and Ben Sanders, the Montfords and every other parent on the roster, previously on the roster and hoping to be on the roster eventually. He'd never reached so many dead ends in his entire career. He'd even talked to the brain-damaged guy, Shane Bellows.

Judging by his conversation, his inability to follow intricate thought processes, the guy wasn't capable of planning and carrying out a series of crimes.

He also had no motive. Shane Bellows was obviously very fond of Bonnie.

Everyone loved Bonnie. And Little Spirits. Even those who weren't closely acquainted had heard only good things about the day care.

There was a little grumbling from various people who'd done business with some of the nearby establishments, due to the traffic jams at drop-off and pick-up times, and sometimes because of noise, but certainly nothing negative enough to be termed resentment, let alone the darker motivations that would drive someone to criminal acts.

In his super cab pickup, rather than the cruiser that sometimes garnered attention he didn't need, Greg drove out of town, two boxes of groceries on the seat beside him.

He made his biweekly drop-off to Hugh Francis, a hermit who'd helped him solve the ten-year-old mystery of his father's carjacking.

And then, still incognito, he drove a little farther, pulling into the parking lot of the Kachina Grounds casino.

It was the first time he'd been back since Beth's breakdown there the previous September.

Triggered by a piano player on stage in the casino, his wife had started to recover her memory that night. She'd suffered a frightening loss of emotional composure as a result.

They'd also been attacked. They'd walked unknowingly into the middle of a drug deal in the back parking lot.

And later that night, he and Beth had shared their first kiss.

Hoping to dispel the cloud of unease that had settled over him, Greg concentrated on that kiss as he entered the casino.

He was on a fool's errand; he knew that. But he had no other stones to overturn at the moment and, at least for him, activity was always better than idleness.

When he'd dropped by to see Mike Diamond

Tuesday at noon, the first day of April, Diamond's secretary had said her boss had taken the afternoon off. Either playing a hunch or giving in to desperation, Greg had played his sheriff card—giving the impression that his need to find Diamond had an air of urgency. He'd learned that while Diamond hadn't told his secretary where he could be reached, he often spent his free time at the casino.

As Greg had told Beth, he didn't really suspect Diamond. Didn't make sense that the man would sabotage his own property, especially when he had a deal pending. However, even remote possibilities were worth checking out.

The casino was swarming with people, mostly senior citizens from what he could tell, waiting two and three deep for slot machines. Greg weaved his way through them, eyes alert for the man he'd come to see, at the same time trying to stay inconspicuous.

He didn't want Diamond to know he was there. If by some chance, the man had something to hide—

"Hi, Sheriff!"

Turning, Greg saw Mr. and Mrs. Bob Mather, Sr., sitting together at a pair of quarter slot machines.

"Bob! Clara! Good to see you!" Greg moved to stand behind them, glancing around as he did. "Any luck?"

"Clara just hit the spin for a thousand," Bob said, grinning at his wife. The smile Clara Mather sent her husband almost made Greg envious. In all the years these two had been married, life's hardships had not dimmed their love the slightest bit.

It was the same look he used to intercept between his sister and her husband when they'd been so wrapped up in each other they'd forgotten he was around.

''Congratulations!'' he told the older couple, hoping he and Beth shared that look—and that they'd still be doing so fifty years from now.

And what about Bonnie and Keith?

After chatting for a couple of minutes, Greg excused himself, slowly casing the casino. The Mathers said they hadn't seen anyone they knew. But then, they might not know Mike Diamond.

And they hadn't been through the entire room.

By his second go-round, he was ready to call it quits. Ryan was getting his two-year molars and hadn't been feeling well. Greg was anxious to get home and see what he could do to distract the little guy.

Then he saw him. With his back to the casino, Greg hadn't recognized the Shelter Valley landowner until he'd taken off the cowboy hat Greg had never seen him wear before.

Instincts buzzing, Greg pulled a dollar from his pocket and fed it to a quarter slot machine that had just become available.

Diamond wasn't wasting his time on slots. Or Bingo. Or Keno. Or even the sports club. He was sitting at a poker table. A high-stakes poker table.

Greg pushed the Bet Three button and looked around the casino. Diamond was at the highest-stakes table in the place.

And by the looks of the chips in front of him, the number of cigarettes in the ashtray, the empty drink glass and the state of his finger-ruffled hair, he'd been there awhile.

"You done, mister?"

A tiny, elderly Indian woman with wrinkled skin and gnarled knuckles gazed up at him.

"Ah, no," Greg said, glancing at the machine. He hadn't won anything, but he had a quarter left. He pushed the Bet One button and put his knee on the stool.

The woman stood patiently behind him, apparently taking him for an early leaver.

Greg pulled another dollar from his pocket. Fed the machine. And watched Diamond. The man studied his cards, his shoe bobbing nervously on the stool's foot bar, and pushed an entire stack of chips to the betting line.

The woman behind Greg cleared her throat. Hardly looking at the buttons, Greg pushed one— and watched the game going on a quarter of the way across the room.

The dealer threw a card. Scooped up Diamond's chips. As Diamond moved, Greg saw how few chips he had left. Greg ducked his head, preferring, especially now, not to be seen by Diamond, who'd stood up to leave.

A slot machine was clamoring, bells ringing so loudly Greg was getting a headache. A moment later, deciding Diamond had had enough time to get out of there, he got up to leave.

And turned to see the dealer scoop up the bill Diamond had just laid on the table and count out another stack of chips. Diamond had apparently stood up to get more cash, presumably from the automatic teller close by. One thing was certain: that had been no small bill.

"Jeez, mister, look at what you done!" the weathered old woman practically shouted at Greg's shoulder.

The irritating noise was coming from his machine.

Greg had just won five thousand quarters.

"You take it," he said, as he pushed the old woman to the stool in front of his machine.

"If this is an April Fool's trick, mister, you're one sick bastard."

Greg leaned toward the woman, speaking directly into her ear. "It's no April Fool's trick, just your lucky day." With a squeeze to the speechless woman's shoulders, he walked out.

People were starting to gather around, and the last thing Greg wanted was to draw attention to himself.

Besides, he might've hit a jackpot that really meant something.

He'd bet his badge Mike Diamond had a gambling problem.

Not that it made damaging his own property any more plausible—unless he was so desperate he was trying to force Bonnie to move. Maybe losing the sale was worth it if he could jack up the next tenant's rent. His sister had mentioned a bathroom leak the previous month. Had that been more than an accident, as well?

Greg just might be jumping to ridiculous conclusions. Then again, ridiculous had led to answers more than once in his career.

For now, he had a job to do.

CHAPTER EIGHT

"CURRENTLY WE'RE DOWN-LINKING about fifty percent of our programming from satellite," Martha said, her brow creased in concentration as she sat back on her side of the two-cushion couch in the deserted studio.

Elbow on the arm of the couch, Keith studied some of the numbers she'd already given him. "So that means our catalog of digital media currently provides less than ten percent."

Analog and MPEGs were both at twenty.

"Right."

"We're a digital cable station with full production capabilities."

"Yes."

"And half of what we do is coming from Philadelphia, Germany and Japan?"

"Right."

Ankle across his knee, Keith asked, "How much from Philadelphia?" as though he expected good news.

"About five percent."

"Damn." The Philadelphia Public Broadcasting Company, from which they purchased satellite downloads, at least produced programming in English.

"The good news is that most of the German and Japanese stuff is on overnight." Martha's grin helped. But only a little.

Caught up in the administrative issues, like getting the money, federal licenses and cable company partnerships, he'd lost sight of MUTV's inventory over the past year. Martha had just taken over as program director after a couple of years spent volunteering on scripts and productions while she worked with the theater. She'd only now finished a thorough investigation of the station's programming inventory.

"I promised one-hundred percent original programming within two years," Keith muttered.

"I know."

"We have a hell of a lot of work to do."

Martha tossed her clipboard between them. "I'm ready."

The tension gripping his chest eased noticeably. He stared at her. Here was someone he could *count* on. With his life scattering about him, that meant a lot.

Martha tilted her head. She'd gotten a haircut the previous weekend, had it textured, she'd said. He liked the sassy windblown look.

"It's late. You should probably get home to your kids," he said, disappointed.

"They're not home."

Neither was his family. Because it was Wednesday night, Bonnie was at church choir practice with Beth, and Greg had taken Katie and Ryan to a face-painting extravaganza at Wal-Mart.

He and Martha had put in a long day. Having been called in at six that morning due to a malfunction in the TiRac system, they'd been at work for more than twelve hours already.

"We could map out a general plan if you'd like, just to have something to come back to in the morning." She was smiling, didn't look tired at all.

"Don't you want to get home?"

"I have an empty house waiting for me. Tim's at ball practice, followed by a pizza party, and the girls are with Ellen at the mall in Phoenix. But if you need to go home…"

Keith tried not to be affected by the calm in her eyes. "No, Bonnie and Katie are out, too. I guess we could make a start."

"Great." She picked up her clipboard, flipping to a new page.

"But only if we order in something to eat."

Martha laughed. "You men, always thinking about your stomachs."

Keith had intended to stand up. Find a phone. Call for pizza. Instead, he soaked up the amusement on Martha's face. It was honest. Real. So unlike anything he'd seen at home lately.

God, he missed the easy laughter that used to light up Bonnie's eyes. He missed his wife so damned much.

"Have you ever felt like you were wasting your life?" He hadn't planned to ask the question.

Martha shrugged, her shoulders slim in the white, short-sleeved pullover she was wearing with her jeans. "Yeah. Doesn't everybody?"

Shaking his head, Keith debated continuing the conversation. "I don't just mean fleeting thoughts," he said. "Has there ever been a time in your life when being who you were was not enough?"

"Yeah." She answered slowly, watching him.

"There has?" He hadn't really been expecting that. Martha seemed so sensible.

But then, until recently, so had Bonnie.

"Yeah." Martha brought her leg up to rest it sideways on the couch; it was only inches from his ankle.

"What did you do?" He regarded her intently.

She took a while to answer him. The question was personal. Maybe too personal. Something was happening between them. A distance diminishing.

He could tell exactly when Martha made the decision to eliminate the distance altogether.

"I didn't do anything," she said, surprising him again. "I was everything I thought I'd wanted to be. A wife. A mother. An active citizen of Shelter Valley. When the dissatisfaction started, I ignored it. Just kept reminding myself that I had everything I'd always wanted. And I'd busy myself more and more with the house, the kids, volunteering. And eventually it worked. Sort of."

"What do you mean, sort of?"

"The feeling that life was passing me by went away, but I think part of me did, too. I was a wife, a mother. Somehow, though, I'd lost myself during those years."

"Is that when you went to work at the theater?"

She shook her head. "I told you, I didn't do anything. Todd did."

"What'd he do?" Keith hadn't known Martha's

husband well. And what he did know, he sure as hell didn't respect.

"He left me. Which was a huge eye-opener."

"And that's when you got the job at the theater?"

Another shake of her head. "For a while after that, all I did was obsess about escape."

"From Shelter Valley?"

"Yeah, *and* from life."

She looked down at her hands. "At first, I was just shocked, busy getting through every day, minute by minute. I don't think I dared look far enough ahead to *want* anything. Or maybe I just wasn't capable of feeling anything at all, including anticipation or hope for the future."

"The bastard should be shot."

She looked up. "Yeah, I went through that stage, too, spending hours imagining his painful death."

In another lifetime, Keith would have grabbed her hand. Squeezed. Held on. Just for the comfort of one human being connecting with another.

But in this life he was a married man.

"Then, about six months after he'd left town, the dust had settled and I looked at my life, at what I still had."

Martha grimaced. She grabbed the clipboard, held it to her stomach, wrapped her arms around it. "I was almost forty years old. With four self-sufficient kids who still needed me but were already setting out on lives of their own."

"And *that's* when you got the job at the theater."

His gaze met Martha's as he waited for her answer.

She grinned. And he did, too.

"Eventually," she said. "I was already writing a script for Becca Parsons...."

She told him about the Save the Youth program Becca Parsons had instituted a few years before and how her friend had invited her to participate. Keith already knew she'd studied theater and performance arts at Montford, but had left college to get married before she'd ever earned a degree. The next year, she'd directed Becca's production, which had led to her job as theater project director.

"And now you feel like you have a life," Keith said when her words dwindled away.

She nodded slowly. And he wished he understood.

How did directing theater projects even begin to compare with motherhood? Men could direct projects and develop programs and manage any number of things—as could women—but they could never give birth. That belonged only to women, and surely it was the most significant act any human being could ever accomplish.

"Thank you." Clipboard to her chest, she smiled almost shyly.

"For what?" *Whoa, man, don't even think about it.* Martha might be attractive and intelligent and right here, focused on him. But he was a married man.

"To begin with, for listening. I'm just now realizing how long it's been since I've had the chance to really talk. You know—about the stuff that goes on inside even if you refuse to acknowledge it."

"I want to listen," Keith said, telling the truth. "I wish I could do more to help."

"Well, that's the second thing," Martha said, sliding forward on the couch. "You hired me. With all the viewers we reach, you're giving me the chance to make a difference in a much larger way than I ever thought I could."

She sat on the edge of the couch, turning to look at him.

Keith held himself rigid. Without even trying to, he'd somehow managed to give Martha something that in six months of endless attempts he hadn't been able to give his wife. A sense of satisfaction. Of hope.

"I sure wish I could help you in return," she said softly, her eyes so warm Keith felt oddly comforted. "You seem to be feeling a bit lost."

Todd Moore was not just a bastard. He was a fool.

And after months of living on the precipice of impending disaster, Keith was tired.

"Bonnie's looking for more out of life than I can give her."

"Has she told you that?"

"Well...sort of."

"She wants to leave you?" Martha sounded shocked. Horrified.

He sat forward, elbows on his knees, hands clasped. "She says not, but I honestly don't know anymore."

Martha leaned toward him. "What did she say?"

Keith explained as well as he could, although he didn't understand what he was saying.

"All I can say is, if she's feeling this way, she needs to do something about it," Martha answered after a minute, her expression serious. "That sense of emptiness doesn't disappear, it just hides inside you where it can do all kinds of long-term damage.''

She softened the truth with a squeeze of his hand.

Keith didn't know what to think, so he thought about that hand holding his, calmed by its warmth.

Martha smiled at him. ''Just hang in there, Keith. She'll get through this. Bonnie's a smart woman and she loves you. You need to have faith in that.''

Meeting her eyes, Keith nodded. She was right. Bonnie, their marriage, their love, deserved his faith and more.

They stood, eyes still locked, dropping hands slowly.

And went home.

AFTER HER CONFERENCE, the van was taking her back to Shelter Valley much too quickly. Bonnie wasn't ready for the two days of exchanging ideas, learning, networking and absorbing new information to be over. Her adrenaline was flowing too fast for Shelter Valley's pace.

She hated that. Hated that she had to go back. Hated that her life in Shelter Valley couldn't be what she needed it to be.

And when she thought about her husband, waiting at home for her, and her baby girl looking forward to her return, she hated herself. How could she possibly not be satisfied with them?

She'd been offered the chance at a directorship with a national program that set guidelines and provided funding for shelters and educational facilities for homeless kids. Several times during the past two days she'd been encouraged to apply for the position. Not only by people she met, but by the hiring committee itself—after they'd attended her "standing room only" workshop.

She'd turned them down.

And as the miles rushed past, she was mourning the loss of what might have been.

"GRANDMA, YOU CANNOT possibly feed three people three meals a day in three different places!"

"I'll ask you to remember that I am the one with seniority here, young man," Lonna said as she watched Keith install her new scanner the following Sunday. "Which makes *me* the boss."

The old woman was sitting in one of two floral upholstered armchairs in her living room. Bonnie sat in the other, her heart going out to her husband. And to the woman who was fighting for the right to live her life the way she wanted to. The way she'd chosen for herself.

"I know you're the boss," Keith grumbled, lying on his back as he ran a cable behind the desk. "But that doesn't mean you can ignore the dictates of time. Or your own physical boundaries."

"It means I make my own decisions and that's that," Grandma said, her face set.

Keith sat up. "And I'm supposed to sit here and watch you kill yourself?"

"And what's the point, young man, of being alive if I can't really live?"

As she glanced back and forth between them, Bonnie's smile was absent. Keith, giving up his Sunday to help his grandmother, presented such a wonderful picture to her as he sat there on the carpet, the jeans and polo shirt he'd changed into after church outlining his muscles and his slenderness, a look of pure frustration creasing his brow.

She watched Grandma in her navy slacks and polka-dot blouse, her nylon-clad feet in navy pumps even in the comfort of her own home. The stubborn set of her jaw and lips was at odds with the vulnerability in those sharp blue eyes.

Keith lay back down, screwing the two sides of the cable plug into the back of the hard drive.

"My friends and I have been watching out for each other since we were children," Lonna said, her gaze boring into the bottom of Keith's soft leather loafers. "Through broken toys, bad grades, dating, college graduation, broken marriages, babies, your grandfather's death, the death of my son. We certainly aren't going to stop now."

"I'm not asking you to stop caring, Grandma, or even to stop doing. I'm just asking you to realize that you are only one woman, and you're seventy-six years old." Keith's muffled words were interspersed with an occasional grunt. "What's going to happen to all of them when you collapse from overwork? When you fall and hurt yourself? Or have a stroke?"

Bonnie saw what her husband did not—the brief flash of fear in the old woman's eyes.

"I'm going to go when it's my time," Lonna said, voice as strident as ever. "And when that happens, the good Lord will provide. Until then, I have to do everything I can for others."

Sitting up, Keith bumped his head on the desk.

And didn't swear, at least not out loud. Bonnie wanted badly to hug him.

"Grandma, I cannot allow—"

"Hey," Bonnie interrupted before their argument could erupt into a full-fledged fight. "I have an idea."

Two pairs of angry eyes turned her way.

"I know there are a lot of stay-at-home moms in this town who'd be willing to do a meal a week. And probably more. Why don't you organize them, Grandma? Put out requests, talk to Pastor Edwards and Becca Parsons…"

"Bonnie, you're talking about a lot of work," Keith began.

"…talk to your grandson who could put a public-service announcement on the newest local cable station," Bonnie said, interrupting her husband a second time.

"You might just have something there." Lonna was sitting forward, her expression eager.

"When I was at the conference in Phoenix this week, I sat next to a woman at lunch who's the director of a women's shelter. Her mother is ninety-one and still lives on her own, although she can't cook anymore. This woman was telling me about the Meals on Wheels program they use. I've heard of it of course, but never really knew much about it. All the food is cooked in one place and then volunteer drivers take the meals around at specified times each day. With enough volunteers, which would be easy to come by in Shelter Valley, you could start our own version of Meals on Wheels."

"I only have three friends in need," Grandma

said, sitting forward, "but I'm sure there are more. You're a smart young woman, Bonnie, and you're right—Shelter Valley is long overdue for something like this. I'll get started on it this afternoon. I can coordinate, get cooks, drivers…."

Grandma had crossed over to her desk and was writing in a spiral notebook.

"In Phoenix they run the program out of a hospital. The cooking's all done in the kitchen there."

"We don't have a hospital," Lonna murmured, "but we don't really need anything that big. And if our program grows, we can always use the church kitchen."

"We might even be able to work something out with the kitchen at Montford," Bonnie said as the thought occurred to her. "I don't know about weekends, but they're certainly there from breakfast to dinnertime every day during the week."

Whatever way Grandma decided to work things out, the idea was a good one. Bonnie was so caught up in the possibilities, she forgot all about her husband still sitting on the floor by the computer. Until he stood up.

He was frowning. Avoiding her eyes. He wanted Grandma to slow down, to stop taking on the care of all her friends. Not to run another program.

With a sinking stomach, Bonnie wondered if she'd just given him one more thing to be angry about.

"I wish you'd think about this some more, Grandma," Keith said, closing his bag of cords and sundry other computer items. "Anyway, you can't start this afternoon. We were planning on taking you home for dinner.'' It was pretty well understood that dinner with them was the real reason Lonna had called him over in the first place. ''Greg and Beth are already there with Katie and Ryan. They're expecting you. You're Ry's only grandparent, too, you know.''

Looking up from her pad, Grandma's eyes softened perceptibly as she glanced from her grandson to his wife. ''You're sure I won't be intruding on you young folks?''

Every Sunday for almost seven years, and still she had to ask. ''We're positive.''

''Well, then.'' She set the pad down and picked up the purse that had been waiting on the edge of her desk. ''I guess since we've been without a program for a hundred years, one more day won't hurt. I already did breakfast this morning, and Grace's daughter is in town today and said she'd see that everyone got dinner.''

Lonna talked and planned all the way over to Bonnie's house. Keith contributed nothing to the conversation.

CHAPTER NINE

SHANE WAS LANDSCAPING the following evening when Bonnie walked outside with Beth and Ryan and Katie.

"Are you sure you want her?" Bonnie asked, glancing at her little girl, a miniature of herself with those green eyes and riotous black curls, tightly clutching her aunt's free hand.

"You come," Ryan said, settled on his mother's hip, nodding down at Katie.

"Yes, Ryan," Katie said, looking up at her mother, her little brow puckered with worry at the thought that she might be denied a dinner of macaroni-and-cheese with her cousin.

"I really don't mind." Beth laughed. "I never should've told Ryan in front of Katie that I was making macaroni-and-cheese for dinner tonight, instead of Wednesday. I'm really sorry about this."

"No!" Bonnie assured her sister-in-law. "I'm happy to get some time to myself. I just feel bad for you, dealing with the two terrors on your own."

"Since we don't have even one terror between us, I'll be fine," Beth was saying, lowering Ryan to the ground so he could climb into the back of his mother's new Ford Taurus. "Besides, Greg's working late and I get lonely in that house when it's just Ry and me.''

Shane was watching as she got Katie's car seat from the van and loaded it into Beth's car. She waved at him.

Dressed in jeans and a flannel shirt with the sleeves rolled up, he looked like something straight out of a celebrity magazine. Dark hair, rugged and gorgeous…

''Hurry, Mama!'' Katie jumped up and down on the pavement beside her.

Beth helped her buckle the seat in. ''Maybe you and Keith can have some time alone,'' she said, sending her friend a warm smile.

''Keith and Martha are ordering in dinner again and working late.'' Bonnie related what she'd just heard from her husband when she'd called about Katie going home with Beth. ''They're trying to come up with enough programming ideas to fill fifty percent of their airtime and be ready for viewing within a year. In two years, they're supposed to be at a hundred percent.''

The kids were in their seats and demanding dinner, each egged on by the other so that the little voices were getting louder and shriller by the second, preventing any reply Beth might have made.

''I'll have Keith pick her up on his way home.'' Bonnie raised her voice to be heard.

Beth nodded and climbed behind the wheel, her composure unaffected by the children's noise. A woman who'd lived through hell, but found her own piece of heaven.

Bonnie felt tears in the back of her throat as she watched them drive away.

THERE WAS REALLY no reason to hang around. Other than another letter from Mike Diamond to avoid, there was nothing pressing in the office. And no plans to make for Little Spirits, when she didn't even know if there'd *be* a Little Spirits this time next year...

"Hi, Bonnie."

Spinning on the asphalt, Bonnie smiled at Shane. His interruptions always seemed to be perfectly timed.

"Hi! How's your day been?"

"Good." He leaned on the edge trimmer he'd just run around the perimeter of the property. "Now that I've learned my way around and I've got a routine, I finished everything on my list faster than I thought I would, but that's okay. I just wrote a note to remind myself to schedule more things per day."

It was a long sentence for him. And with only a hint of the deliberateness with which he usually spoke, reminding Bonnie of the young man she'd loved so desperately in high school. A man with a plan.

"Do you have to work a certain number of hours a day?" she asked, squinting into the setting sun. In spite of the balmy April day, she was starting to feel warm in her black stretch pants and short-sleeved sweater.

"No." Shane's gaze met hers and then wandered away.

"Oh. That's good." It was a lame reply but all

she could think of. She sensed that he was no longer interested in discussing his schedule.

"Why didn't you leave?" he asked, nodding toward the drive Beth had just exited.

"Katie wanted to go home with Ryan."

He continued to watch the road. "Annnd...you annnd...Keith can...have dinner...alone." His speech was suddenly awkward, slow and a little slurred.

His embarrassment was painful to watch.

She shook her head, wishing there was a way to reach Shane, to tell him he was fine just as he was. That he still had a full life ahead of him.

But she wasn't completely sure that was true. The whole thing was so damned sad.

"Keith's working late."

"You'll be alone for dinner."

Bonnie wondered if she could get Shane involved in sports, if he'd be able to handle the chaos of a Shelter Valley men's baseball game.

"I don't mind. I can go for a longer jog," she said, shrugging.

"Will you eat dinner first?"

Grinning, Bonnie patted Shane's forearm. "I'll grab a sandwich or something," she assured him. "Don't worry, I'll eat."

His eyes settled on hers. "I eat alone every night and I could share with you," he said. "Because I eat alone every night." He frowned and shook his head. "Sorry."

"For what? Wanting to share your dinner is nice, Shane."

Still shaking his head, he said, "I repeated myself."

"Don't worry about it." She smiled at him, holding on to his forearm this time. "I'd love to share your dinner, Shane. If you have enough, that is."

"Mrs. Tandy always makes too much."

"Probably so you'll have leftovers for lunch."

"I throw it away."

"Why?"

He looked down again, shifting his feet, though he didn't move the arm she held. "Too many notes."

"Notes?"

"To keep track of how old things get."

Because without notes there'd be no way for him to remember which night he'd eaten what.

Grabbing his hand, she pulled him toward the shed where the groundskeeping tools were stored. "You could date them," she told him, already thinking up a system that would be clean and simple. A calendar by the refrigerator and stickers on the counter that he could easily affix each night. Or maybe he could just have Mrs. Tandy put stickers on the containers when she made dinner.

Shane put away his tools one at a time, seeming to know automatically where everything went. And then, still without a word, he retrieved the lock, slid it into the outside latch on the shed and squeezed it shut.

"You're going to have dinner with me," he said as he turned around and stood there, hands hanging at his sides, looking lost.

"Yes, I am." Bonnie grinned, taking his hand.

"And we're going to set up a system for you to put dates on your leftovers," she told him.

"That will be good." Shane started to walk, pulling her with him. "Thank you."

She'd planned to drive the short distance to Shane's apartment, but when he strode off with her in tow, she didn't have the heart to stop him.

Instead, hand in hand, she walked home with him.

"I DON'T KNOW about you, but I'm beat." Martha sat back in the upholstered metal chair, a stack of recently closed folders on the round table in front of her.

"You're incredible," Keith said, trying hard not to notice how his employee's nicely shaped breasts filled out the white sweater she was wearing.

Bonnie had had a sweater on that morning, too. The peach-colored one he'd bought her the previous Christmas.

"We've accomplished far more than I thought we would," he continued. "This is great stuff." Together, with the help of suggestions gathered from students, they had two hours of original children's programming slotted daily, a couple of student-generated game shows, some interactive classes that would need FCC approval, plus a talk show hosted by Montford students to discuss world issues of importance to young adults. There'd also be a second talk show, hosted by members of Montford's continuing-education program, discussing issues of interest to senior citizens. And—one of Keith's favorites—they were hoping to have a coffeehouse, in the style of old New York coffeehouses. The set would look like an intimate club, and each week there'd be different artists performing everything from instrumental music to poetry readings. Anyone with talent to share would be welcome.

Their production students would be given opportunities to create impressive résumés that could help them break into the television production field.

And MUTV was going to be a station people wanted to watch.

"We might even win an award or two," Martha said, standing, slowly gathering her things.

"I'm happy just to be able to air everything in English," Keith told her, holding open the door of the conference room for her. He turned off the lights behind them.

Because it was dark and the parking lots mostly deserted, he walked Martha to her car.

"I hope you get home before your kids," he said as he opened her car door.

Tim, her star pitcher was, as always, playing ball. The two middle girls were at a friend's house planning a surprise party, and Ellen was working at Wal-Mart, which was why Martha had been able to stay late.

"Me, too," she said, smiling in spite of the tired look in her eyes. "Otherwise I'm going to have to nag them to pick up everything they threw on the floor when they walked in, and I hate that."

"Them throwing things on the floor?"

"That, too," she said, placing her purse on the seat and turning to give him a quirky grin. "The nagging," she said. "I hate having to be the bad guy all the time." She shook her head. "That's the dad's job, you know?"

Laughing, Keith said, "No! I didn't know."

"Yeah, well, it is."

Thinking of Katie, he could have argued. "I never thought about that aspect of being a single parent," he said, instead. "Not having anyone else around to play the bad guy now and then."

She leaned back against the car. Keith rested his arms along the top of the opened door.

"I think, aside from the loneliness, it's the part I hate most," she said, sighing.

Keith couldn't easily read her expression beneath the shadows cast by a parking lot light that should've been brighter. But he could see the glistening in her eyes.

"If there's anything I can do…"

He had no idea what that would be, but he meant the words. Completely.

"Better watch out," she murmured. "With four teenagers, I might just get desperate enough to take you up on that."

"I hope you do."

She stared up at him. Keith withstood the scrutiny. And then, apparently satisfied, she nodded.

Pleased with their mostly silent arrangement, he nodded back.

"So how are things with Bonnie?" she asked softly. Keith had assumed she'd just climb in her car and go.

"Okay."

Her girls would be home soon.

"Just okay?"

He debated avoiding the question. And then wondered how he could expect her to lean on him and still retain self-respect if he didn't let her give a little support in return.

"She's still distant."

"With Katie, too?"

He wished he had an answer for that. "She's a wonderful mother," was all he could come up with. Because she was. And because he owed Bonnie some loyalty. "Bonnie was made for motherhood. She never seems to run out of patience or encouragement, no matter how many times she has to tell Katie something or show her how to do a task. She always seems happiest when she's tending to her little ones."

"Then maybe that's your answer," Martha said, leaning her head against the top of the door frame. "Suggest another baby."

When he didn't respond, she asked, "Do you want more children?"

"Yeah. One, at least."

"There you go, then."

Keith brushed at the gravel beneath his foot, the sound of the small pebbles against his shoe reminding him of a horse walking. On a hot summer day. With him in the saddle.

And Bonnie beside him.

With a picnic lunch—and a blanket to lie on—packed in the saddlebags.

"She doesn't want another baby."

"You've asked her?"

Keith tried to read Martha's gaze in the darkness,

wondering how far he could take this and not cross a very dangerous line. "Yes."

Martha straightened, the door only partially between them. "She said no."

"Not exactly." He slid his hands into the pockets of his Dockers, staring down at ground he could hardly see. But that didn't matter. His mind held a very clear vision he wasn't going to escape from. That of his wife, wet and hot, digging into the toe of her high-heeled shoe. And worse, he couldn't escape the memory of the sheer panic he'd seen on her face.

"She just won't have unprotected sex."

He was glad of the darkness now. And the door that stood between them.

"So she *has* said no."

He swallowed. Needing to share the pain that was draining him, trying to understand things he couldn't make sense of. Things Martha might be able to help him understand.

"I think she *wants* to want another baby," he said slowly. "Maybe part of her really does." He looked up at Martha, who watched him silently, her mouth a straight line. "Or it's just because she thinks I do."

"Haven't you ever talked about it before now?"

"Yeah," he said, his voice getting louder. "She's always wanted a big family. She's Shelter Valley through and through."

And everyone cracked jokes about how big the families were in Shelter Valley.

"So maybe you're just misunderstanding something...."

Keith felt a sudden anger inside him. Anger that

had been building for months. Anger that made him clench his jaw and raise his chin a notch.

"Misunderstand that when I'm ready to make love to her, she runs for protection? That she'll stop cold right in the middle to grab a condom?"

He was shocked when he heard the words. Regretted them immediately.

He had to hand it to Martha. She didn't flinch. Didn't seem offended, disappointed. Her expression, what he could see of it, seemed to be filled with encouragement. Understanding. Empathy.

"Oh."

But Keith couldn't just leave the situation hanging there, half-told, between them.

"It's not that I want her to have a baby because *I* want one." He didn't think he was doing a very good job of explaining. "I mean I do, but only if she does."

Martha nodded, grabbed the door, setting her hands next to his arms, resting her chin on her hands. "I understand."

"I think what's making me feel so threatened is that she's always wanted more children, and the sudden change is confusing."

"Maybe she's just busy at work and doesn't feel now is a good time."

Maybe. He didn't think so.

"Her inability to even try has pretty well convinced me that she doesn't want to be that committed to me. Doesn't want to be more tied to me than she already is."

"You think she's got the idea of leaving in the back of her mind."

Keith wished he could read Martha's expression, needed to see in her eyes the truth of her words.

"Yes."

She stood, lifted a hand to his face. "I think she's a woman who's searching for the ground upon which her life is built, Keith."

"But the ground didn't shift."

"Maybe not, but that doesn't mean she realizes it." Her hand dropping back to the car door, she continued, "And maybe the ground *did* shift," she said, adding a new thread of fear to the dread that had become Keith's constant companion. "Maybe something in Bonnie changed and she's just finding her footing again. Give her time, Keith. Believe her when she tells you she loves you."

He stared at her. "How do you know she tells me that?"

"Because if she wasn't giving you something to hang on to, you wouldn't still be there."

Keith wanted to kiss her.

She got into her car and drove away.

CHAPTER TEN

SHANE DIDN'T SAY much on the way home. He walked the few blocks to his apartment, his movements definite and full of purpose. When he got there, he climbed the stairs and dropped her hand.

"This is nice," Bonnie said, pleased to see a planter overflowing with some kind of purple flowers on his landing. There were no cobwebs or dust piles, and the building had a fresh coat of paint. "I didn't realize you lived so close."

Pulling a single-fold leather wallet out of his back pocket, he opened it, slid out a key and unlocked the door. He held it open an inch or so with the toe of his tennis shoe, and then, before going into the house, put the key back in the wallet and his wallet back in his pocket.

"I'm sorry, what did you say?" he asked, glancing over his shoulder at her, his palm flat against the slightly open door.

Bonnie blinked. "Just that I didn't realize you live so close."

He nodded. "I don't drive."

She'd wondered. And wondered, too, if they were going inside.

"Maybe someday," he added, and it took Bonnie a moment to figure out he was talking about driving.

''The doctor thinks you'll be able to drive again?'' she asked, relieved.

''Around Shelter Valley.''

Turning back, Shane pushed the door open. Looking to either side, he left her standing there while he turned on a lamp in the living room. And then went to the stereo, pushing buttons without seeming to even notice them. A Phoenix jazz station came on.

''Excuse me.'' He passed her, heading back outside. She heard his footsteps on the wooden stairs.

Was she supposed to follow him? Feeling uncomfortable, Bonnie waited just inside the opened doorway.

Shane's heavy step was on the stair, coming closer. He stumbled once. And when he entered her line of vision, she frowned.

''What's wrong?''

He was sweating. His brows were raised and drawn, as though he'd been frightened.

''I forgot the mail,'' he said, going back inside, a couple of white envelopes clutched in his fist. ''I can't come upstairs without getting the mail.''

''Okay.''

''I have to close the door now.''

Bonnie wondered if he thought she had to leave before he could do that. Her presence, or something, was obviously throwing him.

''Should I go?''

''You didn't eat dinner yet.''

''I know, Shane, but if you need me to leave, I can get something to eat at home. It's what I was going to do, anyway.''

''No. You said you were having dinner here.''

Okay. So apparently he wanted her to stay.

She moved farther into the room, hoping he'd close the door.

He did.

"Was there something bad in the mail?"

"No."

Shane went to the lamp he'd switched on earlier, reached as though to turn it on, then seemed to realize he already had. He moved on to the stereo, nodding his head a couple of times before walking to a desk in the corner, where he carefully separated the envelopes and slid them into folders neatly labeled on a rack.

His shoulders were less taut as he turned. Bonnie smiled at him—and tried not to stare at the wall behind his desk. There must have been more than a hundred Post-it notes, all covered with Shane's strong, masculine writing.

"I'm sorry."

Coming still farther into the room, Bonnie cocked her head. "For what?"

"I was nervous with you."

"I didn't notice," she said, fingers of one hand crossed behind her back to excuse the half-truth. She'd known he was tense, but not that it was directed at her. "What did I do?"

"Nothing." He stood beside the desk, watching her.

As far as she could tell, he hadn't once glanced around his room, reacquainting himself with home as she always did when she came in after being gone all day.

Fighting an urge to cradle him in her arms, she murmured, ''What upset you?''

''I came upstairs without the mail.''

She didn't understand the problem, although she was trying her damnedest. She assumed it had to do with his need for routine.

Hands at his sides, Shane stood there looking gorgeous in jeans that fit his athletic hips and legs to perfection. His broad, muscled shoulders and chest were impressive, too, even hidden behind the loose flannel shirt.

''But you have it now,'' she told this man who was so perfect in appearance, yet so damaged beneath the surface.

''Because I cannot remember,'' he said slowly, obviously speaking with difficulty, ''I have to learn habits.''

He paused. Bonnie could see from the concentrated look on his face that he was trying to formulate thoughts. She remained completely still. Quiet.

She hurt for him and the effort such a simple function cost him.

''Before I could live alone,'' he continued, sounding more like the intelligent man and less like the lost little boy, ''I had to learn habits to keep my life on track.'' Despite his relatively articulate remark, he spoke with painful slowness.

He grimaced. Now that she'd spent more time with him, Bonnie was beginning to discern patterns. He didn't like it when he repeated himself.

That he knew, and cared, she found astonishing.

It meant that the man he'd once been was still in there someplace. Didn't it?

"The habits ensure that I take care of myself." Eyes lowered, he turned slightly away from her.

"If I don't get the mail on my way up, I'll forget. And then I don't pay my bills."

"You pay your own bills?"

Shane's shoulders stiffened again, his back straightening as he faced her. "I am not completely imbecilic," he said.

She could have slapped herself for her insensitivity.

But in spite of everything, Bonnie grinned. That was the old Shane talking. And God, she'd once adored that man.

"I know you're not, hotshot," she said, reverting without thought to the nickname she'd once used so naturally.

Shane grinned back, his brown eyes meeting hers. For an instant, they were sharing the same thought, the same memory.

And it was good.

"How about that dinner you promised me?" she asked him, gazing around the room, appreciating the methodical neatness, if not the starkness of the decor. A nice couch, hunter-green leather, a couple of matching chairs that were big enough to swallow her, and an expensive-looking three-piece oak table set.

There was nothing on the walls.

No area rugs to give life to the sterile beige carpet.

No implements on the tiled fireplace hearth.

Here was something she could do. Add color and

warmth to his home. Already her mind was spinning
with decorating ideas, little things like plants—no,
wait, he'd have to remember to water them…

"Do you want to see the bathroom?" Shane
asked.

"I'd love to see the rest of your place, if you don't
mind showing me."

He said he didn't mind, but his movements were
stiffer than normal, slower, his speech sporadic at
best as he showed her the kitchen, the spare bedroom
that was completely empty except for some boxes,
the guest bathroom. He spoke only after she did, and
then in one or two words, usually just to express
agreement with whatever she said.

Whenever they exited a room, he looked nervously back toward the kitchen.

"We can go eat now if you'd rather," she said
when they left the guest bathroom.

Shane shook his head, though his brows were
drawn together. "I want to show you," he said.

And then, with another glance toward the kitchen,
he added, "Just a minute."

Leaving her in the hall outside the bathroom, he
went to the living room, returning with a notepad
and pen. He scribbled quickly, then pocketed both.

"Okay," he said, his mouth relaxed again. "This
is my room."

The bedroom set was obviously masculine, ex-
pensive. A king-size bed with little storage doors
built into the headboard. There were matching night-
stands, a tall dresser, a bench under the window. All
in light oak.

"Did you bring the furniture from Chicago?"

"Yes."

He was standing awkwardly in the doorway, his hands rubbing up and down his thighs.

Turning back to the room, a space devoid of any color or life, Bonnie couldn't help imagining the man who'd picked out this furniture, and the life it had witnessed while still in Chicago.

She felt a pang of envy.

For the women who'd known him? For the man he'd been?

For herself because, as much as she'd loved him, she'd never seen him at his best?

"Bon-nie."

His voice was loud. Staccato.

She whirled to face him. "What?"

"I want to know—" He tried the next word, but emitted only a breath. And then, with effort, he finished the sentence. "Why I didn't love you enough."

"What?" Bonnie repeated, heart pounding, all too aware of the thoughts she'd just been entertaining. She had no idea how to answer him. Or even to whom she was speaking.

The injured man-child? The successful businessman? The high-school football star?

"You and I," he said, still standing in the doorway. His hands, now hanging at his sides, were clenched. He was frowning, his chin tight, determination in his face. "I know you loved me."

Bonnie swallowed. "Yes."

"I left."

"Yes."

"You cried."

"Yes."

"Why didn't I love you enough to stay?"

It was a question for which she had no answer. A question that had once tortured her unmercifully.

Knees unsteady, Bonnie wanted to sink down on the end of that big mattress.

"How do you know you didn't?"

And how could it possibly still matter to her?

For years she'd comforted herself with the belief that it had been his wanderlust that had taken him from her, not anything to do with her. She'd found some peace in believing that he'd loved her, but his life had forced him to leave Shelter Valley.

And hers had forced her to stay.

"I know because I remember."

Had the whole thing not been so sad, Bonnie might have laughed at the irony. Here she was, standing with an ex-boyfriend who couldn't remember to get his mail, but could still remember not loving her.

"I just don't know why," he muttered.

She shrugged, upset, confused, wondering how to navigate such unfamiliar territory.

"I don't know, either, Shane," she finally said. "I guess I just wasn't the type of girl guys like you fell in love with. You were going places. I wanted to stay here."

She recognized another, more immediate irony. Wasn't she, in a sense, describing Keith and her today? One of them hearing the call for more than life in Shelter Valley could provide, while the other, with equal intensity, couldn't imagine ever leaving.

With the tip of his tongue peeking through his lips, Shane seemed to ponder her words.

"I think I should serve dinner now."

Bonnie was startled. He seemed to be completely unaware of the tension sizzling around them. Between them?

Or had she just imagined that, for a second there, they'd been ex-lovers trying to recapture what they'd lost?

Giving herself a mental shake, Bonnie followed him out to the kitchen. She'd let Keith's paranoia about the man's intentions get to her. Shane was a handicapped janitor struggling to get through each day, and she, a former friend over for dinner.

A friend who was there to help him, not to find closure for her own emotional history.

"AND THE NICE BIG BEAR who forgot a lot wrote himself a note about the dinner waiting in his cave, reminding himself to set the table and get drinks for his guests while the dinner was warming over the fire. That way, he didn't have to worry about forgetting and having all the other bears laughing at him…"

Keith stood in the hall outside the nursery Wednesday night, listening to his wife's sweet voice as she spun one of her imaginative tales for their daughter. Katie had been a newborn the first time Keith had been treated to this side of Bonnie. It had been a 3 a.m. feeding. He'd stood outside the nursery and fallen in love with his young wife all over again as she'd brought make-believe worlds to warm and vibrant life.

It was late, as Katie had insisted on staying up until Bonnie got home from choir practice; by now, the little girl was probably already fast asleep. Bonnie would be rising soon, gently tucking the quilt around Katie's shoulders and up under her chin, smoothing dark curls away from her forehead, before leaning down to kiss her cheek.

Keith walked quietly away.

BONNIE WENT IN to work Thursday with Lonna on her mind. She'd just spoken to Keith's grandmother that morning, and preliminary reports on the meal program were good, but she had a feeling that things could quickly get out of control. Already Lonna was hearing from others in the community who wanted to be added to the list of meal recipients. So far, she was taking anyone who expressed a need, but had said this morning that qualification guidelines would have to be established.

Some kind of donation system or funding plans would have to be initiated, too.

Bonnie moved through the quiet rooms, Katie trotting beside her. Turning on lights, glancing over the children's art, which was plastered to walls, reading over charts filled with names and stars, Bonnie worried that she'd unleashed an avalanche in her attempt to lighten Grandma's load.

"Katie wants to color," her daughter announced, pulling her hand free to scamper into the three-year-olds' classroom.

"Okay, but only with these crayons on this paper," Bonnie said, setting the little girl up at a toddler-size desk with a box full of jumbo crayons and several sheets of white art paper. Over the past few months, Katie had made several attempts to cover the walls with her artistic expressions.

"Okay, Mommy." The child nodded with utter seriousness as she climbed into the tiny chair and set to work.

"Come show Mommy what you've made when you're done."

"Okay, Mommy."

With a grin, Bonnie continued her opening rounds, checking to be sure each room was ready. She loved these early-morning times alone in the day care with Katie.

She'd hate to lose them. Ever.

Rounding the corner into the nursery, she flipped on the light, her gaze automatically seeking out the cribs to ensure that the linens were fresh.

She stopped in her tracks.

Inside the nursery, the floor was covered in a pile of crumbled plaster and dust. Looking up, taking in the two-foot-square hole in her ceiling, she could hardly believe her eyes. The pile on the floor was wet, as was the area around it, as though there'd been water gathering above until the weight of it had forced the ceiling panel to give way.

"Must have used quality materials when they built this place," she said aloud. This was not a problem, just a nuisance. A phone call and it would be taken care of.

Except that she'd been making an awful lot of phone calls of this sort lately. With one mishap after another, it really was as though the fates were trying to tell her something.

But what?

That it was time to move on? Or just move out?

Or was it just a series of completely unrelated mishaps with coincidental timing?

By the time Jennifer, Sharlyn and the other teachers began to arrive, the mess in the nursery had been swept away and deposited in the trash bin out back. And although the ceiling had not fallen near any of the cribs, for safety's sake, Bonnie had wheeled them all out of the nursery and into the little room by her office. It was generally used only on the rare occasions they had a sick child at Little Spirits.

That was when Katie presented her with three pieces of paper covered with dark little splotches of bold color and told her they were apples.

And the parents who started to drop off their children began to express concern about all the incidents at Little Spirits. Even Phyllis Sheffield and Randi Foster, Bonnie's friends, made pointed jokes about leaving their children in a facility that had been racking up a fair number of insurance claims.

Time was apparently running out. Either Bonnie had to get serious about staying put and having the place gone over with a fine-tooth comb while she launched a public-relations campaign to diminish public fear about the unsolved fires—or she'd better begin making other plans.

"WHAT DID YOU FIND?"

Greg stood as Deputy Burt Culver came into his office, a file in his hand. Greg had continued to follow up every lead, half lead and non-lead on the two

The Harlequin Reader Service® — Here's how it works:

Accepting your 2 free books and gift places you under no obligation to buy anything. You may keep the books and gift and return the shipping statement marked "cancel." If you do not cancel, about a month later we'll send you 6 additional books and bill you just $4.47 each in the U.S., or $4.99 each in Canada, plus 25¢ shipping & handling per book and applicable taxes if any.* That's the complete price and — compared to cover prices of $5.25 each in the U.S. and $6.25 each in Canada — it's quite a bargain! You may cancel at any time, but if you choose to continue, every month we'll send you 6 more books, which you may either purchase at the discount price or return to us and cancel your subscription. *Terms and prices subject to change without notice. Sales tax applicable in N.Y. Canadian residents will be charged applicable provincial taxes and GST. Credit or debit balances in a customer's account(s) may be offset by any other outstanding balance owed by or to the customer.

If offer card is missing write to: Harlequin Reader Service, 3010 Walden Ave., P.O. Box 1867, Buffalo NY 14240-1867

NO POSTAGE
NECESSARY
IF MAILED
IN THE
UNITED STATES

BUSINESS REPLY MAIL
FIRST-CLASS MAIL   PERMIT NO. 717-003   BUFFALO, NY

POSTAGE WILL BE PAID BY ADDRESSEE

HARLEQUIN READER SERVICE
3010 WALDEN AVE
PO BOX 1867
BUFFALO NY 14240-9952

GET FREE BOOKS and a FREE GIFT WHEN YOU PLAY THE...

Lucky 7

SLOT MACHINE GAME!

Just scratch off the silver box with a coin. Then check below to see the gifts you get!

YES! I have scratched off the silver box. Please send me
the 2 free Harlequin Superromance® books and gift for which
I qualify. I understand I am under no obligation to purchase any books,
as explained on the back of this card.

336 HDL DRRL   **135 HDL DRR2**

FIRST NAME	LAST NAME

ADDRESS

APT.#	CITY

STATE/PROV.	ZIP/POSTAL CODE

7	7	7	**Worth TWO FREE BOOKS plus a BONUS Mystery Gift!**
🍒	🍒	🍒	**Worth TWO FREE BOOKS!**
♣	♣	♣	**Worth ONE FREE BOOK!**
🔔	🔔	🍒	**TRY AGAIN!**

Visit us online at www.eHarlequin.com

(H-SR-01/03)

DETACH AND MAIL CARD TODAY!

fires at Little Spirits and had come up completely empty.

After the casino trip, he'd given Diamond to Culver. Culver was the best investigative detective he knew.

"All those trips Matilda Diamond takes to see her ailing sister..." Culver began. He tossed the file on Greg's desk, dropped easily into the chair in front of it.

"Yeah?"

"She's not visiting her sister. For the past three years she's been checking herself in and out of a mental institute in Phoenix."

His deputy named the high-priced hospital and Greg whistled. "Checking herself in?" he asked, brows raised as he picked up the folder.

"Yeah." Culver sat forward, elbows on the arms of his chair. "She's accumulated one hell of a lot of medical bills, Sheriff," he said, using the more respectful title for his superior, as he always did now. The days of "Greg" and "Burt" had ended months before when Greg had held Culver's career, his life, in the palm of his hand. And given it back to him.

Greg glanced through the folder. "Insurance is covering them, right?" he asked.

The uniformed deputy shook his head. "Admittance isn't prescribed."

Standing, his gun a reassuring weight against the thigh of his uniform slacks, Greg settled on the corner of his desk. "Has she got an addiction problem?"

"No."

"What, then?"

Culver shrugged. "Depression, I guess, although that's not official. Either no one knows or no one's talking."

Patient confidentiality could be a barrier to information. If the investigator wasn't Burt Culver.

Always a remarkable sleuth, Culver had a sixth sense that had been honed with impressive results over the past months. Probably his way of atoning for the lapse in judgment that could have cost him his career.

Greg met his deputy's gaze. "The man gambles at the high-stakes tables, has huge medical bills to pay and an unstable wife."

"Classic 'first crime' evidence." Culver slid naturally into the deduction process.

"He needs a large amount of money."

"The property deal in Phoenix is legitimate. And lucrative."

"He could easily have reached the point of being desperate to see it go through," Greg said.

"A gambler, lying about his wife's illness. It's an MO that fits amateur criminal activity."

Greg nodded.

"Diamond gets rid of Little Spirits and the deal goes through."

Leaning back, Culver rested an ankle across his knee. "Either he scares Bonnie into leaving, or the fires worry her clients enough that business drops off...."

It made sense, except...

"He's not going to damage the property that's his meal ticket."

"There wasn't that much damage."

"Only because we got lucky. The Kachina Fire Department hit the scene in record time. Things could've been much worse."

Greg told Culver about the fallen nursery ceiling. "And a bathroom flooded not too long ago," he added.

"Any sign of tampering?"

"None that I know of, but Bonnie had both fixed before calling me. Paul Belango did the jobs for her, and while he said he didn't notice anything, he hadn't been looking for evidence, either. The bathroom was the result of a clogged toilet and the ceiling had been holding water due to a loose pipe joint. Both things could be just normal wear and tear."

"So, back to the fires. What if the building burned down? Diamond could still sell the property to his Phoenix developer. There'd be insurance money, too."

"Insurance is only going to cover the cost of the original building—surely not as much as the sale that's already pending. And a property sale isn't going to net nearly as much as the current deal."

Dropping his hands, Culver peered up at him. "You got any other ideas?"

His deputy already knew the answer to that.

"What about Bonnie?" Culver asked.

"What about her?"

"You said your sister doesn't want to sell. Could she be doing this to make the building less desirable, losing Diamond his sale?"

"Forget it." Greg stood. "In the first place, Bonnie would never do anything like that. She'd lose her business first.

"Second, she was in Phoenix the night of the craft-room fire. And third, her business is as much at risk as Diamond's sale. Parents are starting to get uneasy."

Greg could have added a fourth. He wasn't sure his sister cared enough about Little Spirits anymore to keep it going, even without Diamond's threat. She certainly wasn't desperate enough to resort to criminal activity to save it.

Which left him with a crime against a member of his own family, and no leads.

A déjà vu experience he could have done without.

CHAPTER ELEVEN

SHE COULDN'T SLEEP. Bonnie tried to sink into the mental image that normally relaxed her—the field with soft cool grass, trees rustling, a blue sky overhead and a light breeze against her skin. But she couldn't lie still.

The alarm clock LED screen glowed red in the darkness of the master bedroom—1:33 a.m.

Eyes closed, she tried counting sheep, but had trouble picturing the sheep jumping over hurdles. Sheep didn't do that very well, did they? They didn't really do much of anything that she knew of, except mill around and it was hard to get an accurate count of a bunch of milling sheep.

Keith was behind her, on his side of the bed. A million miles away. A stranger.

And little Katie. God, how she loved that child sleeping so innocently in her bed down the hall. She'd be sprawled sideways in her bed by now, with the covers kicked off.

If the classic sheep-counting maneuver wasn't going to work, were there any faraway places she could escape to? At least in her mind? She'd always wanted to go to France. But not without Keith.

New England was beautiful. Rolling hills. Huge old trees. The homes and the history. The water.

But what would she do there? She had more beauty than she could ever behold right here in Shelter Valley.

The LED display changed again. She had to be waking Katie up in less than four hours. Get her fed and dressed—which took at least an hour because she didn't like to rush her daughter—and then off to another day of watching her teachers work with blessedly happy little kids.

Mike Diamond's secretary was trying to pin her down to an appointment. Probably because Bonnie wasn't responding to the landlord's letters.

She wondered what Greg had found out about the fires.

How about Geneva? She'd heard there were beautiful mountains there. There were beautiful mountains surrounding Shelter Valley, too, and if she drove a little bit north, toward Sedona, the mountains were spectacular. She didn't need to go to Geneva for mountains.

And the long flight would be daunting....

Keith moved and she held her breath, hoping she hadn't disturbed him.

He'd been working extremely long hours. And still helping her out with Katie and the house. And running back and forth between their home and Grandma's. He'd even done a meal delivery that night. She'd delivered the other two. But then, she was a regular driver on Grandma's list now.

She was also a huge pain in the butt to her wonderful husband. She absolutely could not let her restlessness disturb his sleep.

But did he have to be so damned perfect? Didn't

he know that by being so perfect he'd set up a standard that was impossible to live up to? Even if he didn't have a meaningful job right there in Shelter Valley, he'd still find a way to be satisfied with what he had.

Why in hell couldn't *she* be just as satisfied? Lord knows she was doing her best.

Ireland had fantastic rolling green hills. Great accents. And bars. With free-flowing taps of interesting ales and lagers.

Still, there was that long flight to consider....

Though, if she was going for accents, Australia would be the place. Then again, that was halfway around the world....

She couldn't bear to be away from Keith. Even if he *was* too perfect.

And would she change one single thing about her husband? Perfect or not, she loved him.

He wanted them to have another child. He actually thought a baby would solve all her problems.

Something touched her side and she jumped so hard she bumped into the headboard.

"Shh. It's okay." Keith's whisper was soft against her skin as he pulled her more fully against him.

His voice wasn't slurred with the dregs of sleep. She wondered how long he'd been awake.

Expecting him to push his hips against her, Bonnie waited. And tried not to cry. She wanted so badly to make love with her husband. But she was terrified of having sex with him. Of where it might or might not lead.

She was scared to death of driving the wedge between them any deeper.

A minute passed and he didn't push. He wasn't sleeping, either. His breathing was too controlled.

Slowly, not wanting to disengage the arm around her, she turned, snuggled into his chest.

And started to relax when he let her stay there. He kissed the top of her head. His breath remained controlled—none of the little hitches that signified sleep.

"We have to be up in a few hours," she whispered eventually.

"I know. I keep telling myself that."

"So why aren't you sleeping?"

He shrugged, his chest hair tickling her face with the movement. "I have no idea."

"Me, neither." There wasn't any one thing on her mind. Nothing in particular that she was brooding about.

"Anything new?" he asked unexpectedly.

"I heard Becca and Will Parsons are adopting a baby." Bonnie smiled. "A little Korean boy. If all goes well, they're going to fly over at the end of term to get him."

She hadn't talked to Becca yet, but Phyllis had told her the news that afternoon.

Keith was quiet and she realized, too late, her mistake. She'd brought up the subject of babies again. Becca Parsons wanted a second one badly enough to adopt.

"I hear Junior Smith is thinking of retiring as mayor." Her husband's voice was even.

"We hear that every time he's up for reelection."

"I think he means it this time. I was talking to Freda today, setting up an appointment with Will to go over production plans and possible funding ideas, and she said Junior bought some horse property outside of town. She also said Becca's planning to run for mayor next fall."

"No kidding?" Bonnie would have lifted her head to see his face, but she was too comfortable right where she was.

She'd missed gossip sessions with Keith.

"You really think she'll do it?"

"I hope so. She'd be great."

"Shelter Valley's first female mayor."

"Can you think of anyone better suited to the job?"

"Other than Grandma?" Bonnie giggled.

"I'm surprised *she* didn't tell us about this."

"Maybe she doesn't know yet."

"You think there's anything in this town that Grandma doesn't know about?"

Yeah. She didn't know who'd set the day-care fires.

Though she had plenty to say about the fact that Greg hadn't found any answers yet. That was Grandma. Expecting everything at once.

Mostly from herself.

"So you and Martha are ready to run your plans by Will?" She hadn't realized they were already at that point.

"At least for a first-round look." The rumbling of his voice was reassuring.

"That was fast."

"Martha's got some great ideas. And a valuable

understanding of public-television goals and para-
meters. We also got some good stuff from my kids.''

Keith had told her that he was polling his students
for ideas; she hadn't known he'd already received
feedback.

''I'm glad Martha's working out so well.''

''Me, too. You were right. She was the best
choice.''

Bonnie moved a little closer. Laid her head completely on his chest. Matched her breathing to the
steady rise and fall of his.

''How's she doing with the rest of her life?'' Martha's kids were older, so Bonnie didn't have much
to do with the other woman. Most of what she knew
came from Phyllis Sheffield, who was one of Martha's closest friends.

And Becca Parsons of course. She and Martha had
been best friends since college. Maybe even before.

Some of Bonnie's tension returned when she realized how long it was taking Keith to answer her.

''I'm not sure how she's doing,'' he finally said,
relieving her of a worry she wasn't ready to acknowledge.

The relief was short-lived as he continued, ''On
the surface, she's doing fine. I just worry about her
some. She's all alone raising four teenagers. Seeing
to their needs in true Martha style and without com-
plaint. I wonder who sees to *her* needs.''

Bonnie wasn't sure she cared who saw to Martha's needs. As long as it wasn't her husband.

''Does she date at all?'' she asked, hoping the answer was a resounding yes. Hoping that Keith's only
knowledge of the woman's circumstances came from
the Shelter Valley gossip mill—or perhaps an over-
heard conversation between her and someone else.

"No."

"She's got a lot of support from girlfriends." *She doesn't need* you, *Keith.*

And Bonnie didn't need the thoughts suddenly clogging her mind. Jealousy wasn't becoming. And it was out of character for her.

But Keith and Martha had been spending an unusual amount of time together lately. Bonnie had been able to ignore the irritating little doubts at the back of her mind—for the most part, anyway—but she and Keith weren't at the best place in their marriage. And—

"I'm sure you're right," he said. "But it's got to be hard, you know, with four teenaged kids."

"Maybe we could have them over for Sunday dinner," she said. "Look how much being part of a family helped Beth feel less alone."

If you can't beat them, join them?

"I'm not sure four teenagers will want to have dinner with a bunch of old folks."

"Maybe not. But Martha can come. And maybe the kids will, too. Katie would sure love to have them here. And if they spend any time with Grandma, they'll be asking to come back."

Cantankerous though she was, Grandma had that effect on people. Especially teenagers. She always had.

"I'll ask," Keith said. "Thanks."

"For what?"

"Caring."

Yeah.

TWO DAYS AFTER Bonnie had shared his sleeplessness, Keith left work early for a meeting with his wife and her brother. Greg had called the meeting to discuss the day-care situation. Keith was glad to be getting somewhere with that.

The fires themselves had been small; it was the idea that more could be coming that bothered him.

Or maybe it was just that concentrating on the fires diverted him from thinking about whatever else was troubling his wife.

Hands in the pockets of his tan Dockers, the sleeves of his black cotton shirt rolled up past the elbows, Keith let himself into Little Spirits just after one on that Wednesday afternoon.

Though he could hear muffled sounds coming from the three- and four-year-olds' rooms, the huge playroom outside Bonnie's office was peacefully quiet. As were the one- and two-year-olds' rooms. It was nap time at the day care.

A time that used to be Bonnie's least favorite. He wondered if it still was.

Waving at a couple of the teachers who were talking quietly in the hall, Keith walked to his wife's glassed-in office.

Still a few feet down the hall, he heard her talking to someone. She wasn't happy.

"I am still under lease and if I choose not to respond in any way at all for the next two years, I am perfectly within my rights...."

Keith waited to hear who was on the receiving end of her "don't mess with me" tone of voice.

And when no reply was forthcoming, he realized she must be on the phone.

But not for long. She made it clear that she was not going to be pressured into doing something she wasn't ready to do.

And then hung up.

A woman who no longer cared, who had one foot out the door, didn't fight like a she-cat protecting her cubs, did she?

Keith felt a little better as he turned the corner into her office.

THE FEELING DIDN'T last long. And the meeting wasn't about the fires.

"Look, you two, what you have is precious. Too precious just to let it slip away." Greg, sitting forward in one of the two chairs in front of Bonnie's desk, wasn't getting the hint he and Bonnie had both given him.

To leave things alone.

"You adopt a kid and suddenly want to play father?" Keith asked him, half grinning. And half not.

He appreciated what his brother-in-law was trying to do, felt grateful for his support, but the problem was his to handle.

And Bonnie's.

Greg ignored him, turning to Bonnie. "You've got to get past this notion that you don't matter, Bonnie. It doesn't make sense."

"Just because you don't understand doesn't invalidate the way I'm feeling. And remind me to thank your wife for her loyalty."

"Don't bring Beth into this. She's a good friend to you and you know it. She's just worried. And if she's going to choose who to be loyal to, I would hope it'd be her husband.''

Bonnie raised her chin. ''And does she agree with you? She thinks I should just get over myself?''

Keith leaned forward.

Greg sat back. ''No.''

''Well…''

''But that doesn't mean you should throw away your whole life for—''

''Let her be, Greg.'' It was the same old thing. They'd been at this for half an hour and were getting nowhere.

His brother-in-law swiveled to face him. ''She's my sister, and I'm not just going to sit here and watch her screw up—''

''Let her be.'' Keith was deadly serious.

''But—''

''Whether Bonnie stays or goes, whether we stay married or not, is between Bonnie and me.''

''She's not thinking straight and—''

''She has a right to her own views. And frankly, I don't want her staying because she feels she has no other choice. I want her to stay because she's made the choice to do so.''

''Excuse me, I'm right here.'' Bonnie's lips were pinched.

''You sound as though you wouldn't be shattered if the marriage broke up,'' Greg shot back.

Keith understood his brother-in-law's frustration. He'd been dealing with his own for months.

''That's between Bonnie and me, as well,'' he said now, his sharpness a result of his own growing anger. He could have told Greg just how "shattered" he'd be. But the time for that was past.

Greg's chair scraped against the floor as he stood. "I hear you've been spending a lot of time with Martha Moore down at the station."

"Greg..." Bonnie stood, too.

As did Keith. "We're going to leave that right there," Keith said through gritted teeth, standing nose to nose with the sheriff of Shelter Valley. "Before this goes any further and damages a relationship that I value more than most."

With one last glance at husband and wife, Greg nodded, then turned slowly and left.

Keith wasn't far behind. But not before some of his anger spilled over onto his wife.

CHAPTER TWELVE

"WHY ARE YOU CRYING, Bonnie?"

Running a hand through her springy dark curls and wiping away the evidence of her tears, she smiled up at the handsome man leaning on the wall surrounding Little Spirit's outside play area. "I'm not crying."

"I'm pulling weeds out here," Shane said from the other side of the five-foot cement-block wall. "I heard you sobbing." His words were slow, almost childlike.

It would be easy to confuse him, to distract him. But that would be cruel.

"I'm just having a bad day," she said, instead.

"Your husband was here today."

"During nap time, yes," she said.

"Your office window was open."

Bonnie stared up at the dark-haired man, at shoulders that had once ruled a football field. That athletic prowess had won him scholarships to the best schools, providing the opportunity for Shane Bellows, son of a destitute family, to get the education he needed to rise to the top.

"He yelled at you."

"Not really at me," she said. She should be getting to church for choir practice, not sitting in one of the swings in a deserted play yard crying. Keith had taken Katie home with him when he'd gone.

"He's just frustrated because I want to do some other things."

"What things?"

"I don't *know* yet." The blue skies and sunshine above, the perfect mid-April day with its warm temperature and balmy cool breeze, were a balm to her troubled spirit.

"You want to leave Shelter Valley?" His tongue seemed to tangle with the words.

"No," she replied instantly, needing to wipe the worried look from his eyes. But also because she knew the words to be true.

She loved Shelter Valley.

But kids loved their parents and the home they grew up in, and still needed to spread their wings eventually.

She pushed off the ground with one foot, swinging back and forth enough to create a slight breeze against her heated and damp cheeks.

Shane spoke again. "You said before that things were different here."

"When did I say that?"

He frowned. Looked down until all she could see was the top of his head.

"I don't know when," he finally admitted.

Bonnie's heart reached out to him.

She wondered what T-shirt he was wearing that had blue shoulders. She didn't remember seeing him in it before.

"I think you might be remembering the conversation we had after the first fire," she said quietly.

"Things have changed. You said that."

Sympathy in her eyes, Bonnie smiled at him. "You're right."

"But…you like Shelter Valley." He had to work so hard to get the simple sentence out, to complete a thought.

"Yes."

And when he said no more, just continued to stand there, leaning on the wall looking at her, Bonnie just kept right on talking.

"Keith and I seem to have reached an impasse." Scuffing the toe of her tennis shoe in the dirt, she swung slowly. "He doesn't understand what I'm feeling, so he's taking it personally." She stared up at Shane, wondering why she was telling him these things.

"I understand how you feel, Bonnie."

"You do?"

He nodded. "And I want you not to leave Shelter Valley."

Him and everyone else.

Bonnie sent him a smile that was part grimace. "You'd just find someone else to chat with if I did," she told him.

"No, Bonnie." He shook his head, his close-cut dark hair in contrast with the earnest-little-boy look on his face. "For the first time since the accident, I feel sort of whole again. Because of you." His voice was even, controlled. There it was, the hint of the man he'd once been.

"I sure don't know what I've done."

"You care."

Yeah. She did. A lot. About him. About Keith and

Katie. And Greg and Beth and Ryan and Grandma and pretty much everyone else in this town.

LONNA HAD NO IDEA what was going on at Sunday dinner, but she didn't like it.

The family members were in their usual seats, Ryan and Katie on separate sides of the table in booster chairs, Keith and Bonnie at either end, Greg and Beth across from each other, and Lonna next to Katie.

Bonnie's chicken enchiladas were perfect, the salad crisp, and Lonna could still smell the chocolate cake that had come out of the oven shortly after her arrival.

The only thing missing was the chatter. Other than tending to Ryan, Greg concentrated on the food on his plate. Bonnie was so intently focussed on Katie, you'd think the child was a newborn.

Beth smiled at anyone who met her eyes—which wasn't happening often. She broke what seemed to Lonna an interminable silence. "I thought Martha and her kids were going to be here today," she said.

Bonnie leaned over to wipe cheese sauce from the side of Katie's mouth, pushing a lock of dark hair behind the little girl's ear.

Cutting an enchilada with his fork, Keith said, "Tim had a ball game. She promised to be here next week."

"She bringing those kids of hers?" Grandma asked. Now, there were some young folk who could use a Nielson family dinner.

Assuming this one wasn't starting a new trend.

"At least Tim and the two younger girls."

"Make your party casserole, Bonnie. The kids always like that."

Bonnie smiled. Nodded. She was a good girl.

But not a particularly happy one.

In a couple of long gulps Keith finished off the water in his glass, glanced down the table at the pitcher sitting in front of his wife and put his glass down.

That blond hair of his was touching the collar of his polo shirt again. Why couldn't he understand that a man looked much more respectable with short hair?

She bit back the reminder that he needed a haircut. Lonna had been fighting with him about the length of his hair since junior high, and today did not seem like a good time to resume the argument.

She swallowed a bite of food, an uncomfortable experience with the acid rising from her stomach.

Peering at the children of her heart, assessing each one, Lonna settled on Greg first. "You got something bothering you, Sheriff?"

Greg's steely gaze met hers. With a lift of her chin, Lonna met his challenge to mind her own business.

"You might say that."

Bonnie's fork made a loud screech along the bottom of her plate.

"Me do it," Ryan told his mother as she attempted to stab a piece of chicken with his toddler-size fork. The little guy was adorable with those soft blond curls and baby cheeks.

Silently Beth handed over the fork.

"So who's the culprit and what'd he do?" Lonna asked.

"Like this, Ry," Katie said, stabbing her plate with great exaggeration. Her fork came up empty.

The sheriff of Shelter Valley, dressed in jeans and a white polo shirt, pushed his half-full plate away and rested his forearms along the edge of the table. Without turning her head, Beth looked at her new husband, her mouth in the straight line that gave away nothing.

Lonna's indigestion increased.

"I don't know who the culprit is," Greg said slowly, glancing pointedly at his sister.

"Leave me alone, Greg," Bonnie warned. And in a lighter tone, "Eat your dinner. I made it especially for you." She smiled, but the brightly colored T-shirt she was wearing didn't seem to suit her as much as it used to.

"Why's he mad at you?" Lonna stared from one to the other.

"Dinner's good," Greg said. "Thanks."

"Why's he mad?" Lonna asked again, more sharply this time.

"He's just being a guy, Grandma." Bonnie turned back to Greg. "Aren't you?"

He conceded with a bowed head. But the glance he sent his sister seemed to be warning her that while he'd drop things for the moment, he wasn't letting her off the hook.

Bonnie placed her knife and fork on top of the half-eaten enchilada in the middle of her plate.

"So what's bothering you besides things that are none of your business?" she asked Greg. She put the lid on the sour cream. Gathered up the empty rice bowl.

"Where you were the night of the first fire."

Bonnie's head whirled around so fast her short dark curls were flung against the side of her face.

"You think *I* had something to with the fires?"

"Of course you didn't," Lonna declared.

She looked at her "almost" grandson, waiting for him to deny his sister's charge. He did not.

"Assuming I was even the kind of person who could do such a thing, why on earth would I sabotage my own business?"

"I have no idea why, Bon," Greg said, rubbing his forehead. "Insurance money maybe? That's what Culver's going to think. Or to make the building less valuable so the sale will fall through?"

"You can do better than that, Sheriff," Bonnie said. "All I have to do is refuse to move and the deal will fall through."

"But Diamond's going to apply more pressure, making it pretty difficult for you to continue to refuse."

"It would still be easier to say no to my landlord than become an arsonist."

"So maybe you and Keith need the insurance money."

"Are you asking if we do?" The quiet tone of her voice did nothing to diminish the anger in her question.

"Not today."

"Of course they don't," Lonna inserted, giving up on her food, as well. "My grandson just got promoted. Everybody in town brings their kids to Bonnie. Any fool can see they're doing just fine.''

''Thank you,'' Bonnie said with a brief glance at Lonna. Her gaze returned to her brother. ''But you're going to ask, aren't you?''

''No. Just leave it.''

Lonna had a feeling this fight wasn't about the day-care fires at all.

''I'm a grown woman, Greg. I don't need you cleaning behind me.''

''I don't think you're responsible for the fires, Bon,'' Greg said, his face softening. ''But we're fairly certain it's an inside job, and you're the first person anyone's going to look at.''

''Down!'' Ryan's baby voice interrupted with gusto.

''Katie can get down, too,'' Katie added earnestly.

While Greg helped Ryan, Bonnie wiped Katie's mouth and hands and lifted her down from her booster seat.

''You two stay in the family room,'' she told the pair as they tore off together.

''Why are you so certain it's an inside job?'' Keith asked, his brow drawn as he glanced from sister to brother. He hadn't eaten much, either.

''We aren't certain, but both times the fires have been in places that wouldn't really hurt the day care. A supply closet. A craft room. Nothing that's going to slow business down.''

''That could be pure chance,'' Keith said.

Lonna didn't know what to think. She was just glad the kids were talking to each other.

''It's highly unlikely that book of matches just

sailed through the supply closet vent by accident,'' Greg said. "And the angle the rocket had to be at to make it through the craft-room window..."

"That pretty much means someone had to be doing it deliberately." Keith stood, carrying glasses over to the sink.

"And that the person in question would have to know the layout of the day care."

"It could just be some disgruntled parent," Beth threw in from the sink. "Anyone who's ever left a child there has had a tour of the place."

Bonnie joined her sister-in-law at the sink, loading the dishwasher with rinsed dishes. "Greg's already been through everyone who's ever been on the roster."

"What about Diamond?" Bonnie asked. Lonna collected the rest of the dishes from the table, scraping off the mounds of uneaten food. Keith sat back, swishing ice around in his empty glass.

"We're checking on him, but it doesn't make sense, considering how badly he needs this deal to go through."

"Couldn't he be attempting to sabotage Bonnie's business to get her to leave?"

"Possibly, but probably not. In doing that, he'd risk losing the thing he needs the most."

"What about the janitor, Shane Bellows?" Keith asked. Grandma saw the not-so-friendly look Bonnie shot over her shoulder at her husband.

"There's no way Shane would do anything like that," she said. "Not only could he never pull it off, what possible motive could he have?"

"Bitterness?" Keith asked. "An urge to get back at the world?"

Greg shook his head. "I have to agree with Bonnie on this one," he said. "We've talked to him and will do so again, but I don't believe he could do something like this. He can't even follow a conversation."

"Besides," Beth added, "it's obvious that Shane is fond of Bonnie. He wouldn't do anything that would knowingly hurt her."

Lonna knew about the poor boy of course, as did everyone else in town, but she hadn't seen him since his return to Shelter Valley. From what she'd heard, though, he was more lost than violent.

Keith brushed crumbs from the table into the palm of his hand. "You're probably right," he told Greg. "As long as Bonnie has Little Spirits, Shane has access to her."

No one replied to that, but Lonna had a feeling there was plenty that wanted saying.

After a quick peek around the corner into the family room, where the kids were playing, Greg grabbed a cloth and began wiping the table.

"You've been too quiet, Grandma. What do you think?" he asked.

"I think you'll find whoever it is and when you do, he should be strung up."

The kids all chuckled, which eased the tension and her physical discomfort somewhat, but Lonna was still concerned. She'd been planning to move on from Greg to her grandson and his wife, to bring whatever problem had been bothering them out into the open. They obviously weren't having much luck solving it themselves.

But when she opened her mouth to speak, she closed it again. Everyone was smiling, working together, being a family.

She'd leave it at that.

Though she didn't have any herself, Lonna paid close attention to the kids' dessert portions, satisfied to see that everyone did much better with the cake and ice cream than they had with the enchiladas. Maybe things would right themselves on their own.

There was always hope. Always.

"I need to be getting home, Keith," she announced as soon as they'd finished eating.

"But we haven't had even one round of Trivia," her grandson said, pulling the game from the cupboard.

Lonna was tempted. She would've liked to stay. She enjoyed the game, loved being with the kids. But...

"I've got things to do," she told him. "My friend Madeline's daughter has to go back to work, and the job she found is in Phoenix, so she won't be able to get home to prepare her mother's lunch. I need to add her to the meal list." Lonna grabbed her purse before she could talk herself into staying. Even just for one game. "And Dorothy called about a woman she met at the clinic who's recently moved to Shelter Valley to live with her son and his family. She's in a wheelchair and is alone during the day—"

"Grandma—"

She held up her hand. "Not today, Keith," she warned. Her stomach hurt. She wanted to stay and beat the pants off these young people who some-times forgot that she knew so much more than they did.

And she wanted a nap.

She didn't know whether to feel happy or not when, without another word, Keith took her home.

BONNIE DIDN'T NORMALLY run on Sundays, but Keith expected her to that night. Tensions had been high most of the day, which meant she'd need the release exercise seemed to bring her.

He found it ironic—in a humorless way—that he was getting to know this new woman who'd taken possession of Bonnie well enough to predict her ac-tions.

She told Katie a bedtime story before she left. One of her originals, which she created on the spur of the moment, instead of reading one of the many books they'd bought the child.

It was another story about the bear who wrote himself notes. This time the bear made a new friend and found out he could still help people even though he was pretty forgetful, because he could still listen and that was a big part of being a friend.

Keith liked the big old guy. But then, he liked all of Bonnie's characters.

Afterward they walked down the hall together, leaving the little girl sleeping soundly in her horse-and-rainbow room, tucked beneath the princess sheets. The past few hours had been good.

And he had work to do that would take care of the rest of the evening. Logistics to lay down for a new Sunday-morning religious series they were

launching in another month. The time slot had been
offered to any church that wanted it, first come, first
served, in one-hour segments.

Bonnie grabbed her tennis shoes from the hall
closet, getting ready to leave.

The first piece in the series was a question-and-
answer program offered by Pastor Edwards. Keith
and Martha would be meeting with him the next day
to firm up the show's schedule.

"It's nice out. You want to sit outside for a
while?" Bonnie was looking at him.

She had her shoes on, but no socks. No running
gear. Just the designer jeans and brightly colored
T-shirt she'd had on all day. Though he generally
slipped into gym shorts and a T-shirt at home when
the weather warmed up, Keith hadn't changed out
of the Dockers and polo shirt he'd worn that day,
either.

"Sure," he said.

He slipped on the sandals he kept by the garage
door.

Work could wait.

"We're really lucky, you know, to have a place
like this," Bonnie said as they settled on a high-
backed cement bench by the pool in their backyard.
She pulled up her knees, feet on the bench, as she
leaned her head against the wall.

Damn, she was cute.

"Yeah." Keith sat comfortably beside her, missing the days when he would've put an arm around
her. "But we've worked hard for it."

Her head moved along the cement in the semblance of a nod. She was staring up at the starlit sky, her throat bare and fragile-looking.

He'd give a lot to know what she was thinking.

Keith described the religious program he was going to be working on the next day. She made some good suggestions.

She asked if he wanted a glass of sun tea. And went to get it when he said he did. Keith lit a fire in the cement pit in front of them. It wasn't really cold enough, but he didn't much care.

"Grandma sure was feisty tonight." Bonnie settled back on the bench.

He poked the fire with a stick, sending sparks up into the night. "I'm worried about her. She's doing too much."

"I've always expected that I'd grow old in this town, with all the friends I've shared a lifetime with. But I never really pictured our bodies giving out on us. Or thought about how difficult that would be."

Sitting forward, elbows on his knees, Keith played tag with the stick and the flame. "I'm beginning to think Grandma's going to kill herself trying to keep up with all her commitments. She's incapable of saying no."

"She'll be okay." Bonnie didn't sound too worried.

"She's seventy-six years old."

"And if you take away the things that matter to her, she's not going to make it to seventy-seven. Everybody needs a purpose. Grandma's always needed a dozen."

She was right. But Keith was having a hard time seeing Lonna so tired and slow-moving—behavior that was the antithesis to everything he'd always known her to be. The rock of Shelter Valley. Of his life.

The one person in the world who could handle anything.

"She's doing exactly what she needs to be doing," Bonnie said. "I think it would kill her to stop."

He poked the fire some more. She stared silently out into the night. They sipped their tea.

CHAPTER THIRTEEN

A WHILE LATER Bonnie asked, "Does Greg really suspect I set those fires?" Her voice was uncharacteristically docile.

"I don't think so," he replied. "Do you?"

"Not really, but I can see why he'd put himself through the misery of asking just the same."

"Because of Beth."

"And Deputy Culver, too. Trusting people he loved cost your father his life."

Glass on the bench beside her, she lowered her chin to her knees, her arms wrapped around her legs.

She appeared to be contemplating the ground.

Alternating between an odd kind of repressed anger and a vulnerable, sappy love state, Keith stayed beside her, growing more uncomfortable as the minutes filled with a silence he didn't understand.

He loved her so much.

And, his darker side chided him, he was still a man and there was only so much imploring that a man could do. His own self-respect wouldn't allow him to...to act like a puppy begging for scraps from the table.

Glancing over at her, he ached to pull her into his arms. He ached for the rights he used to have, which had somehow slipped away from him.

She sipped her tea. Rested her chin on her knees again. Stared at the fire.

Did it mean anything that she'd chosen to be with him rather than go running?

He remembered the first time they'd sat out there like that. They'd pulled a lounge chair up to the fire and slept there all night, cuddled in each other's arms.

Now they usually slept on opposite sides of the bed.

How had they lost each other?

The fire crackled. The night grew chillier. Keith put on another log, his glass long since empty.

"Is it me, Bon?"

"What?" Her eyes were warm when she glanced at him, but she looked as though she'd been a million miles away—while he'd been right there with her.

"Whatever this is between us. Is it me? Something I've done? Something I'm not doing?"

"Of course not!" Her hand encircled his forearm. "You're wonderful, Keith."

He didn't know about that, but it hardly mattered, in any case. No matter who or what he was, it apparently wasn't right for her.

That thought, a constant companion, ate away at him like acid.

"There must be something I can do, or do differently. Some way to help…"

He was a man of action. The stagnancy of waiting, the idleness while his life drained away, was wreaking havoc with his mental equilibrium.

He had to try. Because he couldn't take this much longer. He deserved better.

And so did she.

Bonnie slid her hand up under his arm, moving closer until she was hugging his arm with both hands, laying her head on his shoulder. "You're doing it," she whispered. "You're still here."

He wasn't proud of the obscenities that ran through his mind.

She wanted him to go on waiting. To continue exactly as he'd been doing. Loving her. Needing the promise of forever. And wondering every single morning if this would be the day she left.

She buried her face against his shoulder and it was only then that he realized she was crying.

SIX-THIRTY IN THE MORNING, and the air reeked of smoke. Wearing white cotton drawstring pants, a bright orange shirt and tennis shoes, Bonnie jumped down from her van. She released Katie from the car seat behind her, then grabbed her bag and purse—and the envelope of insurance forms she'd filled out over an early cup of coffee before dawn.

"Pee-eew. Stinks." Katie said.

"Yeah, thank goodness it's not us this time," she said to the toddler. "It's probably somebody burning weeds."

The air wasn't cloudy, the building wasn't smoking. There were no sirens, spiraling lights or fire hoses. No bustling men or official-looking clipboards. Little Spirits and the surrounding area was peaceful. Quiet.

Until she stepped inside.

"*Pee-eeeww!* Stinks, Mommy!" Katie said, grabbing her nose.

Dropping everything except her purse, Bonnie swung Katie up and ran back to the van, strapped her in. She grabbed her keys and her cell phone, hit the automatic dial to Greg's house and before her brother's sleepy voice even came on the line, she was speeding out of the parking lot.

"THANKS FOR BRINGING the doughnuts. I should've thought of that," Keith said around a mouthful of glazed pastry.

Martha chuckled. "You're a man. It's not your job."

"I'm not a chauvinist." He grinned back. "I can do doughnuts." His program director looked great, in spite of the fact that it wasn't yet seven o'clock on Monday morning. Her navy slacks and matching jacket were for their meeting with the pastor in a few hours.

More and more, Martha was a breath of fresh air in a very cloudy life.

He picked up the agenda she'd handed him, along with the box of doughnuts, when she'd come in moments before and taken her seat at the round table in one corner of the studio. A large wall of equipment, analog, digital and MPEG players, computers and screens separated them from the rest of the room.

"I didn't say you were a chauvinist, I said you were a man. And in my experience, men have a tendency to think that food just appears at opportune moments."

Her black hair was short like Bonnie's, but straight. He preferred Bonnie's wayward curls, but on Martha, straight looked good.

"Some of the best chefs in the world are men," he told her.

"A cooking show. Of course!" Martha said, scribbling. "We can launch it with some kind of cooking contest, and the winner will be the show's host, at least for the start-up."

A pen replacing his doughnut, Keith jotted some quick notes. "An hour-long show," he suggested, "with factoids thrown in—the best chefs, best restaurants in the world, dining etiquette..."

"And some health tips, too, like giving caloric content or cholesterol levels for the day's dishes."

"This is good!" Keith grinned.

"*We're* good, partner." Martha thrust her hand across the table and Keith shook it, held on only long enough to give her fingers a grateful squeeze.

"I'm—"

"Keith?"

He froze. Then yanked his hand back as though he'd done something wrong. Turned.

"Bonnie?"

"Hi, Daddy, it stinks, pee-eew." He barely registered Katie's toddler gibbering.

His wife was standing by the wall of equipment, their daughter in her arms, taking in the cozy sight of Martha and him with their hands clasped.

There was absolutely no reason for him to feel guilty.

Or sick.

"What's wrong?" He stood quickly.

"There's been another fire."

Thoughts of his program director, of their meeting and MUTV fled as it dawned on him that Bonnie's presence meant much more than her witnessing Martha Moore and him alone together.

"At the day care?" he asked, grabbing Katie and sliding his free arm around Bonnie as he led her to the couch along the wall.

"Yeah," she said. "It's okay—again, not much damage—but they're thinking something more serious was intended this time."

He hated that he felt good having Bonnie come to him with her troubles. Needing him. He didn't want her that way, wasn't a man who had to have someone dependent on him to make him feel important.

"Greg's already been there?"

She nodded.

"We drived fast, Daddy." Katie was flipping the lobe of his ear back and forth.

"A fire truck's there now, but the flames had already burned themselves out before I arrived. The fire was started in the Dumpster, but Greg thinks a fuse had been run inside through the dryer duct. The laundry room has some smoke damage." She was glancing between Keith and Martha, who'd turned to face them but was still in her seat at the table. "He thinks that whoever set the fire intended the flame to travel along the fuse and into the dryer, which would've created an explosion."

"Can I color?" Katie asked.

Keith shook his head, removing his daughter's fingers from his hair. Katie liked to twist the hair at his collar around her finger, but didn't stop when the curl got tight and started to pull strands from his scalp.

"Greg *thinks* there was a fuse?" he asked his wife.

"It only just happened, so he doesn't really know what's going on, but there were ashes in the Dumpster. Smoke in the laundry room. Part of a burnt fuse on the ground outside the dryer duct. And no other sign of fire."

"I don't like it."

Katie was yanking the ends of Keith's tie, trying to wrap them around her neck. He slid a finger between the material and his own neck.

"Greg doesn't think I need to close Little Spirits. He just wants another half hour to go through the place."

"Can she have a doughnut?" Martha asked, looking at Bonnie.

Bonnie smiled, though her smile was a little off, and nodded. Katie squirmed down and took off at a run to the table.

"I want to know who's doing this," Keith said, tired of feeling impotent.

Bonnie's intelligent green eyes were shadowed. "I know. Me, too."

Taking her hands, only vaguely aware of Martha and Katie across the room, Keith tried to put everything he felt and couldn't say into a look. He wanted to tell Bonnie to go home, to stay away from all the things pulling at her, to be happy.

And not to worry about him and Martha.

Except that home seemed to be one of the things pulling at her. And Martha was someone he needed right now.

KEITH WAS QUIET on the way to the church. Not certain what right she had to interfere, Martha watched the familiar sights go by and said nothing.

Students and other staff had already begun arriving by the time Bonnie left that morning, giving Martha and Keith no opportunity for personal conversation.

Her friend wasn't doing well, though. That much was obvious, especially to one who'd been through the hell of a forever kind of faith becoming shaky. In her case, the faith hadn't just been shaken, but broken.

She hoped the same wasn't in store for Keith.

Sharing this time with him, these problems he was experiencing in his marriage, was painful but also oddly soothing. She was seeing a side of men that, after her years with Todd, she'd considered only a fantasy.

It did her good to see Keith's compassion. To witness the deep emotion, the love and loyalty he felt for his wife. His patience and ability to forgive.

PASTOR EDWARDS had said he'd meet them in the vestibule. He wasn't there.

"You're sure he said ten o'clock?" Glancing at his watch, Keith frowned.

"Positive."

It had been almost two years since she'd visited the church—since Todd had left her to run away with one of his students—and she didn't like being there now.

"Maybe we should go check his office," she said, heading off in the direction she remembered a little too well. She'd come here several times during the initial shock of Todd's defection.

Back when she still had hope they could salvage their "till death us do part" relationship.

"Something bothering you?" Keith asked, increasing his pace to keep up with her.

She liked him in a tie. It suited him. As did the tapered charcoal dress slacks he was wearing. Bonnie Nielson had to be struggling pretty badly to be messing up with this man.

"Last time I was here was with Todd."

"Attending church with the kids?" His voice was softer, warmer than it had been since Bonnie left.

"Going to counseling with Pastor Edwards."

"I didn't realize you guys went to counseling."

Tensing inside, trying to ignore the burning pain that still accompanied some of those memories, Martha shrugged. "Just that one time. But it was long enough for Todd to announce that he had no interest in making our relationship work, that he wanted a divorce, that he already had plans to marry Stacy."

"God!" Keith said. Then, looking around a little sheepishly at their surroundings, he muttered, "Sorry."

She could always count on Keith to take away the sting. Martha smiled. "No need to apologize to me," she said.

"I wasn't."

"Oh."

They turned the corner, entering the shorter hall where the church offices were.

"So why did he agree to counseling if he wasn't willing to try?"

"He said it was so I'd have assistance when he told me it was over."

Keith snorted. "That was big of him."

His support was nice. In a healing kind of way.

The pastor's office door was open a crack, but there was no sound from within.

Knocking, Keith pushed open the door, peering around its edge, Martha right behind him.

"Oh, my God."

She wasn't sure who said the words. Or if they both did.

Maybe even three of the four people present uttered the cry. The fourth, Emily Baker—married, slim and beautiful, mother of two Montford students—gasped. And pulled her blouse together over bare breasts.

Her bra, obviously a front-clasp kind and probably wispy with lace, was dangling around her shoulders beneath the back of her blouse.

Keith stopped short. He stood, feet apart, hands on his hips, shoulders straight. "I don't believe this."

"I…it's not…"

Pastor Edwards's voice faded away.

Because of course it was.

CHAPTER FOURTEEN

DISBELIEVING, KEITH STOOD and stared speechlessly at the minister who'd guided this town for more than two decades.

Until he couldn't stand the sight before him. He turned away.

"We'll come back later."

"No! Please!" He heard the pastor's voice behind him. Keith slowly spun around.

"I…we…" With an intimate glance that saddened Keith, even while he could empathize with the deep caring it conveyed, the minister included the Baker woman in whatever he was about to say. "We're sorry."

He straightened, regarded Keith and Martha. "I'm going to ask you to keep this to yourselves."

"How can we do that?" Keith said incredulously. "You're supposed to be an example to the entire community!"

Pastor Edwards nodded, chin forward. He wasn't denying anything, wasn't making excuses. And while Keith was disappointed beyond measure, he also respected the older man's attempt to acknowledge what he'd done.

But to ask them to hide it?

Keith shook his head. "You're also a married man," he said.

"I know. And..."

"And you're married, too!" Keith interrupted, pinning the lovely Mrs. Baker with an angry glare.

Keith wondered if Martha was remembering her last meeting in this office with Todd.

"I'm sorry," Edwards said again, his voice low. "More sorry than I'll ever be able to make you understand."

"We both are." It was the first time since her initial gasp that he'd heard a sound out of the Baker woman. He wished she'd do something with the bra clumped beneath her shirt.

It was hard to find any kind of sympathy, compassion or forgiveness with that evidence hanging there so blatantly.

Pastor Edwards hadn't just been caught in a surprise kiss, he'd been feeling up one of his parishioners in the office where God's spirit was supposed to preside.

"How long has this been going on?"

Keith glanced at Martha when he heard the accusation in her voice.

She looked awful. Ashen. Her eyes dull.

Edwards and the other woman shared some intense silent communication and then, when Emily Baker nodded, Edwards said, "Since before Christmas."

Emily Baker had been in charge of the church's annual Christmas pageant—a wonderful show this year that had included singing and acting and used elaborate sets and original music, calling on Shelter

Valley's most talented citizens. The program had told the story of a savior in modern times, appearing in a ghetto neighborhood. It had run for two weeks and brought hundreds of people in from Phoenix and the surrounding area.

They had a digital recording of it on file at the studio and planned to show it during the holiday season this year.

"You're having an affair," Martha said.

Neither of the accused had an answer to that, which was answer in itself.

"And you want us to look the other way," Keith burst out, "come to church and pretend that when you talk to us about the commandments and living good Christian lives, it all *means* something?" He was a little surprised at the vehemence driving him. He'd never been a very religious man.

Unlike Bonnie. And then he remembered...

"My God, man, my own wife came to you for counseling!"

That was when Edwards bowed his head.

"I'm sorry," the pastor said again, eventually raising his eyes, though his shoulders remained slumped. "I expect to pay for my sins. And will spend the rest of my life atoning for what I've done."

"Then why in hell are you doing it?" Actually Keith didn't want to know. Didn't want to continue this conversation for another second. What he wanted was out.

But with fear churning inside him, he stayed there, as though hoping for answers he didn't think existed.

Some understanding that would bring order to the world again.

Was there some outside force that awaited even the best people—his wife, Pastor Edwards—taking control of them against their will? Forcing them to do things so contrary to their character they would never fully recover?

And if the preacher could fall prey to such sins, couldn't a layman like Keith? Or for that matter, a woman like Martha?

Edwards shrugged, glanced at Emily and then away. "I've spent my entire life in the service of others," he said. "All my decisions have been based on my standing in the eyes of the community—and of God. Even the movies I watch, the books I read, the language I use, have been carefully chosen to reflect my calling."

Shifting from one foot to the other, Keith shoved his hands in his pockets. If the sacrifice was too much, Edwards should've left the ministry....

"Even the choice of who I'd marry was made based on what kind of woman would make a suitable pastor's wife."

Martha leaned against a big leather armchair. Keith hoped to hell she was okay.

"And until a few months ago, I'd been satisfied with that, with having a...practical marriage and focusing on the needs of my parishioners. And then I found out what I'd been missing."

"Your spiritual vows were that dispensable?" Martha demanded, her voice shaking with emotion.

Keith had an urge to pull her against him, to lend her his strength.

"No!" Baker and Edwards said at once.

"Please don't think we fell into this lightly," Emily Baker said. Tears flowed down her cheeks, nothing melodramatic, no sobs, just quiet tears that touched a chord of sympathy in Keith.

"Or that there was some point where we actually *decided* to…to get involved," she added. "I haven't been unhappy with my husband all these years. We've got two great kids. When I fell in love with Bruce, no one was more shocked than I was. Except maybe him." She exchanged a sad smile with the pastor.

"We fought this thing from the very beginning." Pastor Edwards took over the story. "We went through weeks where we wouldn't even look at each other."

"And then, after one of those periods, we met accidentally," Emily continued. "In the storeroom above the garage out back. Seeing him unexpectedly like that…I started to cry."

"The next thing I knew, I was holding her," Edwards said.

"And that's when you decided a clandestine affair was worth the cost?" Martha asked.

"That was only a couple of weeks ago," Emily told her.

"This is the first time we've been together since then," Edwards insisted. "And I can promise you, it will be the last."

Studying the woman, the couple, sensing the struggle and pain they were suffering, Keith felt his shoulders ease, his heart begin to soften.

"I asked for your silence only so we could make

our reparation privately," Edwards said. "My wife is going to be hurt enough by this. I'm begging you to let her at least have the comfort of pride left intact."

"You're not going to leave her?" Martha asked.

"Of course not. Emily and I have made a mistake, but God forgives those who are willing to repent and forsake their sins. I've lost much in these past weeks, but I have not yet, I hope, lost my life. My wife is a good woman. One with whom I've built that life. One for whom I care deeply."

"I can't even believe I'm in this situation," Emily said, shaking her head. "No matter what this looks like, I'm a moral person. There's no way I could live a clandestine life." Her gaze met Edwards's. "Not even for love. I can't face a lifetime filled with the remorse and recriminations—the self-loathing—of the past few weeks."

Martha sat on the arm of the chair, listening.

"I'm ashamed to admit that the happiness I've discovered with Bruce was too strong to deny, but I can promise you the guilt of these past weeks is stronger."

"Our only conversations, until today, have been to guard ourselves against this ever happening again," Edwards said. "Emily is very active in the church and has a right to the spiritual sustenance she gets here. We were confident we had our, er, personal issues beat."

"I've got a couple of teenagers at home," Emily whispered, a plea in her voice and in her eyes. "Please let us set this right in private."

Keith glanced over at Martha and when she nodded, turned back to the guilty pair.

"Fine," he said with a single nod of his head, finally able to take his hands from his pockets. They weren't itching to strangle someone anymore. Or hit something.

He waited while Martha made arrangements to reschedule the morning's meeting and then, at last, he was out of there.

The clean fresh air was a relief, but Keith still felt unnerved. He would've bet his life that Edwards, a man he'd known since he was a teenager, would not only choose *not* to commit adultery, regardless of his physical and emotional desires, but that he wasn't capable of it.

And if *he* was capable...

"It's horrible, isn't it, to discover that faith can always be broken?" Martha asked quietly as they drove through streets that had been home to both of them most of their lives.

"Yeah."

A horrible lesson to learn when he was trying to have faith in a woman he didn't even recognize anymore.

ONE OF BONNIE'S TEACHERS, Aubrey Winston, the most recent addition to Little Spirits staff, quit her job on Monday. She was young, new in town and, after the last fire, too nervous to stay at the day care.

Sorry to lose an employee, especially for that reason, Bonnie nevertheless took over as the second teacher in the one-year-olds' class until she could hire a replacement. She'd forgotten what it was like to spend so many hours virtually alone with people who were still too young to talk.

To add to the stress, Keith had been more distant than ever since she'd interrupted him and Martha on Monday, and she hadn't had the chance to have it out with him. In the classroom all day, she'd had to stay late each evening to take care of management details.

On Thursday afternoon, three days after the fire, when Becca Parsons came in to volunteer, Bonnie thankfully gave her Aubrey's position for the rest of the day, grabbed her purse and left the building.

She had no plans. No destination in mind. Other than a sojourn for peace and regrouping. But she wasn't really surprised, either, when she ended up at the building that housed the new MUTV studio.

She went in the back way—not that she was expecting to happen upon anything unexpected.

Alan Rafkin, Keith's long-time technical engineer, came out of a door ahead of her.

"Hey, Alan." Bonnie smiled.

"Bonnie! Good to see you." Then he frowned. "You're not at Little Spirits. There isn't any more trouble, is there?"

"Just playing hooky for an hour," Bonnie replied, grinning.

Alan, a sixty-five-year-old bachelor, had never needed the day care's services, but it didn't surprise Bonnie that he knew about her troubles.

"Keith's in the studio," Alan told her.

"Thanks." Bonnie smiled again, shoving her keys in the back pocket of her black designer jeans as he headed off in the opposite direction.

She followed the twists and turns down hallways and around corners, remembering the day the previous September when she and Keith and a group of students had made the trek a hundred times or more, helping with moving in.

She'd passed Keith in the hall that many times, too. It didn't seem to matter what she'd said that weekend, she'd made him laugh. As though she were the wittiest woman alive.

She couldn't remember the last time she'd made Keith laugh.

Was that because she'd lost her wit? Or he his sense of humor?

He was alone, sitting at the computer used to update the bulletin board that ran on MUTV during every half-hour commercial break. One of his full-time employees, Camilla White, usually sat there.

Keith's hair, always a little long, needed a trim. Something Bonnie usually did for him. He was wearing the tan jeans she loved and a plaid shirt with the sleeves rolled halfway up his forearms.

Bonnie's stomach quivered. God, he looked good.

Sometimes it was hard to believe he was hers. Who'd ever have thought that plump Bonnie Richards, nurturer extraordinaire, the girl dumped by the high-school quarterback, would end up with the greatest-looking guy in town?

And who'd have guessed she'd screw it up?

"Where's Camille?"

"Sick." He spun around. "Bonnie! Is everything okay?"

The immediate crease in his brow, the shadowing

of his eyes on seeing her, made her wish she hadn't come.

"Everything's fine," she said, fidgeting with the hem of her collared T-shirt as she came closer, sat sideways in the chair next to him.

All week there'd been one thing on her mind. More than the most recent fire at Little Spirits, more than her loss of an employee and possible clients, or Grandma Nielson and her friends, or even her own dissatisfactions, what had been bothering her was the cozy scene between Keith and Martha. The scene she'd interrupted.

"I had a chance to slip away and thought I'd see if you could get free for an hour."

He studied her for several seconds before saying, "Okay."

"You can leave?"

His attention reverted to the computer screen with its blinking cursor. And then he checked his watch.

"I guess," he said hesitantly. In the old days, he'd always been eager for their trysts. Had told her they were the most important part of his days.

But then, it had been a long time since she'd offered. Maybe he'd forgotten.

They walked out to the football field and beyond, until they were forging a path through undeveloped desert.

"I had another letter from Mike Diamond this morning."

"I thought your mail doesn't come until noon." He was walking far enough away that their fingers didn't even brush.

"It came by overnight express."

She glanced over at her husband's bent head. Just how intimate were he and Martha Moore? Was her discovery of the two of them prompting this withdrawal?

"He's raising my rent. Adding the cost-of-living increases he hasn't charged in the past five years."

"Can he do that?"

"I think so."

"How much will it be?"

She told him. Watching their feet step on the hard dusty ground, one foot and then another. In unison.

At least there was something about them that still was.

"There'll be less profit of course, but you can afford it."

If she wanted to.

"I have a feeling this is just the beginning," she said, her mind only half on the conversation. "He's going to make my life hell until I go."

"Eventually he'll lose that offer and need you to stay."

She'd thought of that, but wondered how desperate Diamond would get first.

"He offered to pay me twice that if I leave now."

Keith nodded. "A relocation fee."

"He's coming in next week."

Her husband's head shot around. It was one of the few times he'd looked her in the eye all week. "You agreed to the terms?"

"No. He's coming for an inspection."

"What?"

"The lease allows it. He's just never done it before."

"You think he's going to be looking for things to give you a hard time about?"

"Don't you?"

"Probably."

Hands in his pockets, Keith stopped, faced her.

"Why did you come here?"

"You've been so distant all week…" She needed to rail at him. But she couldn't. As far as she knew, he'd done nothing wrong.

"Just preoccupied."

She could leave it at that. The part of her spinning out of control begged her to leave it at that.

"You want to talk about it?" she asked, instead.

Bonnie hardly breathed, waiting for his reply. Prepared to hear what a paragon of virtue and good works Martha was or—maybe worse—to be told that her husband no longer wanted to share his troubles with his wife. She crossed her arms behind her, squeezing her hands together.

When it finally came, the reply was nothing she could have dreamed up. Ever. It was that ludicrous.

Pastor Edwards and Emily Baker?

"There's no way," she said with complete certainty. "You must've seen wrong."

"I stood there and watched her button her blouse, Bonnie."

"So maybe she hurt herself, needed a Band-Aid, just had surgery. Something." As farfetched and nonsensical as her reply was, Bonnie spoke with complete sincerity.

"Her bra was still hanging behind her."

CHAPTER FIFTEEN

BONNIE SANK onto a boulder, chin to her chest, and peered sideways at her husband.

"Has the whole world gone mad?" she whispered.

"It's sure seems that way lately."

She remembered the day not so long ago that she'd gone to see the pastor. Emily Baker had been out in the hall, waiting to go in after her. But according to Keith, they'd claimed that they hadn't been alone together. Nothing was making sense.

For the first time in years, Bonnie ached for her mother's arms around her, enclosing her in a world where some things were solid and sure.

"If you can't trust your preacher, who *can* you trust?" she muttered.

Apparently Keith didn't have any answers, either. He sat down beside her. "Bon? Is there someone else?"

"What?" Turning her head, she stared at him. What on earth was he talking about? "You mean, with me?"

He nodded.

"As in a man?"

"Yeah."

Mouth open, she just kept staring. "You're kidding, right?"

Rubbing a hand through his hair, he sighed. "I know you wouldn't be seeing anyone, but it does occur to me that there might be someone you…have feelings for."

The idea was almost as preposterous as Pastor Edwards and Mrs. Baker.

Was Keith projecting his own desires onto her?

"I love *you*." She wanted no doubt about that.

"Good people don't ask to fall in love at inappropriate times, but sometimes it happens, anyway," he said. "We can't always govern our hearts."

Oh, God. Her face felt hot. And then cold.

"I work with toddlers all day," she reminded him. "Where on earth would I find a man to ruin my life over?"

He, on the other hand, worked with a lovely and competent assistant….

"A father, maybe."

"Whatever else I might be unsure of," she told him emphatically, "I've never had a moment's doubt about my love for you. Why would I struggle so hard to be content with my life here if not for you?"

Elbows on his knees, his gaze was focused in front of them as he nodded.

She didn't want to ask. But had to know.

"This is really about you, isn't it." Never in a million lifetimes would she have thought they'd be having this conversation.

"Uh-uh." He shook his head. But didn't meet her eyes.

''I saw you with her, Keith. I saw the look in your eyes.''

A look she'd believed was reserved for her. And she wasn't going to cry, dammit.

''You're talking about Martha?''

''Is there anyone else?''

''Of course not.''

''But there is her?'' She sounded like a nagging, insecure wife.

''Not in the way you mean.''

It was time to let this drop. To trust her husband.

''So you can honestly tell me you feel nothing for her? At least, nothing more than you feel for any of your other co-workers?''

He paused.

The dust smeared before her eyes, becoming one big pool of beige. Her stomach churned.

And then he turned to her, his gaze accusing. ''What is it with you, Bonnie? I'm not allowed to have friends? You've never been this way before.''

He was right. To a point. She'd never been jealous because he'd never given her reason to be.

''I just don't want you spending time alone with her,'' she said. ''Look what happened to Pastor Edwards.''

Keith stood up abruptly. ''No, Bonnie, you don't get to change the rules,'' he bit out. ''Our relationship has never been about ownership and it's not going to start now. I'm not a possession. You do not choose who I may befriend and who I may not.''

Bonnie was momentarily shocked speechless. She stood, but found she couldn't head back. Not yet. ''Does that mean you can have an affair and I've got no say in the matter?'' she asked after moments of unfriendly silence.

"Of course not.'' The anger appeared to have left him as suddenly as it had come. His gaze, holding her own, softened perceptibly. "I just never thought there'd be room for doubt between us.''

"Like I said, the world's gone mad.''

"Yeah,'' he said, his arm touching hers as they started back.

"So how do we protect ourselves?''

"I don't think we can,'' he replied sadly. "The truth of the matter is, people change. Hearts change. Minds change.''

By *people* did he mean her? Or him?

She supposed it didn't matter.

Because he was right.

NOTHING MADE SENSE.

"What've we got in common here?'' Greg asked, though he and Culver had already gone over the evidence—what little there was—several times.

"Three fires,'' he answered himself while his deputy looked over notes.

"But all set differently,'' Culver muttered.

"And we can't rule out the flooded bathroom and fallen ceiling panel.''

"Those could've been normal wear and tear, just like your sister thought.'' Culver looked up at him.

The two men, both in uniform, were meeting in Greg's office. Greg leaned back with an elbow on the arm of his chair behind his massive desk; Culver, an ankle crossed over his knee, sat in one of the chairs in front of it.

"If this *is* an inside job, the john and the ceiling could easily have been tampered with.''

"I checked out the other tenants this afternoon,'' Culver said, eyes narrowed. "No one else is having any structural problems.''

"The day-care portion of the mall was built first.''

"Only by a few weeks. They all opened at the same time.''

Dropping his arm, Greg stood up. Paced once around the room. Settled on a corner of his desk. They'd had deputies driving by the day care more often, but so far there'd been absolutely nothing to report.

"Who do you suspect?'' he asked.

"Because nothing fits any kind of MO, the way I see it we have three choices,'' Culver said.

"They are?''

"We're dealing with someone really stupid—''

"An amateur.''

"That's a given. But this is either a stupid amateur who'll eventually get caught. Someone with an ax to grind, who isn't smart enough to fight his battles in a legal way.''

Greg nodded. "Number two?''

"It's a really smart amateur who's making us run in circles. Maybe a kid who's in it for the challenge.''

Harder. But definitely a possibility.

"Or?''

"Or it's an inside job, meaning Diamond or your sister.''

Everyone else at Little Spirits had alibis. Except the janitor, who couldn't remember where he'd been.

But in his case, his lack of memory *was* his alibi. And that checked out with his physician.

"My sister doesn't have a strong enough motive."

"I agree."

Greg was damn glad to hear that.

"And while Diamond has the motive and no verifiable alibi, he says he stands to lose, not gain, by these mishaps, and I believe him. It doesn't make sense that he'd sabotage his own sale. He admitted to the gambling problem, by the way. And to being in debt past his ears."

Once again, Greg agreed. He also trusted his deputy's instincts.

"If it's either of the first two, the strikes are going to get more dangerous, do more damage, possibly even during the daytime when Bonnie's got kids there."

Culver laid a hand on Greg's shoulder as he passed him on his way out. "We'll get him, Sheriff. We always do."

Yeah. Before or after Bonnie got hurt?

BONNIE RAN INTO Becca and Bethany Parsons in the grocery store Thursday after work. She had Katie in the cart and needed to get home to make dinner, but wanted to know how the afternoon had gone.

"You'd left before I got back," she told her friend as the two little girls struck up a toddler version of conversation. "Did the one-year-olds wear you out?"

"No." Becca chuckled. "I had a meeting with Junior Smith late this afternoon."

"So is it true that you're running for mayor?"

Becca glanced around, as though to ensure they were alone in the aisle. "I haven't decided for certain, and I won't until we get home with the baby, but Will's encouraging me to go for it."

Bonnie grinned, truly happy that life was turning out so well for a woman the town had counted on for more than twenty years. "When do you leave to get him?"

Becca named a date and then rattled off several things they had to do before they'd be permitted to bring their new son home.

"How old is he?"

"A month."

"Does he have a name?"

"Will wants to name him Randall—after his little sister, Randi. I think he should be Will, Jr."

"So, you'll have this decided sometime before his first birthday?" Bonnie asked, smiling.

The girls were both hungry and restless, and after another moment of congratulations, Bonnie pushed her cart up the aisle.

"By the way..." Becca called behind her.

Handing Katie an animal cracker from the box the little girl had grabbed from a display, Bonnie turned. "Uh-huh?"

"I saw Lonna this afternoon. Apparently she's got a couple more people calling her for meals."

Bonnie had spent the evening before with Keith's grandmother. "Yeah. And now they're talking about visits, too. When I left last night, Grandma was working up a tentative chart to schedule volunteers."

Something else Bonnie had to worry about. Her attempt to help grandma meet her goals might very well be the death of the older woman.

"You know," Becca said, pulling alongside Bonnie again, nodding as Bonnie asked if Bethany could have a cracker. "There's money available for community programs. I used some to start up our Save the Youth group. Maybe Lonna ought to think about writing a grant proposal."

"To hire help, instead of relying on volunteers?" Bonnie asked. That would sure solve one problem. Volunteers weren't always the most reliable people to have on staff and every time one didn't show, Lonna had to step in.

"Sure," Becca said. "Or fund a party once a month."

"Or maybe even rent a facility for everyone to get together for bridge games or craft projects."

Katie swung her feet, kicking the cart. Bethany joined in.

"We'd better go," Bonnie said, holding her daughter's feet still when the little girl disobeyed her plea to stop.

"The grant money's there," Becca said again as she wheeled her cart away. "Think about it…"

Bonnie nodded. If she could get Grandma some real help, that would be one huge relief.

HE COULD HARDLY WAIT for Katie to go down, had to bite back impatience when the almost four-year-old insisted on dressing herself after her bath. Which, by Katie's definition, included choosing what she was going to wear. It took them twenty minutes to convince Katie there was a reason for pajamas; the little girl had opted for her swimsuit first, because it was her favorite garment. She'd occasionally tried to wear it to church.

And then she'd lobbied adamantly for her favorite pair of shorts and a Christmas sweatshirt that had been too small at Christmastime.

If it hadn't been for Bonnie's laughter while she supervised, finding logical answers for every one of Katie's arguments, Keith might have pulled rank, intervened. He was all for skipping the bedtime story, too. Especially when Katie asked for the Dr. Seuss classic *Green Eggs and Ham.*

There were just some times a guy was beyond "Sam I am."

And this was one of them. Keith had to convince his wife that he still wanted her. And make sure he convinced himself, too.

"Daddy read." His daughter's request surprised him. Bonnie was generally the parent of choice for that task.

"Yeah," Bonnie added, still smiling. "Daddy read."

And so, while inside he was screaming *no,* Keith started in.

But his mind wasn't on the odd, skinny creature with the ugly face who refused even a taste of green eggs.

All afternoon, ever since Bonnie had left MU to go back to work, he'd been unable to shake the feeling that he and Bonnie had turned some corner, that they were on a road he'd neither chosen nor wanted.

Somehow he had to get them off.

He tried like hell to mimic the voice of the skinny little creature. And glanced up from the pages to find his wife watching him.

He continued reading.

Katie was on her lap, and Bonnie stuck out her tongue at Keith over the child's head.

Had he been mistaken? Had that day's conversation broken down barriers rather than erect them? Was his plan to solidify his relationship with his wife not even necessary? Had he misread things that badly?

God, he had to get off this roller coaster.

He read on, hoping each time he looked up to see his daughter's eyes drifting shut, or better yet, to find them closed.

Bonnie was still wearing the black jeans and tight tan-and-red shirt she'd had on that afternoon. Keith itched to get under that top.

Sex might not be a cure-all, but it could sure as hell make you feel better.

The next glance showed him what he wanted to see.

Katie Marie Nielson had fallen asleep.

HE'D MEANT to talk first. To clarify that while he couldn't tolerate Bonnie's ultimatum that afternoon, he and Martha were not having an affair. He'd never even kissed the other woman.

But he was kissing his wife—outside their daughter's bedroom door.

Before they'd even made it down the hall, she'd wrapped her arms around him. "Kiss me."

Her face was lifted, her eyes wide in blatant invitation.

Keith lowered his head. One kiss.

And then they'd talk.

Her lips opened even before his did, her tongue dancing lightly along his lips. Fire shot through him.

There wasn't anything light or dancing about the way his tongue explored her, no pretense that this was anything but bone-deep need. The need to reassure himself that he would not, like Edwards, jeopardize his self-respect for the momentary comfort Martha might offer him.

He heard a moan. And a moment later, realized it had been his own.

"I'm hot…" Bonnie licked his lower lip.

"Mmm-hmm," he mumbled against her mouth. He wasn't ready for the kiss to end. Was tired of thinking.

His breath was no longer steady, but then, neither was hers.

God, he loved this woman.

That had never been in question.

"Touch me." Her words were a whisper.

She grabbed his hand and he held on, squeezing her fingers, wanting a way to hold on to her, their marriage, as easily as could hold that hand.

"We need…"

"Shh," she said, bringing her finger to his lips while she rubbed her breasts against his chest. "I know. We need—" she kissed him "—to move—" another kiss "—out of the hallway."

They should. But he was afraid that if they moved, reality would intrude. He kissed her, instead.

"Come on," she said, pulling him toward the other end of the house, into the family room, grabbing a throw off the back of the couch and tossing it on the floor.

"I need to feel you inside me." She looked up at him, her green eyes shadowed with passion. He saw there, in her gaze, an emotion he'd missed earlier. Desperation.

She had something to prove, as well.

He followed her down to the hastily thrown blanket, unfastening his pants as he went.

"KEITH?"

"Ye…" His voice broke. "Yeah?"

Bonnie rolled onto her stomach, still naked. They were both lying on the blanket in the family room.

Keith didn't think he could move yet. Lovemaking hadn't been that intense in a very long time.

"Why did you pick me?"

He opened his eyes. "Because I loved you."

"But why me?" she said frowning. She was up on her elbows, unselfconscious about her nakedness. "You're gorgeous, you have an impressive education, and even then you had a great job. You could've had any of a dozen women in town, not just a chubby girl like me."

He'd been stuck on the "you're gorgeous" part and only tuned in again when he heard "chubby."

"You weren't chubby."

"I was, too." She nodded her head for emphasis.

Shifting to his side, Keith propped himself up on one elbow, holding her gaze. "You were all woman, with curves that enchanted me."

"You must have been blind."

"No, I knew exactly what I was seeing, and I wanted that woman so badly I couldn't sleep nights."

"So you're disappointed with the new skinny me?"

"I think the past hour pretty much answers that." He traced the crease between her brow. "Why do you ask?"

She shrugged and flopped down, her chin on the arms she'd folded in front of her. "Today, when I came to see you at school, I was struck by how lucky I was that someone as gorgeous as you chose someone frumpy like me. My type, or the type I was then, usually got the geeks with glasses."

He wondered if, now that she was trapped in a life that didn't give her enough challenge, she still felt so lucky. And was afraid to ask.

"Speaking of today," he said, drawing a finger down her spine, "I want it clear that there is nothing sexual between Martha and me."

She laid her head on her arms. "Okay."

There was no perceptible difference. Nothing to indicate that the barriers were going back up.

"You're sure?"

"Yeah."

"Because, you know, a great thing about you and me is the trust we've had from day one. It's allowed a freedom that not many couples have."

She lifted one hand to her chin.

"Yeah."

"We've always been able to have friends without there being a threat to our relationship."

Her chin rocked gently in the space between thumb and forefinger. "You're telling me you and Martha are friends and that you intend to remain that way."

He must not have explained well enough. "This isn't about Martha and me, Bon, it's about *you* and me."

"But you *are* still going to be friends with her."

He started to see red again. "Yes."

"Why?" Sitting up, Bonnie lifted a corner of the blanket up and pulled it around her. "What is so compelling about her that you can't forgo her friendship even now, when we're already facing so many challenges?"

Keith took a deep breath. Slid into his briefs. Calmed himself enough to talk rather than fight.

"It's got nothing to do with her," Keith said, although he supposed if he slowed down and really thought about it... "It's about our marriage, and whether or not we want it to be a cage or a window. Are we going to be so insecure with each other that we can't interact with anyone else?"

"Tell me what she gives you, Keith."

"She's a friend. She gives me support. I give her support. That's it."

"And I don't give you support?"

"Of course you do! But does being married mean we can only get that from each other for as long as we live?"

"No." It wasn't an empty agreement, or given for sake of keeping the peace. She spoke confidently, looking him straight in the eye.

But she knew him too well. Knew there was more.

He could tell by the almost calculating look in her eye as she watched him.

"I'm *enough* when I'm with Martha." He hadn't meant the words to escape. Hadn't really, before now, formed a coherent thought out of the nebulous emotions that had been swarming inside him for months.

Bonnie frowned. "What does that mean?"

"When I'm with her, I can relax, knowing that she's satisfied being there. I don't have to wonder what's wrong with me, what I'm not providing." Surprisingly it felt damn good to voice the thought.

"What do you want me to do, Keith? Tell you that I don't yearn for more out of my life? It would be a lie."

"So then leave!"

"I don't want to leave. I love you. And Katie. And Shelter Valley and everyone here."

"Maybe you don't want to go because you just haven't had any better offers."

"Yes, I have."

Keith's heart stopped. "Who from?"

She told him about a job offer she'd had at the conference she'd attended several weeks before. And her refusal to even consider it.

"Why?" he asked, losing much of the fire that had prompted his words.

"Because I don't want to leave you."

Keith didn't know what to say. If she stayed, she'd be unhappy. If she left, he would be.

And if he went with her?

"Are you in love with Martha?"

"What? No!" He wanted to pull his wife into his

arms, escape back to the earlier part of the evening, when all that existed was the love between them. "I told you, it's not like that at all. I swear to you, Bon."

"Okay."

Keith was pretty sure she finally believed him. But he was beginning to fear that, for them, "okay." might never come again.

CHAPTER SIXTEEN

SHANE WAS WITH BONNIE in the day care kitchen when she found the broken glass. She'd come in on Saturday as she sometimes did and he'd been outside at the other end of the property, raking some gravel, in case he got to see her.

And because the gravel had to be raked.

Someone had broken a window in the kitchen.

"I don't believe this." She sounded scared.

And that surprised him. The other times stuff had happened, she'd taken it in stride.

"It's just…a broken…window." Speech without spitting was hard today.

Instead of her usual nice colorful clothes, she was in black workout pants and a tight short black top with a T-shirt over it.

He could see the black top under the T-shirt. It was nice on her breasts.

"I have exercise clothes, too," he said slowly, carefully. Maybe if she didn't think about the glass… "They came with me from Chicago."

She was moving around the room, inspecting the hole in the window, looking over the massive countertops and around the huge stove.

"I don't use them here," he said. She'd like him

better if he were in his bike shorts. He had a good body.

"I have to call Greg."

"Why?" Shane frowned. "I'll sweep it up."

For once she didn't notice him.

He'd spent hours waiting around for her, and now this. Shane had no idea what to do. He didn't have his bike shorts. And...

Things settled inside him when she turned and smiled right at him.

But then she ruined it.

"He'll kill me if I don't call him," she said.

"Look at this." She picked up something from the floor across from the window, brought it over to him.

"It's a rock." As big as a softball.

"Someone threw this through the window."

She sounded really surprised, and Shane's head started to hurt.

Dammit. She was confusing him.

"I'm sorry."

"Oh, Shane." She looked up at him. For her it was a long way up. Her eyes were wide open and warm. He liked them that way. "Don't be sorry," she told him in a voice so soft he wanted to hold it inside him. "It's not your fault."

"But you're upset." He struggled to voice his thoughts. To have clear thoughts. He'd been expecting a better day.

"Not at you," she assured him.

Shane believed her. "Okay."

"I'll have to show this to Greg," she said, turning

the rock over. ''Oh, my gosh!'' She sounded like she might start to cry.

''What?''

He needed to leave now. The day was just bad.

''There's something stuck on the back of this.''

He peered over at the ugly gray stone. ''Yeah.''

''Is it explosive?''

He glanced at it again, but didn't want to. He had to go. Maybe not even sweep up the glass first. He shrugged.

''I have to call Greg.''

This time she sounded very scared.

''I'll stay with you until he gets here, Bonnie.''

And he'd clean up the glass for her. Then he had to go.

WHILE THE REST of the world worshiped, Keith sat home on Sunday. Or rather, he wandered around his empty house unshaven and undressed except for an old pair of exercise shorts. He'd expected Bonnie to stay with him after he'd told her about Pastor Edwards, but she'd had a solo in the service and didn't want to let the choir or congregation down.

'You're a bigger man than I am,'' he'd told her as she'd strapped on Katie's patent-leather shoes and ushered the child out.

She hadn't replied. But then, conversation between them had been infrequent the past couple of days.

Mostly because of him.

What was the point in talking when words with Bonnie inevitably brought anger, instead of solutions?

The phone rang, a welcome interruption from thoughts quickly growing morose.

"I thought you'd be home."

How had he known the caller would be Martha? She rarely called him at home.

He settled back into a corner of the couch, an ankle crossed over his knee, head back against the cushion.

"You couldn't stomach it, either, huh?" he asked. They'd never really talked about that morning in Edwards's office, other than to reschedule the program.

"I sent the kids."

"Bonnie took Katie."

"I couldn't tell them why I wasn't going."

"Bonnie knows."

"We can't not go to church for the rest of our lives."

Couldn't he?

Not completely sure anymore, Keith didn't say anything. Faith was a personal thing. To each his own.

"I just wanted to let you know that the kids and I are going to take a rain check on dinner."

He didn't blame her. Martha knew things were rocky in the Nielson household.

"Anytime. Just let us know when," he said. Because, in spite of everything, he really wanted her to come.

"Would next week be okay?"

"Sure. I'll tell Bonnie."

They could have hung up then.

But she asked about his weekend. He told her about the most recent hit on the day care. A rock with some kind of explosive attached that could have done extensive damage if the rock had hit so that the powder had detonated.

"The attacks are getting more serious."

But whoever was doing this was resorting to pretty chancy methods.

"Is Bonnie still planning to open in the morning?"

"Yeah, Greg's on top of things. And the attacks all take place when the facility's completely empty—not just Little Spirits, but the connecting businesses, as well—and of course, none of them have been touched."

"At least whoever's doing this appears to be targeting the day care itself, not Bonnie or the kids."

The water in the pool glistened beneath the intense Arizona sunshine. Normally Keith loved the blue skies that were so typical here.

"For now."

"I've heard a couple of people mention finding other places for their kids until this all blows over."

"Bonnie's lost a few, but not enough to warrant closing. A lot of people in this town count on her."

He'd always loved that about Bonnie.

He continued to stare outside.

"You don't sound good."

"I'm fine." Did that sound convincing enough?

"It's okay if you don't want to talk about it, boss, but don't insult me with lies."

He sighed. Wished life was simpler.

"I think Bonnie might be leaving."

"*What?*"

Unable to stand the blue skies and sunshine another second, Keith closed his eyes.

He told Martha about his last real conversation with his wife. The one in which she'd told him about the job offer.

"If she turned it down, why would you think she's leaving?"

"Because she couldn't quite hide the resentment she felt at having to do so. It would've been a great opportunity for her."

"Maybe it's time to ask her for a divorce."

His eyes shot open. He sat up. "What did you say?"

"I think you should ask her for a divorce."

That was what he'd thought she'd said. And the last thing he'd expected to hear.

"You're supposed to be buoying me up here," he muttered.

"I can see I've done a swell job of it so far."

She'd helped him a lot. She had to know that. Elbows on his knees, he stared at the floor. The rug had a couple of stains from Katie's juice spills, but it was a hell of a lot easier on the eyes than the blinding cheerfulness of a sun that wouldn't stop shining.

"If nothing else, the conversation would shake Bonnie up," Martha said after she gave him an opportunity to reply—which he opted out of. "Force her to make a decision."

"I don't want a divorce."

"If you ask her," Martha continued, irritating the hell out of him, "and she's shocked and horrified, you'll have the answer you want. You'll know she's still yours.''

"And what if she isn't?" He felt claustrophobic at the thought of it.

"You'll still have your answer," she said.

Keith wished he'd never answered the phone.

"Not the one you want, but at this point it sounds as if any answer would be better than none at all."

Didn't the woman know when to quit? Still—although he remained silent—he held the phone to his ear.

"You need to be able to move forward, Keith."

She was right about that.

"I'm not asking for a divorce."

"Because you're afraid she'll give you one?"

He refused to answer that.

"Because if that's the reason, that's exactly why you should ask."

Martha's voice, uncharacteristically soft, urged him to think about what she'd said. And then she told him she'd talk to him the next day.

Keith didn't say a word.

LONNA LAY IN BED Tuesday night too keyed up to sleep. Or too exhausted to sleep. She wasn't sure which.

She should get up and put one of her favorite Doris Day movies in the VCR. The chipper blonde was always good company. Except that she had to be up to start breakfast in five short hours and knew she had to rest. Late-night movies were something she had to pass up for now.

Lonna closed her eyes, but when she did, the vision of Alice Morsi crying that afternoon was right there to greet her. Alice had lived in Shelter Valley since her marriage sixty years before and was now considering moving into one of those assisted-living places in Phoenix.

Though she could no longer drive, Alice didn't really need the assistance, but since her husband had died the previous fall, her kids had been after her to sell the family home. Until recently, Alice had been fighting them, but she'd said that after so many lonely days and nights, she wasn't sure there was a reason to fight anymore.

For anything.

It sounded as though Alice was moving to Phoenix to die.

And all, as far as Lonna could tell, because she was lonely.

Eyes open again, she thought about the grant money Bonnie had mentioned after dinner on Sunday. She'd offered to help with the writing of the proposals.

Lonna had gratefully accepted. But she was beginning to see that a little money, a get-together once a week, wasn't going to be nearly enough to stop up all the holes in the lives of her friends.

BONNIE DIDN'T GO to choir practice the following Wednesday. She just didn't have it in her to go, considering what she knew about Pastor Edwards. She'd seen the pastor with his wife on Sunday and she'd had to look away.

Driving home from Little Spirits, she tried to shake off the day she'd had at work.

"Katie, please stop kicking the back of Mama's seat," she said for the third time—and only after taking a long, slow breath.

"I'm hungry..." Katie drew the word out into a wail as only a child can.

"Sweetie, you know Mama's going to make dinner just as soon as we get home."

"I'm hungry *now*."

"Too bad." Her sharp reply must have surprised Katie as much as it had Bonnie, because the little girl fell silent.

Keith had beaten her home. She'd hoped for a couple of minutes to recuperate from her day before facing another evening of trying to pretend that everything was all right between the two of them.

"You look like you've had a rough day," her husband greeted her at the kitchen door.

"The only fingerprints on the rock were mine and Shane's." She watched to make sure Katie made it into the house, setting down her bag and purse on the first available surface. The floor. "I got a twenty-minute lecture on not touching anything at a crime scene. And I was lucky. Greg subjected poor Shane to a much longer version."

"He works after hours," Keith said from where he stood at the sink rinsing cooked lasagna noodles. "He could easily come upon evidence."

Bonnie stood, empty-handed, by the door, staring at those noodles. She'd been planning to make macaroni and cheese.

"You said you were going to make lasagna tonight, right?" Keith asked, turning toward her.

"Yes!" She began to collect ingredients. "The hamburger's thawing in the refrigerator."

It didn't matter that, all the way home, she'd been imagining the hamburger in a pot with macaroni and cheese. Keith was helping her, being a family, and she wanted that far more than an easy supper.

Turning off the water, he leaned back against the sink. "So what else happened today?"

He was trying, thank God. She'd been afraid he was giving up on them.

Bonnie put the hamburger on to brown, chopped some onion and grated a clove of garlic.

"Other than two kids vomiting, Katie throwing the biggest tantrum I've ever seen from her and Bo's parents telling me that until the vandal at the day care is caught, they're pulling him out of Little Spirits?"

"But where will they take him? Bo's grown up with you. He knows you guys, responds to you. He's not going to be happy anywhere else."

"But he'll be safe," Bonnie said.

A crash sounded from the other room. Dropping her grater in the sink, Bonnie raced off ahead of Keith.

"Katie wants *Bambi*."

Visions of her darling drenched in blood quickly gave way to the defiant glare staring up at her from angelic features. Katie stood on top of the television set, surrounded by an entire shelfful of movies. Bonnie turned around and left the room.

Keith would be the better parent at the moment.

"Katie, you know you aren't supposed to touch that shelf," was how her husband started.

Bonnie's version would have gone more like, "Katie Marie Nielson, what are you doing on top of that television?" in a voice that could've been heard down at the courthouse.

She'd had a call that day from Dan Gentile, a man she'd met at the conference in Phoenix. He was the CEO of a nonprofit organization that ran high-quality, secondhand stores all over the country for lower-income families. He'd offered Bonnie the national directorship of the children's division.

KATIE GOT LASAGNA in her hair. After pronouncing it yucky. Which it was, because Bonnie had forgotten the ricotta. Keith got a call during dinner and still hadn't returned to the kitchen by the time Katie wanted to get down. Which she couldn't do without immediately going in for a bath.

Leaving the dirty dishes covered with drying, caked-on food, Bonnie took her daughter to the bathroom, turned on the faucet and put her in the tub. Only after splashing water all over the floor did Katie submit to a dunk and a shampoo. And then she refused to allow Bonnie to dress her in her pajamas.

That wouldn't have been so bad, except she also refused to dress herself.

"Katie Marie, you may *not* run around the house naked."

"Katie go to bed."

"You may not go to bed naked. You'll catch a cold."

"It's not cold under my blanket," the child said in her little voice, missing her "r" in the way Bonnie found particularly adorable.

"It's not nice, either," Bonnie persisted, remaining patient with difficulty.

It took forty-five minutes to get the little girl dressed and settled in her bed.

And Bonnie, expecting that Keith would have finished eating and cleared away the dishes, traipsed out for a cup of tea before collapsing in the family room in front of the television.

The kitchen looked exactly as she'd left it, with Keith's uneaten dinner congealing on his plate in the middle of a table littered with food that had been pretty disgusting when it was still fresh. Six months ago Bonnie would have tackled those dishes with a cheerful heart and a fullness of spirit. She was a wife. And a mother. Exactly what she'd always wanted to be.

And still wanted to be.

She stacked the dishes. Carried them to the sink, removing the pans she'd put there while making dinner. She turned on the water, grabbed the scrub brush to rinse the dishes. And used her shoulder to dry the tears dripping softly down her face.

"Sorry, hon." Keith came back in just as she was getting to the pans.

"You couldn't have put that call off until after dinner?" She didn't know who was more horrified by her waspish tone. She or Keith.

Bonnie ached to wrap her arms around him and take away the sting. Except that she thought it would probably require a lot more than that to undo the damage they'd managed to inflict on each other.

"Our satellite went off the air."

"You pay technicians to take care of stuff like that."

She winced. A woman who wanted her husband to massage her shoulders the way he used to after she'd had a hard day should not harp at him for something he couldn't help.

She scrubbed at the pans, washing them herself rather than placing them in the dishwasher, because she thought it might be therapeutic.

Keith hadn't said a word. She was afraid to turn around. To see the look on his face. Or worse, to find him gone. So she kept scrubbing.

And then he spoke.

"WE NEED TO TALK."

Chest tight, certain he was bringing himself more unhappiness, Keith stood his ground. He had to take charge. Put a stop to this endless waiting. Forget about holding on to a faith that was flimsy at best.

Bonnie took one look at him, nodded and wiped her hands.

As if on cue, they went into the living room. A place reserved mostly for the occasional formal event. Bonnie sat at one end of the beige silk couch, perched on the cushion's edge.

Keith took a chair. A deep breath. And then plunged in.

"I need to leave," he said calmly, forcing himself to look her straight in the eye. "At least for a while."

The qualification was unnecessary. Stepping backward when he had to run forward.

Bonnie didn't say anything. Just sat there, staring at him. He couldn't read her thoughts anymore.

"I'm just not cut out for this, Bon. I'm happy here, in this house, this life. And as hard as you're trying to be, you're not. I don't see how anything's going to change and I can't go on day after day waiting for the other shoe to drop. I can't keep walking through my days with this awareness that I'm not enough to make you happy. That the life I can give you is not enough."

She didn't argue. Didn't say anything. Just continued to sit there, staring at him. Keith had no idea what to do next.

How did one leave a wife? he wondered. He wasn't angry, didn't have the energy to storm out.

Should he just get up and go?

Could he tell her how much he loved her?

Bonnie bowed her head, her black, riotous curls a temptation and a sadness to him. He'd expected to have the right to run his fingers through those curls, to wake up beside them for the rest of his life.

"I'll go."

Her words shocked him so much that for a second there he thought his heart was ripping in two.

"I'm the one who started this whole thing," she said, her voice eerily steady. "I should be the one to leave."

Keith had to struggle to breathe. What had he thought? That once he'd called her bluff she'd come to her senses? Confess her undying need for him? Beg him to stay?

He couldn't have been that foolish. Could he?

He didn't think so.

Bonnie stood. Left the room.

So what *had* he been expecting?

Keith honestly didn't know. But it sure as hell hadn't been this feeling of paralysis. As if he didn't have the strength to stand. Or the will to think.

Where was anger when he needed it?

Life as he'd known it was ending.

He didn't have a script for the rest.

KEITH WAS STANDING by the garage door when Bonnie, suitcase rolling behind her, came into the kitchen.

"Where will you go?"

"I have a room at the Holiday Inn in Wickenburg." She named the nearest town.

Hands in his pockets, he nodded. He was still wearing his slacks and tie and looked so good Bonnie could barely make herself take another step.

She glanced down the hall toward Katie's bedroom door.

How was she ever going to do this?

Should she say goodbye to Katie? Or just go? Which would be kinder?

She glanced at Keith, needing him so desperately. Needing his help and support to find her own strength. He met her gaze, but there was no recognition there.

"You'll bring her in the morning?" she asked hoarsely.

"Yes."

She had to make it out to the van. That was all she had to do for now. Just find the energy to put one foot in front of the other until she was in her van.

"I'll call Grandma tomorrow," Bonnie told him. "I'm sure she'll come stay until we figure something out."

He nodded. She had no idea what he was thinking.

"This'll be hard enough on Katie without wrenching her from her own home, her own bed, her routines...."

She was babbling. She had to get out of there before she begged him to let her stay.

"I'll have my cell phone."

At the door she looked toward the hall one more time. She couldn't leave her baby girl. She just couldn't.

So she'd call Dan in the morning and say no? Say no to any future opportunities, as well?

She couldn't stay. Not when she was so filled with frustration. She was starting to take her dissatisfaction out on Keith. And Katie.

Still, she couldn't walk out on her baby girl.

Or Keith. Love for him burned through every pore. And guilt, for hurting him. Fear that their life together wasn't enough for her. And anguish at the thought of spending one day without him.

Keith and Katie were part of her. She belonged with them.

"Just go." His voice penetrated the fog.

So she did.

IN THE END, Bonnie spent the night at Little Spirits. And was up and ready long before the first parent arrived.

Keith. With Katie.

"Mommy!" the little girl cried, darting to Bonnie, her little arms clutching Bonnie's legs.

Tears—and questions—in her eyes, Bonnie looked up at Keith.

"I'll be by to get her after work."

He turned and walked out.

CHAPTER SEVENTEEN

THINGS WERE GOING to hell in a handbasket. Lonna Nielson had no idea where that cliché came from, but neither did she have time to make up a better one.

Her back ached. Her hip ached. And she had ten meals to prepare that afternoon. The young mother who'd agreed to make Friday night's meals had a sick child. Bonnie and Keith were going to be taking Ryan and Katie to Phoenix to attend a stage version of one of those new newfangled educational cartoon shows the kids were so crazy about these days. Only, this one had actors, instead of animated characters.

Greg and Beth were going to Beth's students' first recital at MU—which was where she'd hoped to be. Becca and Will and Phyllis and Matt and Tory and Ben and the Montfords would all be there, too.

Lonna stirred, chopped, browned, took a sip of milk to offset the acid in her stomach and preheated the oven. Everyone on the list was getting baked spaghetti with tossed salad that night. She'd gone easy on the spices; there was nothing in the meal that broke dietary restrictions, and garlic was a cure for most everything.

Except, perhaps, whatever was ailing her grandson and his wife.

Breaking the spaghetti noodles into halves, she dropped them gently in the boiling water, wiped the sweat from her forehead and tried not to think.

Running from her thoughts wasn't something she did often. It wasn't her way. Lonna Nielson had survived widowhood at the age of twenty-seven, made it through the raising of her son and somehow lived through the tragic deaths of him and his wife. She'd conquered demons in her mind and in the world around her, fought battles at work, on the civic front and occasionally at home.

While the spaghetti boiled, she added chopped onions and green pepper, grated garlic, tomato sauce and paste to the ground beef.

As tragic as the Second World War had been, it hadn't robbed her of faith in humanity; it had strengthened her resolve that, against all odds, miracles happened and good could prevail. The Korean War, Vietnam War, Gulf War...

She lifted the big kettle of spaghetti, wincing at the pain between her ribs as she carried it to the strainer in the sink.

Even terrorism hadn't made a cynic of her.

The spaghetti drained, Lonna poured it into the pot of sauce, one hand pressing into her sternum as she stirred with a big wooden spoon.

But this thing between Bonnie and Keith—whatever the hell it was—might just manage what nations at war had been unable to do. If they split up, she just plain didn't want to go on.

So she wasn't going to think about it. Spooning half the spaghetti mixture into the bottoms of four oblong baking pans, she covered it with slices of

American cheese, spooned the rest of the sauce on top and finished off with a final layer of cheese.

She'd told Bonnie she couldn't stay with Keith and Katie this weekend. That she'd already promised to spend the night at her friend Madeline's while her daughter was at a business meeting. It hadn't been true, but when she'd called, Madeline had been thrilled about the extra company. If those kids wanted to screw up the only thing that mattered in life, she sure as hell wasn't going to help them.

Ripping sheets of foil with too much force, Lonna covered the pans of spaghetti, carried them to her oven and slid them inside. An hour, tops, and they'd be ready to go.

She had a job to do.

"I THINK YOU'RE MAKING a huge mistake, Bon," Beth said.

It was Friday after work, and the two women were in Bonnie's office while their kids played in the big room on the other side of the windows.

"You love him."

"I know." Bonnie swallowed back the tears she'd been fighting all day. "I love him so much that I can't keep hurting him. Besides—" she blinked, looking out at her daughter "—I don't think I have a choice anymore. If I didn't leave, he was going to."

"So that's it? You're getting a divorce?"

"I have no idea." Bonnie shook her head, trying to clear away some of the fog. Since she'd walked out of her house the night before, she'd been living in a realm of unreality and shock, battling emotions that had grown nightmarish. "I haven't talked to Keith today, except to tell him Grandma can't come until Monday and to ask him what he wants to do about the show tonight."

"You guys don't have to go. We can explain it to Ryan," Beth said quickly.

Bonnie shook her head again. "No, it's okay. We've been telling the kids about this for months—ever since we got the tickets. It's all they've been talking about today."

"Still—"

"I think it's important," Bonnie interrupted, questioning the desperation with which she was holding on to the evening's plans. Remembering those tickets some time in the wee hours of the morning had finally allowed her to fall into a fitful sleep. "Katie needs to see that her life will go on, that her father and I both love her and are there for her."

The two women looked at each other. Beth was the one who started to cry first.

"I just can't believe this happening," she choked out.

"I know," Bonnie said, glancing toward the children. She had to remain strong for Katie. When her "I can't, either" broke on a sob, she got up from her desk, looking out the window to the parking lot.

She told Beth about the offer from Dan Gentile.

"Are you going to accept?"

Bonnie shrugged. "I told him I needed a few weeks to think about it."

"Does Keith know?"

"I plan to tell him tonight."

Beth joined her at the window, bringing an extra

tissue, and they talked for the few more minutes they had before Keith was due to pick up Bonnie and the kids for the trip to Phoenix. Beth agreed to tell Greg about Bonnie and Keith's separation that night.

Bonnie knew there was no way she was up to her brother's reproof. At least not without a good night's sleep.

"So where will you stay tonight?" Beth asked as they saw Keith's car pull into the parking lot.

"I—"

"You can always stay with us when you bring Ryan home."

Bonnie hugged her sister-in-law, wishing she didn't have to let go. "Thank you," she said. "I may take you up on that later, but for tonight I'm going home."

Beth's eyes lit up as the women broke apart. "You are?"

"Don't look like that, Beth," Bonnie said. "I'm sleeping in the guest room. Keith and I just thought it would be less confusing for Katie since we're getting in so late. And she's been looking forward to this evening for so long...."

LEAVING KATIE with Keith, Bonnie went in to work for a few hours on Saturday. They'd spoken only in brief, polite phrases the night before, even after she'd told him about Gentile's offer, and Bonnie wasn't sure how much more of that she could take. But she was going back home. At least for the evening. She and Keith had already signed up to do the major dinner run for Grandma, who was still at Madeline's.

And her brother, after an hour-long "counseling" session that morning, had made her promise to talk to Keith again. He and Beth were keeping the kids that evening so she and Keith would have the time alone.

In the meantime she had a lot of work waiting for her. While she'd hired someone to teach the one-year-olds—a young woman who'd recently graduated from Montford with a degree in early-childhood development—she still had catching up to do.

She was also in the middle of writing the grant proposals for Grandma. She'd stumbled across some other funding possibilities, as well, and wanted to research those.

A couple of hours into the mound of paperwork, she threw down her pencil. The day before, a registered letter had come from Diamond's attorney, outlining the terms Diamond was offering to buy out her lease. Blue skies and sunshine beckoned through the window in the playroom. A few minutes of fresh air would clear her mind, and then she'd work for another hour or two.

She slipped out the back way and ran straight into Shane.

"Do you work every Saturday?" she asked him as he stood, wearing shorts and a T-shirt, on a ladder caulking a window.

"Mostly, so far," he said slowly. Connecting the line of caulking at a corner, he slipped the gun into a holster at his waist and climbed down from his perch on the tall metal ladder.

Automatically holding the ladder, Bonnie squinted

up at him. "When do you ever get your own stuff done?"

"When I'm not here."

Bonnie started to chuckle and then stopped, not sure if he'd been teasing her or not. It was just such a classic Shane response.

"You'll miss all the college football games."

When he was back on the ground, he glanced at her and then down at his feet. "You remember that I used to watch them." It was the little-boy tone.

Smiling warmly, her first natural response in days, she said, "Of course I remember."

Shane shrugged. "They don't play in the spring."

With a flashback to the insecure girl she'd been in high school, Bonnie felt color rise to her cheeks. "I knew that."

"And by the time the season starts…" He was pushing the words out with such effort he spit a little on the last word and stopped. Then, with obvious difficulty, he started again. "I won't have to work Saturdays," he said.

"Your job is going to change?" Bonnie frowned. Was Diamond so sure he was going to succeed in getting rid of her? And were the new people planning to put Shane out of a job?

He shook his head. "I'm just not good enough at writing my notes," he said, speaking a little more easily. "I don't figure out enough to do each day and end up with work left over on Friday. So I do it on Saturday."

She could help with this one. "When you finish early during the week, why not just take a couple of Saturday's jobs and get them done early?"

Hands in his pockets, Shane rocked back and forth. ''I have to do what the notes say.''

''But if you—''

''I have to do what the notes say,'' he repeated, his classically handsome face lined with frustration.

Spurred on by the knowledge that Shane was a person she still seemed able to help, Bonnie didn't let his frown deter her.

''How about if I sit down with you and we'll plan out your week so that it doesn't include Saturdays, and then we can make notes from the new plan.''

He studied her, giving no indication of his thoughts.

Was that because he was still good at masking them—or because he was having a hard time formulating any?

''I would like to do a schedule with you,'' he said slowly and with obvious effort, ''but I get to see you alone when I work Saturdays.''

Bonnie's stomach flip-flopped. She leaned back against the metal braces of the ladder, her hands on the steps behind her. ''I don't normally work on Saturdays,'' she said.

''But you're always here.''

''Lately, maybe, but it won't always be that way.''

The way things were looking, she might not be in Shelter Valley on Saturdays—or any days—much longer.

''I like being with you, Bonnie.'' His stare had become intent.

Proceeding slowly, she chose her words carefully,

her first and foremost goal not to hurt him. "I like being with you, too, Shane."

"Okay then, good."

Used to people towering over her, Bonnie suddenly grew more aware of Shane's height, the breadth of his shoulders.

Or maybe it was the odd, too-adult look in his eyes. Awkwardness made her search a little desperately for the perfect thing to say.

Who was in charge here? She'd always assumed it was her. Now, though...

"I know you're not happy, Bonnie."

It didn't surprise her that even Shane could figure that out today.

When she didn't say anything, he took a step closer. "I can make you happy."

Did he mean because she liked being with him? Or could he really be saying what she was afraid he was saying? What she'd be certain he was saying if he was whole.

Should she humor him? Or set him straight?

"Right now, you're making me uncomfortable." She opted for honesty.

"I can make you happy."

The repetition, evidence of his handicap, was reassuring.

Until Shane took hold of the ladder on either side of her.

"Shane..."

Continuing to stare at her, he didn't seem to hear.

"Sha—"

She didn't finish because his mouth came down on hers. With all the sensual fire he'd had as a teenager, mixed with a huge dose of experience she hadn't seen in him before. His hard, athletic body pressed her against the ladder, and Bonnie couldn't breathe.

Completely overwhelmed, by the past, by old desires and dreams that were suddenly reality—even if a grossly skewed version—Bonnie didn't immediately push him away.

He opened his mouth over hers, coaxing a response she had no intention of giving, but started to give, anyway. A small part of her clouded mind had the rational thought that kissing must be an instinctive thing, and that was why Shane was still so masterly.

And the rest of her wanted to cry.

SATURDAY EVENING, that first weekend in May, Keith was alone with Bonnie for the first time since she'd walked out two nights before.

Greg and Beth had meant well, keeping Katie, offering them a chance to patch things up.

Keith couldn't believe how much he missed his daughter.

Her nonsensical chatter filled the gaps that were widening between him and Bonnie.

"Just one more house," she said, checking their list. She gave him an address outside town.

"What is this, the tenth?" he asked.

"Eleventh." She turned to lift the lid of the cooler right behind the front console in the van. "Grandma's got a full-blown business going here." Apparently finding what she was looking for, she pushed the lid back in place and faced front.

Keith silently took the next corner. He and Bonnie had already said all there was to say about Grandma. Keith wanted Lonna to slow down; Bonnie was busy finding money so she could expand.

Once free of town, Keith pressed the accelerator a little harder. If they'd been wearing something besides blue jeans, T-shirts and tennis shoes, they could have gone to a dinner show in Phoenix during the time they had to spend together that evening. A show that left no opportunity for even minimal conversation.

He made one turn and then another.

Maybe, when they were through, he'd suggest a drive. It would be a hell of a lot better than returning home to spend the evening in front of the television, quiet except for the occasional comment about a particularly asinine commercial.

When he'd promised Greg they'd spend the evening together, he'd thought it would be preferable to having his brother-in-law breathing down his neck. Now he wasn't so sure.

Slowing, he turned onto a desert road that led to a new housing development about five miles south of Shelter Valley. So far only a few homes had been built, but word was that every lot had sold.

"Isn't that Pastor Edwards's car?" Bonnie asked. She was looking down a narrow dirt road they'd just passed.

Keith threw the van in reverse, backed up. Edwards's car wasn't on the road. It was parked in an alcove off to the side. Even from that distance, Keith could see the shadows of two figures in the front seat.

"They're making out." Bonnie's horrified disbelief mirrored his.

Except his had an unhealthy amount of anger mixed in. "I don't believe it!"

As though viewing a fatal car accident, the two sat there and stared. "It's been less than two weeks," Keith said almost to himself.

"What's wrong with him?" Bonnie's voice was rising.

"I've had enough." Keith yanked open the door of the van. He could hear Bonnie right behind as he ran several yards to the car and wrenched open the door.

"So much for taking care of things," he said, not even attempting to hide his contempt.

"Keith…" The older man didn't recover nearly as well this second time. And then, "Bonnie."

Emily Baker groaned, bent over until her face was almost in her lap. She might have been crying. Keith almost hoped she was.

At least if the woman felt bad about what she was doing, some part of this would make sense.

"Emily and I just…needed to be together." Edwards was appealing to Bonnie.

"I'm sorry," Keith heard his wife say. He recognized that tone of voice. Edwards had no idea who he was dealing with.

But Keith knew.

"You're a woman. I'm sure you can understand that sometimes love is stronger than the best of intentions.…"

Stepping up beside him, Bonnie nodded. Keith waited.

"I also understand how I'd feel if I were your wife," she said.

Edwards turned his head.

"Do you have any idea what you're throwing away?" Bonnie asked, peering in at Emily Baker. "My gosh, Emily, you've got two teenagers still living at home."

"I know," she said, eyes filled with tears. "I've thought about nothing else for weeks. I never expected to fall in love with Bruce. It just happened. And I can't bear to think of living my whole life without him."

"So, just like that, you throw away the lives of at least four people?" Keith shouted.

Yet why should he be surprised? Wasn't that exactly what he and Bonnie were doing? Throwing away lives?

Edwards didn't quite meet his eyes. "Not necessarily."

"I gave you the benefit of the doubt the first time," Keith said, standing close to Bonnie. "I hope *you* understand that I can't do it again."

The man slowly nodded. "Can you give me twenty-four hours to break the news to my wife?"

At the moment Keith hated to give the man anything. "Yes," was all he could manage.

Emily Baker, still bent over, started to sob. It was only then that Keith realized the woman was covering her naked breasts.

BONNIE SAT IN THE VAN as Keith drove, afraid to say a word. Afraid to alienate Keith any further. Life was splintering around her, flying off in frightening directions she could neither understand nor control. She wasn't committing any immoral acts, but was she really that different from Emily?

Following her heart at the cost of the life she'd already built?

Keith parked and Bonnie ran their last meal of the night up to the door, offering to set the table for the older gentleman who answered the door in his wheelchair, taking the couple of extra minutes to do so when he gratefully accepted her offer.

Their marriage woes aside, she needed to talk to Keith. To tell him what had happened at the day care that afternoon. And ask him what to do about Shane. She needed a man's perspective, because her own had certainly been off the mark.

"You're a lifesaver, young woman," the elderly man said, following her into the kitchen.

"I'm happy to help," she told him, surprised by how completely true those words were. She really loved these old people she'd been visiting in the past weeks.

She finished up without hurrying. And then nervously rejoined her husband.

"Can we stop for a bottle of wine and a log, and have a campfire in the desert?" she suggested.

She couldn't bear to go back to the house they were no longer sharing. And anyplace public was out. Other than Grandma, and Greg and Beth, no one knew they were separated.

"We have a perfectly good fire pit at the house."

She noticed he didn't say at "home."

Bonnie swallowed. Hard. These past few days had been so confusing she could hardly think.

"Please?"

He glanced over at her briefly, then nodded.

She rode silently beside him into town.

Twenty minutes later, as Keith climbed back into the van with a couple of bags, he said, "I got zinfandel and a four-hour log. Is there a blanket in the back, or do we need to swing by the house?"

"There's one in the back."

Nodding, he said no more, just turned the van back out toward open road. His silence didn't bode well.

He'd promised Greg that he'd spend the evening with her, not that he'd be open to friendly conversation.

With the help of a flashlight, Keith dug a little pit for the log, then went back to get the wine. Bonnie spread the blanket close enough to the pit that he could tend the fire without having to move.

Darkness had fallen during the short drive out, and once the sun was down, the evenings were still chilly enough to warrant sweaters. Without them, the fire would be just right.

Bonnie broke the silence. "Have you got matches?" She couldn't believe she hadn't thought of that until now. If they had to drive all the way back to town...

"Right here." He pulled a pack out of the back pocket of his jeans.

Ripping off a match, he struck it, holding it away from him as it plumed into flame, lowering it to one end of the paper-wrapped log.

As she watched the flames burst into life, Bonnie's cell phone rang. Keith glanced at her.

"It could be Katie." Which was why she'd carried the phone from the car. She and her phone were inseparable any time she and Katie were apart. It had been that way from the beginning.

Her mind on the moments ahead with Keith, she said hello.

And then went numb. The blood drained from her face. Less than a minute later she hung up the phone, fear tightening her chest. Her throat.

She stared at Keith. God, she needed his strength.

And she was going to have to hurt him again.

"What is it?" His voice was firm, demanding. He was already covering the fire with dirt, although his eyes never left Bonnie's face.

"Grandma," she said, her voice cracked and barely audible, even to her. "She's been taken to Phoenix. They think she had a heart attack."

IT WAS ONE of the longest nights of Keith's life. Most of the time, as he sat in the too-bright waiting room of a too-busy hospital, he felt completely separate from the people swarming around him, separate, it seemed, from the whole of human existence. As though he was on an island alone. And yet, as the hours dragged on with precious few words from anyone who knew anything about his grandmother, Bonnie seemed to inhabit the island with him more often than not.

They didn't talk much. They just sat quietly together. Later they were joined by Beth and Greg, who must have dropped off the children somewhere.

Coffee appeared. He didn't remember having any.

Someone offered him a pillow. Someone in a pair of green scrubs.

What a ludicrous thought. As if he could sleep at a time like this.

He took the pillow for Bonnie.

And then noticed that she'd been offered one, as well. She wasn't using hers, either.

Beth said something about calling Martha. And Jennifer Grayson, the teacher of the three-year-olds at the day care and Bonnie's longest-standing employee. She moved to a far corner of the waiting room, a cell phone at her ear.

Greg sat and read a magazine, though whenever Keith glanced his way, he caught his brother-in-law staring, seemingly, at nothing.

Life was hell. Love was hell. Most of all, dying was hell.

CHAPTER EIGHTEEN

GRANDMA DIDN'T DIE.

After a night that lasted days, the doctor finally assured them that her heart was strong and healthy—for a woman of her age. As far as he could tell, she'd been suffering from a severe case of indigestion.

And exhaustion.

He intended to keep her for at least a week, to make her rest, to keep her hooked up to a monitor just in case and to run some tests.

Keith stayed in Phoenix to be close to her. Bonnie returned to work—and home, since Keith wasn't there—on Tuesday, leaving Katie with Greg and Beth after work every day so she could make a run to Phoenix to sit with Grandma.

With no pastor to turn to, no husband present and accounted for, no Grandma to confide in, Bonnie tackled the issue with Shane herself.

On Wednesday evening. After the last parent had left and before she drove to Phoenix.

She found him in one of the complex's common areas, waxing the floor.

"Can I talk to you a sec?" she called over the sound of the large machine he was guiding back and forth across the floor.

He shut off the machine immediately. "Yes."

And then, before she could figure out a way to begin when she had no idea which direction to take, Shane said, "I want to make you happy again, Bonnie."

He'd given her the perfect opening—if she could figure out what to do with it.

"I'm married, Shane." At least for the moment.

"But you aren't happy."

And suddenly all she could think about was Katie. The little girl made life worth living. From the moment her daughter had left her body and entered the world, Bonnie had felt an incredible sense of love and protectiveness.

No matter what else happened, that mattered.

"I can make you happy." The repetition appeared to be intentional for once.

"I have a daughter, Shane."

Such an obvious truth and yet, in that moment, so profound.

"I have to think of Katie first and foremost," Bonnie said. She was talking to the janitor, but the words reverberated inside her, loud and sure.

Hands still on the bars of the waxing machine, Shane watched her, the expression on his face frozen one moment, confused the next.

He pulled a note out of his pocket. Read it. Replaced it.

She was probably upsetting his schedule.

She'd promised to help him make up a better one. And hadn't done it yet.

"I'm not going to do anything to hurt Katie," she pressed on, eager to get this done and get out, let him continue with his list of jobs.

His silence made her uneasy. Did he not understand? Or were his feelings hurt, after all?

God, she hated this. All she'd wanted to do was help him.

"Anything between you and me would hurt her, Shane," she told him, speaking to the little boy she saw in him most often.

He loved the kids. She'd seen how gentle he was with them the time or two he'd had to fix something at the day care when they were there. He'd watched them with a grin on his face.

Come to think of it, he'd always been good with kids. Patient with the younger siblings of his friends, working with younger kids during the summer in a city athletic program. She'd always figured it was because he was an only child. Kids were a novelty to him.

And because it fed his ego to be the hero.

He continued to stare at her, as though he expected more.

"Children need stable home lives," she continued. "Especially in a town the size of Shelter Valley. If I do anything that would cause a scandal, it'll affect Katie's whole life."

Like leaving the child's father wouldn't?

"Okay."

Shane turned the machine back on.

"Okay?" she called over the loud humming of the waxer.

"Okay," he called back, and started to move in the slow, rhythmic motion she'd interrupted.

Apparently she'd been worrying about nothing.

He probably didn't even remember the kiss that had been making her sick for days.

Life.

Would she ever understand it?

"HOW WAS YOUR DAY?"

Keith looked relatively rested in the jeans and short-sleeved shirt she'd packed for him earlier in the week.

"Good. Yours?"

"Fine."

"Grandma seemed to be in better spirits."

"She's pissed off at me for making her stay." He tended to his food and the napkin on his lap, not her.

"Yeah, but she's probably secretly glad. She needed the rest."

Bonnie had barely been there an hour when Grandma had shooed them out to have a nice dinner, rather than the hospital-cafeteria food they'd been eating all week. She'd shamelessly played the sick-old-lady card, forcing them to either upset her while she lay there in a hospital bed or spend time together. Bonnie saw through the ploy and so, she was sure, did Keith.

Still, here they were, a separated couple sharing a cozy dinner.

Grandma had been engrossed in a game show, sputtering answers to the idiot contestants, when they'd left. She certainly hadn't appeared the least bit sick or frail.

"Martha called. The crew filmed and aired graduation without a hitch."

"Oh. Good." Montford graduations were usually

a big thing in Shelter Valley, as the town doubled in size with all the parents coming to celebrate. She'd barely noticed the increased traffic.

"How's Katie?"

"Fine. She misses you."

"I miss her, too. But she's probably having the time of her life with Greg and Beth."

"Yeah, but I think she's a little lost without her routine. She was hanging on me all day today."

He nodded. And ate.

Bonnie's mind wandered back to her conversation with Shane. Or rather, the conversation she'd had simultaneously with herself. If she left Katie's father, it would affect the rest of Katie's life. Not just the months the child would spend adjusting, but every day, every year, every holiday and special occasion for the rest of her life.

Was her need to make a difference in the world worth that much to her? Children survived divorce. But did she and Keith have a valid enough reason for putting their daughter through that?

She just didn't know.

"Becca's doing all of Grandma's meal organizing for the next two weeks. And she's got people lined up for Grandma's turns, too."

Bonnie had handed in the grant proposal, but knew Keith wouldn't want to hear about that.

He nodded. Took a swig from the beer bottle in front of him. Chewed. She waited. For what she didn't know. Nothing came.

Was this what they'd come to? Were there so many forbidden and potentially explosive or hurtful topics between them that there was nothing left to say?

And how good could *that* be for Katie? To live in a house filled with silence?

Sitting across from Keith at the California Pizza Kitchen in Phoenix on Thursday night, she wished she could just lie down and cry. Right there, over her pizza.

"Edwards quit his job," she told him.

Not the uplifting topic for which she'd been searching.

Using his fork, Keith scooped up the lettuce and tomatoes that had fallen from his slice of pizza. "They'd have fired him, anyway."

"Rumor has it that he and Emily Baker are leaving Shelter Valley. Together."

"What about her kids? She has two boys in high school, doesn't she?"

"One's in his first year at Montford, but they're both living at home. I assume they'll stay with their father."

"I guess we'll have interim preachers until they hire someone."

That was all he had to say?

"So you think it's right, what they're doing?"

He shrugged, tended to his plate. "It's not for me to say."

Bonnie stopped eating altogether. "But what do you *think,* Keith?" She really had to know. She was a thirty-five-year-old woman in the middle of a crisis and she needed the opinion of the man who'd been her anchor for most of her adult life. "I mean, what they're doing is incredibly selfish."

Keith grabbed a couple of strands of shredded lettuce from his plate. Put them in his mouth.

"What they're doing *is* wrong, in that they pursued their own happiness when they were still obligated elsewhere—living a lie."

"But the end result isn't wrong? Once you're no longer living the lie, it's okay to do anything you want in the pursuit of happiness?"

Keith's shoulders dropped as he scrutinized her. "I don't know the answer to that, Bonnie. Certainly we have a right to happiness."

"But at what cost?" It was beginning to sound as if she was trying to talk her way back into her marriage.

So was she? Had she really determined that was the right decision?

"I think you have to look farther than the here and now," Keith said slowly. "Take Martha, for instance. She was devastated when Todd left. Her kids' lives have been changed irrevocably. But in the long run, they might be better off. What kind of atmosphere would they have provided for those kids—and each other—if Todd had stayed with Martha while he was in love with someone else? At least now those kids live in a home offering them unconditional love. And what kind of eventual effect would it have had on Martha? Knowing that the man she went to bed with every night wished she were someone else?"

"But if he'd never pursued that relationship, she'd never have known."

"You don't think she'd have known something

was wrong? You can't live with a person and not sense that he—or she—isn't happy."

Why did she feel they weren't talking about Martha and Todd Moore at all?

"So you're saying it's kinder for someone to be selfish and pursue his own happiness at the cost of others because in the long run, the others will be happier?"

He shook his head when the waiter appeared, asking if he wanted another beer. "I don't know," he told Bonnie, putting his napkin down. "Who's to say if it would be better to live alone or to live with someone who's not really happy."

"Happiness is a nebulous thing. And it is, to some extent, in our control," Bonnie said slowly, thinking out loud. "Don't you think people can change their thinking, focus on what *does* make them happy? Don't you think that's the right thing to do?"

"I don't believe it's a matter of right and wrong. It's more a question of making the best decision for the greatest number of people concerned."

She didn't know what to say to that.

"Has it worked for you, Bon?" he asked, his gaze penetrating deeper than it had in many days. "Have you been able to make yourself happy by focusing on the parts of your life that you like?"

He knew the answer to that.

And maybe he'd given her his answer, too. He wasn't planning to be the spouse who went to bed every night with someone who wasn't happy to be there.

"Besides," he added as the waiter disappeared with their credit card, "who's to say that Martha, or

Emily Edwards for that matter, are condemned to lives of unhappiness? Maybe there's something else waiting for them just around the corner. Something that never would've presented itself if they were still married.''

"By some*thing* else, do you mean some*one?*"

The waiter returned with a slip for Keith to sign, leaving Bonnie to ponder her question. And his implied answer.

Was Keith already moving on? Mentally, if nothing else? Panic struck her at the thought. His head was bent as he calculated the tip.

He was *her* husband.

And yet, in fairness to him, Bonnie had to figure out why she felt that way. Was it because she wanted him? Or just because she didn't want anyone else to have what she considered hers?

He thanked the waiter, wished him a good evening.

She wanted Keith, loved him to distraction.

Didn't she?

So why wasn't that enough?

"In answer to your question," he said, right behind her as they headed out the door, "it could be either. An opportunity, a person. Martha loves her job, and it's an opportunity she wouldn't have had sitting at home while her kids all grew up and left."

And Martha was still young enough, attractive enough, to fall in love and live happily ever after.

KEITH WONDERED if impasses could last forever. He'd been home from Phoenix for more than a week. He got up every day, went to work, picked up Katie from Little Spirits on the days he had her, came home, did chores, kissed Katie good-night, watched television and went to bed.

On the evenings that Bonnie took the little girl to the Richards home where she was staying, he skipped the stop at the day care, came home, did chores, skipped the good-night kisses, watched television and went to bed.

Katie seemed to be faring all right, enjoying the extra time she got to spend playing with her cousin and finding it a special treat to sleep in the same big bed as her mommy when she was there.

He hardly spoke to Bonnie that week, so he had no real idea how she was doing.

Grandma was back in full swing, adding more people to her meals list, anticipating the grant money she hoped would soon come in. When he'd last spoken with her, she was planning to move a cooking crew into the church kitchen to keep up.

Keith worried about her more than ever—a fact that only irritated Lonna.

"I've just been through every damn test known to man and probably some that aren't yet. I'm healthy as a horse."

"Those tests might've had great results," he told Martha on the Wednesday afternoon not quite two weeks after his return home, "but if she keeps up this pace, we'll be running them all again, with different results. She's seventy-six years old."

He couldn't go through another night like that hellishly long one at the hospital in Phoenix. At least, not any time soon.

"She's going to die, Keith. It's a given. It's just

a matter of the quality of life you allow her while she's here. You want it to be worthwhile, fulfilling, or a waste?''

He stared at his program director, hearing something he had an idea he'd been told many times.

Still. ''It could also be a matter of quantity,'' he told Martha.

''Right.'' She nodded, her face serious. ''What would you choose for her, five years of an unhappy wasted life, or three filled with achievement and a measure of happiness?''

Who are you really thinking about here?

He didn't know where the question had come from. Martha certainly hadn't asked. But once it was in the forefront of his consciousness, he couldn't avoid it.

He wanted as many years as he could possibly squeeze out of his grandmother's life—to put off the day he'd have to say goodbye to her forever. Did that mean he was willing to sacrifice her happiness to gain those years?

His conversation with Bonnie the last time they'd had dinner together replayed itself in bits and pieces. She'd been asking him variations of this same question. At what cost did one obtain happiness?

And could he really be happy with having things his way, knowing he'd taken them at a cost to others?

What else was his wife understanding that he wasn't?

Martha's shriek had him spinning around. Her face was stark white, a complete contrast to the black slacks and blouse she was wearing. She was on her cell phone.

He hadn't even heard it ring.

"I'm on my way."

Her fingers were shaking so badly she had trouble landing on the narrow Off button.

"What's up?"

She stared at him, but didn't seem to hear.

"Martha?"

"Tim was hurt sliding into home. They've taken him by ambulance to Phoenix."

He knew the way. And an idea of what lay ahead. "I'll drive you."

With pinched cheeks and lips that were trembling, she nodded.

KEITH CALLED Bonnie from Phoenix to let her know he wouldn't be picking up Katie that afternoon. He called her again later that night when he returned to Shelter Valley, with Martha and Tim to let her know where he was in case of an emergency. He still hadn't told anyone, including Martha, that he and Bonnie had separated.

As far as he knew, she hadn't, either.

"He's got a compound fracture of the left femur," he told her, tired and yet oddly strengthened as he spoke to her from Martha's house.

Because Tim was thirteen and at that awkward age between adult and child, he'd opted to have Keith with him, rather than his mother, while they set and plastered his leg from just below the hip to his ankle.

"Poor guy."

Keith had always loved Bonnie's easy compassion.

"It's going to be rough for him tonight until the cast sets," he continued. "He's in a lot of pain."

"I can imagine. Did they give him anything?"

"Yeah, but pills aren't going to help him get to the bathroom, and even without the cast, he's too heavy for Martha to handle."

And Tim was horrified at the thought of his mother taking him to the bathroom.

"You're staying there."

"Yeah."

"Will you be home in the morning? Before work?"

"I'll need to shower and get clean clothes. Why?"

She took a long time to answer him.

"No reason. Tell Tim I hope he feels better soon. Good night, Keith."

"Good night."

While he fought twinges of unwarranted guilt, Keith hung up the phone.

And tried not to think too much.

THE KIDS, including Tim who'd taken a pain pill just before midnight, were all asleep in their rooms. Keith wandered out into the living room, hoping to find a shot of something strong and found Martha, instead, going through the paperwork the hospital had sent home with her.

"Everything okay?" she asked, smiling up at him. "You have everything you need?"

"Yes. Fine."

She laid the folder aside. "I thought you'd already gone to bed."

He should have. If he was half as smart as he gave himself credit for, he would have.

"I was hoping to find something that might help me sleep. I don't suppose you have any bourbon around?"

He didn't normally drink the heavy stuff, but nothing about his life was normal lately.

"Sorry." Martha shook her head, sitting, feet tucked beneath her on the couch. "I got rid of everything when Todd left. I was too afraid one of the kids would get into it."

She asked if he wanted some warm milk, instead. He didn't. Hands in the pockets of the slacks he'd worn to work, he wandered around the room, looking at pictures of Martha's kids at various ages, reading the spines of books on the built-in shelf by the fireplace.

"Did you call Bonnie?"

"Yes."

"Is she angry?"

Not sure how much to tell her, he didn't answer.

Martha stood, joined him by the bookshelf. "It's okay, Keith," she said, a hand lightly touching his shoulder. "You don't have to stay. Tim's asleep now, and he's going to have to start letting me help him at some point."

"By tomorrow the cast will have set and he'll be able to maneuver a lot more easily by himself."

"Still, if you need to go..."

He faced her, wanting to tell her that Bonnie had

left him, but he still shied away from the permanency implicit in those words. ''I don't.''

It was late. They'd had a long, stressful day. But he couldn't help noticing Martha's attractiveness. She emanated such energy, an intriguing combination of vulnerability and competence. As though she could handle anything. And yet, needed so much more than she was getting.

''What?'' she asked.

Keith realized he'd been spending far too long staring into those eyes that beckoned him with the promise of unconditional acceptance.

''Nothing.'' He didn't turn away fast enough. ''It's just…''

''What?''

''You're a damned attractive woman.''

A slight tilt of her head was the only surprise she showed. ''Thank you,'' she said.

And then neither of them said a word. Or looked away. Their heads slowly gravitated toward each other. Keith's hands were tucked in his pockets when his lips met hers. And still there when their mouths opened, deepening a caress that had been a long time in coming.

Slowly he pulled his hands free, lifted them to touch her shoulders, to draw her closer.

''Stop.''

With his hands in the air, Keith barely got the word out.

Martha's voice, uttering the same thing at the same time, was much louder.

Bonnie had asked him about right and wrong. He'd just found the answer.

For long seconds they stood there, a couple of feet apart, staring at each other.

"Guess there's no doubt about where that *wasn't* going," Martha said with a grimace.

The last thing he'd wanted to do was hurt her.

"It's not that I don't find you attractive...."

She held up a hand. "I know," she told him, her eyes warm. "Me, too."

They left it at that.

CHAPTER NINETEEN

HE AND MARTHA were the first ones up in the morning. A little self-conscious in his second-day clothes and beard, he sat down at the table and sipped a cup of coffee he didn't really want while she made oatmeal and toast.

"I can't thank you enough for being here," she was saying as she worked in the kitchen. "This was the first time there was nothing I could do to make myself as good as a dad would've been."

She looked cute in her sweatpants and T-shirt, her slim body only a little taller than Bonnie's. "I was glad to be here," he told her honestly. "It felt great to be needed."

He regretted the words as soon as he heard how they sounded. Just because the house was cozy and he felt wanted did not give him cause to think his most private thoughts out loud.

Only intimate relationships permitted such actions.

"You were a godsend," his friend and employee said, facing him, letting him know right then and there that their lapse the night before was not going to change their relationship. "I'm just worried about how much sleep you lost. You have a full day at the studio."

He'd never seen her with her face scrubbed free of makeup. She looked fresh, wholesome, beautiful. Why in hell hadn't some man latched on to this woman?

"Tim was only up a couple of times," he told her, though he had an idea she'd been fully aware of every move her son had made.

But she'd been aware from a distance. The distance they both required.

They'd had a close call.

"Once to go to the bathroom. The other time, I think he just tried to move his leg in his sleep and the pain woke him up."

"You've made a horrible night bearable. Thank you." She turned back to her breakfast. And Keith wanted to sit right there in her kitchen for the rest of his life.

Or at least for a week or two. Long enough to regain some of the energy and confidence he'd lost.

Martha buttered toast, set out plates and bowls, silverware, napkins and jelly. She looked cute.

But she wasn't Bonnie.

KEITH CALLED BONNIE Friday morning. He asked if they could meet—alone—that evening.

Bonnie had felt sick to her stomach ever since.

He was going to tell her he wanted a divorce. That he'd fallen in love with Martha.

And why not? The woman was gorgeous. Impressive. She took her hits and remained standing. If Bonnie were a man, she'd love her, too.

Katie clung to Bonnie most of the morning. Their odd life was starting to take its toll on the child.

Bonnie had nothing but patience for her daughter—and a day full of prayers that she'd somehow be able to protect her little girl from whatever heartache was to come.

She went on with the plan she'd been working on since that Wednesday—when she'd set things straight with Shane—the day life had finally become clear to her.

Life as Bonnie Nielson had to live it.

Bonnie had, over the past ten days, become unshakably certain of what that meant.

LONNA PRESENTED herself in Bonnie's office during Friday's afternoon playtime, just as her granddaughter-in-law had requested.

"I need to talk to you," Lonna said, taking a seat without waiting for an invitation. Her nylons rubbed against her light cotton slacks as she crossed her ankles, reminding her that she was one hell of a woman. Prepared. Confident.

Bonnie had called this meeting, but Lonna was going to take charge of it.

"Grandma, I have some news—" Bonnie began.

"News can wait," Lonna interrupted. "I have some things to discuss with you."

"I'm not up for a lecture," Bonnie said with a tired smile.

"Then it's just as well I didn't bring one with me."

Placing her purse on Bonnie's desk, she leaned forward. "I want you to go into business with me."

"What?" Bonnie's brows rose.

Good. She'd taken the young woman by surprise. Distracted her from all her problems.

Which was the point.

Sometimes it took someone older and wiser, someone who wasn't afraid to butt in, to make the world right.

"I need to get rid of this blasted stomachache and you can help me do it," she said.

Perhaps she should feel guilty about manipulating Bonnie, but she didn't.

Not when the result was going to be the happiness her grandson and his wife couldn't seem to find on their own.

"How?" Bonnie asked slowly.

Her brightly colored top and blue slacks looked nice on her.

"You ever wear nylons?"

"Um, no."

"You should."

"It helps your stomach?"

"No. But it'll help your sex life."

Lonna almost smiled when Bonnie blushed. Maybe later, when her mission was accomplished, she could enjoy that moment.

"Shelter Valley needs an adult day care."

"It does," Bonnie said.

The idea had come to Lonna during the night. A way to help her friends and others without killing herself. And a new challenge for Bonnie to get her mind off whatever had gone wrong in her marriage.

If Lonna hadn't been so damned busy trying to convince herself she wasn't old, she'd have seen it much sooner and saved them all a hell of a lot of misery.

"Shelter Valley has a growing number of residents who can no longer be alone all day, but who still have a great quality of life ahead of them. If we don't do something, they'll end up leaving the homes they love and moving away to someplace that has senior-citizen facilities."

Lonna shuddered. For her, that would be a death sentence.

"We have to open a Big Spirits day care," she insisted.

"You're right."

"I want you to..." Lonna paused. Really looked at her granddaughter-in-law. Bonnie was smiling. "I am?"

"Yep." Leaning over her the desk, she handed Lonna a folder. "This is what I wanted to meet with you about."

Lonna opened the folder, looked over the pages inside and nearly wept. Bonnie had worked up an entire proposal, complete with drawings, financials, confirmed funding.

"You've already heard back on the grant?"

"Not the city one, but Becca assures me it's merely a formality. I found some other sources available to us as long as we stay within certain guidelines."

"You're proposing a dual facility." Amazing. Why hadn't she thought of that?

"Yep," Bonnie said again. "Kids and adults right next door to each other, mingling. The kids will bring vitality and innocence and hope, and the seniors will contribute all the love and wisdom they've spent a lifetime accumulating.''

''We can have bridge tournaments.''

''Every day.''

''And we'll set up a craft room. We could do a holiday boutique, sell our stuff…'' Lonna stopped, realizing that she was thinking of the benefits to herself.

''It won't just be for seniors, Grandma, but for anyone in Shelter Valley who wants to add another dimension to his or her life. That's what the volunteer component is about.''

Her gaze returning to the paperwork on her lap, Lonna nodded. ''I see you have the volunteer program all planned out. I know Madeline would love to do reading time with the kids. And Dorothy, once she heals, will probably be asking to work in the kitchen. She always did make the best pies.''

''There's still a lot we'll have to figure out,'' Bonnie said, her face serious.

Grandma waved her hand dismissively. ''Red tape. We'll plow right through it. I'll bet we could be up and running before the end of summer.''

''There's something else you need to know, Grandma.''

Lonna's stomach tensed. She reached in her purse for one of the antacids her doctor had prescribed. ''What?''

''Keith and I might be filing for divorce. You need to be sure you want to go into business with an ex-relative.''

Hogwash. She hadn't lived for seventy-six years, *fought* for seventy-six years, to end up with more heartache than she could stand.

"Let's leave personal things out of it, shall we?" she asked. And though Bonnie tried several more times, Lonna left that afternoon without having the conversation Bonnie so obviously considered necessary.

FIVE MINUTES past three that afternoon, a small explosion resounded from the three-year-olds' classroom at Little Spirits. Bonnie's desk chair flew behind her, crashing into the wall and toppling over, wheels spinning round and round as Bonnie sped down the hall.

Children and teachers were rushing into the hall from every direction, some crying, some screaming. Some just running as fast as their legs could carry them. They crashed into each other, pushed past anyone they could, many heading in different directions.

Nowhere, in all the chaos, did Bonnie see Katie.

"Get the kids outside!" she hollered to a couple of the teachers. She couldn't find Alice Grayson, teacher of the three-year-olds.

Smelling smoke, she rushed on, frantic now to find her daughter. To know that none of the kids were hurt.

She burst into the room, vaguely aware of smoldering by the finger-painting tables, but only vaguely.

On the floor not far away, Alice Grayson knelt over something Bonnie couldn't see. But she recognized the little piece of fabric she saw from around the toe of Alice's tennis shoe.

Katie's shirt.

AT SEVENTEEN MINUTES past three on the fourth Friday afternoon in May, Keith was alone in his office, trying to concentrate, to create an organizational plan while they were between semesters.

At the moment, it didn't seem to matter. Without Bonnie, nothing mattered. Not Shelter Valley. Not his career or his home or any of the other things that had provided the stability his life needed.

Relieved when the ringing of his phone interrupted work that was completely stalled, he answered it and leaned back in his chair, staring at nothing.

And came down with a crash as soon as he recognized Bonnie's voice.

"Slow down, honey, I can't understand you." Standing, Keith willed her the strength to communicate with him.

"Katie's unconscious!" The words that followed were garbled.

"Breathe, Bon. Breathe."

"I'm trying." He could hear her gulping in deep breaths. "They're with her now."

Blood flowing so fast he could hardly think, Keith assumed by *they,* she meant paramedics. Assuming…

"Where are you?"

"Little Spirits. There was an explosion in Katie's room."

"I'm on my way."

Throwing down the receiver, Keith was out the door, in his car and across town before he'd formulated a coherent thought.

AN HOUR LATER Keith's mind was still reeling, his heart calmer but fairly numb while he helped organize children, calm frantic parents who were arriving in droves after the phone calls Alice and a couple of volunteers had made, answer questions so that Greg and his team could do their work, and keep everyone and everything away from Bonnie, who was holding a very scared but uninjured Katie in a rocker in the nursery.

They'd been very lucky the homemade bomb thrown through the window had not hit the floor another twelve inches closer to Katie or the little girl could have been seriously hurt—if not killed. As it was, the shock had knocked her unconscious; she had a bruise on her head from the fall but was showing no evidence of concussion. Her pupils were dilating as they should and all her vital signs were normal.

And as soon as Keith found out who'd made that bomb, who'd thrown it, he was going to kill the bastard.

BONNIE HAD FINALLY been able to remove Katie's arms from around her neck and slide out of the little girl's bed at home that evening when Greg arrived.

"We've got him," were her brother's first words.

Keith had met him at the door and the three of them stood in the kitchen.

"Thank God." Bonnie sank into a chair.

"Who was it?" Keith asked. Bonnie could feel the tension in him as he stiffened beside her.

She hadn't even thought to ask the question.

"The handyman, Shane Bellows."

"No." Bonnie's face paled. She could feel the warmth leaving her skin. "It can't be."

"Culver found him outside. Bellows was exhibiting signs of intense confusion. Repeating the same thing over and over. Something about you being happy with him. Culver had him searched and found a note in his pocket that detailed today's hit."

"Oh, my God."

She couldn't believe it. All the while she'd been caring about Shane, trying to help him...

"I'm going to kill him," Keith said through clenched teeth.

"No, you're not," Greg said emphatically. And then, more gently, he told Bonnie, "There's more."

She turned to him, waiting.

"Bellows was aiming for Katie."

Bonnie had about two seconds to get to the guest bathroom before she lost what little lunch she'd had that day.

GREG STAYED another hour. As nearly as they could piece together from notes they'd found in Shane's home, that first book of matches in the vent had been a random prank, just as Greg had originally surmised. But Bonnie's reaction to the fire had apparently given Shane the idea that Bonnie wanted out of the day-care business. At the police station, waiting to be taken to a state-run mental facility where he'd be locked up, Shane had told them repeatedly that if he didn't help Bonnie feel happy, she'd leave.

Sick with guilt, Bonnie gave her brother a brief rundown of her talks with Shane and finally, without looking at Keith, about the kiss they'd shared. Her way of handling the situation—by using Katie as a shield to spare Shane's feelings—had almost cost their daughter her life.

They'd found notes that would convict Shane of starting all but the first fire at Little Spirits. These included pyrotechnic instructions, as well as step-by-step agendas he'd written for himself. They'd also found plans for tampering with the pipes at Little Spirits on at least two occasions. One early in the morning. One late at night. They were assuming the first had resulted in the flooded toilet and the other in the fallen ceiling panel.

The assumption was that the mishaps were Shane's attempt to get time alone with Bonnie.

The disturbed boy-man thought himself in love with her and had become convinced that if he could make her happy, she'd return his love. Until she'd mentioned Katie. Shane had seen Katie as a permanent barrier to Bonnie's happiness. And his own.

What she'd been trying to tell him was that Katie was the foundation of her happiness.

Shane, in all his confusion, was facing a long-term incarceration in a state mental facility.

As sick as she felt about him, about what he'd done, Bonnie knew she'd be visiting him there.

In time...

"You coming with me?" her brother asked on his way out. She and Greg had reached a truce the first night she'd spent in his home. He didn't pretend to understand her decision to leave her husband, but he loved her and would be there for her no matter what.

"No." Bonnie shook her head, almost woozy with fatigue. "I can't leave Katie tonight."

She didn't look at Keith, didn't want to see his reaction to the news. At the moment, their talk of divorce didn't matter. She'd sleep in Katie's room if she had to, but she refused to be separated from her.

Or risk her waking up frightened and not finding both parents there to offer comfort.

GREG LEFT. And she was alone with her estranged husband. In the home they'd filled with so much hope. So many dreams.

"I'm sorry I didn't ask you about staying," she said as the door closed behind her brother.

"It's your house," Keith said. "With Katie still so skittish, I would've been more surprised if you'd gone."

Then he just stood there, hands in his pockets.

Bonnie couldn't remember ever feeling so awkward with him. Not even when they were first dating. "When you called this morning, you said you wanted to talk. What about?"

"It's late. You sure you want to get into all that now?"

No. She was pretty sure she didn't. But she gave a noncommittal shrug. "It's not like I'm going to be able to fall asleep any time soon."

Nodding, Keith led the way into the family room, sinking heavily into a corner of the couch. Bonnie settled on the other end, half facing him.

"What's up?" She pretended she was ready to handle whatever he had to say.

"Something that happened with Martha..." He stopped.

Here it came. And she wasn't prepared.

"Anyway, it's really made me think hard about you and me," he went on, "opening my eyes to certain truths I'd somehow missed along the way."

"And?" The one word took all the breath she had.

"I've made some decisions I'd planned to discuss with you."

"About us?"

"Yes."

It took her a minute. Several deep breaths. But she was finally able to say, "Okay, what are they?"

He didn't answer immediately, and every second threatened the flimsy hold she had on her composure. Because she, too, had learned a lot these past few weeks. And one of the things she knew for sure was that his happiness, and Katie's, meant more to her than her own.

She'd get through this for them.

And then hope that Beth and Greg, and the new business, and Katie and Shelter Valley would allow her to pick up the pieces.

"I've realized that if you want a relationship to work," he finally said, "you have to be willing to give up control of your own happiness, but take control of your spouse's."

"What do you mean?"

"I was so busy hanging on to what I needed to

be happy—trying to control *my* happiness and giving up control of yours, making you find it on your own—that I didn't understand the answer was there all along. If I'm thinking about *your* happiness, doing whatever I can to see that *your* needs are met, my happiness is going to follow.''

"Unless I'm a selfish jerk who's busy seeing to my own happiness and not worrying about yours.''

"Granted, but if you were a selfish jerk, I wouldn't be in this relationship.''

She forced back the first wave of tears.

"The idea is, Bon, that if you're looking out for me and I'm looking out for you, we'll be able to find whatever compromise exists to take care of *us*.''

"Because to compromise you have to understand both sides and we're naturally going to understand our own.'' She didn't know how she got the sentence past the constriction in her chest. She really wanted to maintain composure. This was important stuff.

"Something like that.''

"So what are you saying?''

"I'm not sure.'' His grin was sad, self-deprecating and sexy at the same time. "I just know that everything I thought was so important to me—this house, Shelter Valley, my job—mean nothing without you. So if you need to leave all of this behind, I'm ready to go.''

All thoughts of composure fled as Bonnie scrambled across the couch and into her husband's arms. She'd intended to tell him how she felt, about her own discoveries, about the new business she'd committed herself to. But she couldn't stop crying long enough to say a word.

"We'll call a real-estate agent tomorrow, Bon, sell the house. You can accept that job offer or any—"

"No!" She finally joined the conversation. "You love it here. We made plans for our lives."

"You aren't the same woman who made those plans. People change and grow, and when you love someone, you have to be prepared to change and grow along with that person."

Pulling back, Bonnie looked up at him, grinning. "You really have given this some pretty intense thought."

"Yeah, leave a guy alone long enough and you'd be surprised at what he can do."

"Well, a girl can do some pretty amazing things, too," she told him, sitting up. She described her plans for the new day care, Grandma's involvement, the ideas they wanted to pursue.

Keith finally broke in. "We can do a piece on MUTV to help raise awareness and funding." Then he asked, "What are you planning to do about Diamond?"

"Move," Bonnie said. That, too, was suddenly an easy answer. "We need to get away from the aftermath of Shane Bellows," she said. "And if we're going to have a dual facility, we'll need a lot more space."

"Maybe we can find a place tomorrow," he said, rattling off business details about insurances and zoning, obviously trying to ensure as little downtime for The Spirits as possible.

"And what about Gentile?" The hesitancy in his voice was a vivid reminder that they had some rebuilding to do.

"I called him ten days ago and told him he'd have to find someone else."

Keith sat back, removing his hand back from where it had been lying against her leg. "You've known for ten days that you weren't leaving town?"

"I knew I couldn't be far from Katie." Bonnie grabbed his hand, held on to it. "Or from her father."

With one gentle tug, she was back in Keith's arms, kissing him for the first time in too many weeks.

"I thought I'd never have the right to do this again," he said against her lips.

"Always," Bonnie told him, blinking away the tears in her eyes so she could see him more clearly. "I'm yours, Keith. You have every right there is."

He kissed her again. Long and gently. Searchingly. There would be time for strength and passion later. Right now they traveled a different path, one that revealed vulnerability and need—and complete safety for both of them.

Eventually she laid her head against his chest, content to listen to his heartbeat.

"There'll be no more talk of babies until you're ready." He broke the silence, reverting to the subject of their marriage. Bonnie had an idea there'd be many conversations like that in the next days and weeks.

"Give me a chance to get the day care started and I'll be ready. At least for one more."

"You're sure?"

"Completely." Funny how easy it all was when there was clear understanding between them—and unconditional love.

She started to ask what had "happened" with Martha to prompt Keith's new understanding, but decided the answer didn't matter. Just as Keith had trusted her with his happiness, she trusted him.

She had to remember to call the woman with a Sunday-dinner invitation—and make sure she came this time.

Keith fell silent, holding her tightly, and Bonnie settled back against him. They should probably go to bed.

But she didn't want to give in to sleep just yet.

After so much heartache, she needed more time just to lie there in her husband's arms and savor the moments, to be fully conscious of the miracle of life.

And of a love that didn't die.

*   *   *   *   *

1

Another town.

There'd been so many.

But this town, on this cold January day, was the one. It had to be.

She didn't even glance at the dirty snowbanks, the barren trees.

Her dark hair pulled back into a ponytail, Amy Wayne, as she called herself on the road, couldn't take the time to care which fast-food places were being advertised on the billboards she whizzed past, or what the economic atmosphere in this particular Michigan town seemed to be. Depressed. Run-down. Thriving. Prosperous. Gray and broken. Beautiful. She'd seen them all.

She'd come to Lawrence, Michigan, to find her son. Nothing else mattered.

Without taking her gaze from the road, Amy reached for the thermostat, flipping it on defrost to clear gathering condensation from the windows.

A few minutes ago she'd lost sight of the car she'd been tracking all day, but she was intimately acquainted with the fact that county roads went in only two directions. To the next town. Or back.

Her ex-nanny's vehicle was a spruce green, four-door Pontiac Grand Am—purchased after she'd been exonerated, at least by the law, of any suspicion in Charles's disappearance. The car hadn't passed in the other direction, so it had to be up ahead.

And almost out of gas.

As far as Amy could tell, that sedan hadn't stopped for several hours. Which meant its driver would probably be forced to stop in Lawrence.

And Amy was going to be right there when it did.

After almost five months on the road alone, chasing down every hint of hope while the officials investigated everyone Amelia Wainscoat had ever known, Amy would see her son again. Fill her aching arms with his sweet, robust little body.

She'd made only occasional visits home, primarily to deal with business matters. The few people who knew what she was doing, who knew she'd undertaken this search a few weeks after her son's disappearance, wondered about her sanity. But no one had been able to stop her.

Amy could hardly remember what it felt like to be the confident, in-control woman who'd accompanied her son to the amusement park that afternoon so many months before. Some days she could hardly remember what it was like to feel at all.

How much did five-year-olds grow in five months? she wondered, her eyes alert, darting here, there, everywhere at once, ensuring that nothing—no one—got by her. Had he lost that baby fat she and Johnny had loved so much?

The multimillionaire mother might not look so powerful in her department-store clothes and poly-ester-filled parka, with her barely made-up face, as she drove the ordinary black Thunderbird she'd purchased to replace the chauffeur-driven limo she'd left at home. But her slender appearance, still sporting remnants of the sleekness she'd once worn so naturally, was as deceptive as the car she was driving. Over the past months of searching for her abducted son, she and her car had proved just how high performance they were.

They were going to win this one. Johnny had always said she could do anything she put her mind to. He'd told her many times, usually while shaking that gorgeous blond head of his, that he'd never met anyone who could make things happen the way she could.

Of course, that had been B.A. Before the accident. Before she'd known she could take nothing in life for granted. That all the money in the world did nothing for her at all. Bought nothing that mattered.

Her stomach in knots, Amy pressed a little harder on the accelerator, the eight-cylinder coupe sliding only slightly when she rounded the bend. Where was that green car?

She'd lost it twice that day and each time had found it again within minutes. The fates were with her now.

And maybe Johnny was, too. In the past months, Amy had felt an odd closeness to the husband she'd lost. Odd because, in some ways, she felt closer to Johnny after his death than she had during the last few years of their marriage. As though he was watching over her.

In those last years, the one thing that had bound them together was Charles. No wonder she felt his presence, his support, as she dedicated every ounce of energy to finding their son and returning him safely home.

And Johnny had warned her about Kathy. He'd understand why she'd undertaken this search, which others considered a complete dead end.

He'd also understand that she couldn't just sit at home, waiting for the professionals to do their jobs. He'd share her uncompromising need to be out here on the road.

What would her little boy be wearing? He'd always preferred denim. And baseball jerseys. But of course Kathy knew that...if Kathy was the abductor, as Amy firmly believed.

Did Charles have a winter coat?

She should call Brad Dorchester. Let him know she was so close. She was paying the private investigator an exorbitant amount of money for a reason. She'd hired him—a Denver resident—over the perfectly competent detectives in Chicago because he was reputed to be the best in the country.

And she'd promised to keep him informed of her whereabouts.

While the renowned P.I. did not approve of Amy's active participation in the hunt for her son— especially as she was working independently of the official search, driven by her own instincts—he was seriously engaged in keeping track of her and her progress.

And he followed up on every hint, every lead, she might find.

Eyeing her cell phone in the console, she continued to drive.

Dorchester, an ex-FBI agent, and the FBI, along

with various local police forces, had been working around the clock for months. In the beginning, they'd received about a call a minute from people reporting sightings. None of them had turned out to be accurate, but they'd had to check them all.

Charles's picture had been everywhere. On television, posted around the country at police stations, schools, churches. Even in the tabloids.

Another bend in the road.

Still no green sedan.

The town was just ahead. Instead of billboards, she could see buildings. The green sedan might be just around that curve. Amy pressed the gas a little harder.

Where would she and her son stay that evening? Grand Rapids, maybe? Or Kalamazoo? Someplace far from the dusty little towns she assumed Charles had been dragged through all through the fall and into the winter. Someplace where she could get them a penthouse suite and they could order room service and play video games until her little boy fell asleep at the controls and she could pull him onto her lap and never let him go.

Another curve. No car.

Hands trembling, Amy wondered what she'd do if she didn't find him that night.

How could she possibly take this for another day? Or week. Or month.

An insidious burning crawled through the lining of her stomach, settling just beneath her rib cage. Hands clenched around the steering wheel, shoulders hunched in her parka, she admonished herself to stay focused. On the road. On what mattered. She wasn't going to allow doubts. Wasn't going to get discouraged. Charles needed her.

And she needed him, too.

This was the day. The town. She could feel it. She'd never been this close. Never had a lead that lasted longer than the minutes it took to check it out.

Wiping the sweat from her upper lip, she slowed as she approached the town. One motel, a diner, some shops, scattered homes—nothing as formal as a neighborhood—a school that looked a little shabby... Occasional piles of dirty, melting snow.

And a green Grand Am. It turned the corner in front of her.

If you enjoyed what you just read,
then we've got an offer you can't resist!

Take 2 bestselling love stories FREE!

Plus get a FREE surprise gift!

Clip this page and mail it to Harlequin Reader Service®

IN U.S.A.	IN CANADA
3010 Walden Ave.	P.O. Box 609
P.O. Box 1867	Fort Erie, Ontario
Buffalo, N.Y. 14240-1867	L2A 5X3

YES! Please send me 2 free Harlequin Superromance® novels and my free surprise gift. After receiving them, if I don't wish to receive anymore, I can return the shipping statement marked cancel. If I don't cancel, I will receive 6 brand-new novels every month, before they're available in stores. In the U.S.A., bill me at the bargain price of $4.47 plus 25¢ shipping and handling per book and applicable sales tax, if any*. In Canada, bill me at the bargain price of $4.99 plus 25¢ shipping and handling per book and applicable taxes**. That's the complete price, and a savings of at least 10% off the cover prices—what a great deal! I understand that accepting the 2 free books and gift places me under no obligation ever to buy any books. I can always return a shipment and cancel at any time. Even if I never buy another book from Harlequin, the 2 free books and gift are mine to keep forever.

135 HDN DNT3
336 HDN DNT4

Name	(PLEASE PRINT)	
Address	Apt.#	
City	State/Prov.	Zip/Postal Code

* Terms and prices subject to change without notice. Sales tax applicable in N.Y.
** Canadian residents will be charged applicable provincial taxes and GST.
  All orders subject to approval. Offer limited to one per household and not valid to current Harlequin Superromance® subscribers.
  ® is a registered trademark of Harlequin Enterprises Limited.

SUP02   ©1998 Harlequin Enterprises Limited

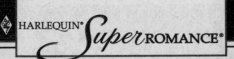

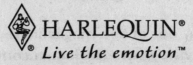

This summer
New York Times bestselling author

HEATHER GRAHAM

&
Golden Heart Award Winner

JULIA JUSTISS

come together in

Forbidden Stranger

(on sale June 2003)

**Don't miss this
captivating 2-in-1
collection brimming
with the intoxicating
allure of forbidden love!**

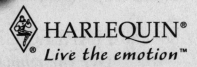

HARLEQUIN®
Live the emotion™

Visit us at www.eHarlequin.com

PHFS

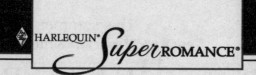

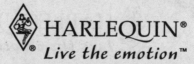

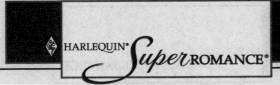

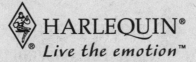

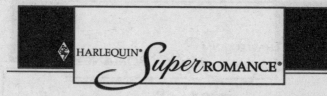

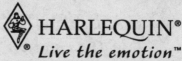

voice of the Holy Spirit, 'You *can* overcome, for I will enable you.' It is enough to make any Christian (at least in his better moments) exclaim with Paul, 'I can do all things in him who strengthens me' (Phil. 4: 13). Without the last five words, that claim might justly be scorned as unwarranted optimism. With them, it amounts to Christian realism. The Christian answer to the perennial problem of moral impotence is the operation of God's power by the Holy Spirit in lives which are totally yielded to Him.

To sum up

The theme of this book is a simple one. It is that in all the questions that may be asked about the moral life, the Christian is driven back to God for the answers. The *meaning of goodness* is to be found in God's character. The only adequate *guide to right and wrong* is to be found in His law, correctly interpreted and applied. The most compelling *motive* in the moral life is the desire to please Him in sheer gratitude for His love. The fullest *pleasure* is to be gained in doing His will. And the necessary *moral power* to turn obligation into action is supplied by His Spirit.

In all these respects Jesus pioneered the way. He not only taught God's law, but exemplified His character, and He still lives to guide and empower those who live in Him. In T. W. Manson's words, 'The living Christ still has two hands, one to point the way, and the other held out to help us along. So the Christian ideal lies before us, not as a remote and austere mountain peak, an ethical Everest which we must scale by our own skill and endurance; but as a road on which we may walk with Christ as guide and friend. And we are assured, as we set out on the journey, that he is with us always, "even unto the end of the world" (Mt. 28: 20).'[1]

[1] T. W. Manson, *Ethics and the Gospel* (SCM, 1960), p. 68.